Bad PUBLICITY

JOANNE SYDNEY LESSNER

Dulcet Press

Also by Joanne Sydney Lessner

The Temporary Detective

Pandora's Bottle

Copyright © 2013 by Joanne Sydney Lessner
All rights reserved.

This is a work of fiction. Names, characters, places, and incidents are products of the author's imagination or are used fictitiously. Any resemblance to actual events or locales or persons, living or dead, is entirely coincidental.

ISBN: 0615777414
ISBN-13: 978-0615777412

Printed in the United States of America
Cover design by Linda Pierro

Published by Dulcet Press
New York
www.dulcetpress.com
info@dulcetpress.com

For Kate, who was there at the beginning and never left

ONE

ISOBEL SPICE STARED AT THE HANDSOME YOUNG MAN slumped over his coffee cup and thought desperately: not again.

She carefully set her tray of melon chunks and assorted pastries on the credenza at the side of the windowless conference room and tiptoed over to the solitary figure at the large oval table.

He'd probably just dozed off. Or maybe he'd passed out. There was no reason to think he was dead just because she'd stumbled across a dead body in an office once before.

But something about the angle of the young man's body was just plain wrong. Isobel gingerly pressed her fingers against the pale, slender wrist. She'd never been good at locating a pulse, even on herself—she'd lied to many an exercise instructor over the years—but somehow she knew that in this case, if there were a pulse to be found, she would be able to find it.

There was nothing. Not even the faintest throb.

Isobel let the man's hand drop back onto the table. His gold signet ring cracked loudly against the wood, startling her. She turned his hand over and was disproportionately relieved to find the ruby-colored stone still intact within its school crest. Isobel gently released his hand and slipped out into the hallway, her panic rising as she gathered steam and burst into Katrina Campbell's office.

"Your client is dead!"

But Katrina's office was empty.

There were several other employees on the lower floor of Dove & Flight Public Relations Isobel could run to, but for several reasons, Katrina was the person least likely to jump to the wrong conclusion. On the other hand, Isobel had to get help. Now.

She dashed back out into the hallway just as Aaron Grossman, a senior account executive, came into view at the far end of the floor.

"Help!" Isobel called, waving him down. "I have to find Katrina! It's an emergency!"

Aaron gave Isobel an odd look and pointed over her left shoulder. Isobel turned to see Katrina, a towering, freckled redhead, coming up behind her from the direction of the small company kitchen.

"Isobel!" Katrina said, drawing closer. "You look like you've just seen a ghost!"

"I have," Isobel croaked. "The body, not the spirit. Come on."

She seized Katrina's arm and pulled her back toward the conference room.

Katrina shook her off. "What is wrong with you?"

But Isobel, who came up roughly to Katrina's shoulder, grabbed her again and propelled her wordlessly down the hall.

At that moment, Aaron emerged from the conference room, his skin paler than usual under his heavy, dark beard.

"Help! HELP! Somebody call 911!"

"Isobel, call 911!" Katrina suddenly seemed to understand, and, breaking free, she ran toward Aaron.

Relieved to be believed, Isobel darted into the nearest office, surprising an eager young junior associate whose eyes grew wide as Isobel relayed to the dispatcher what she had seen.

By the time Isobel returned to the hallway, a small crowd had gathered around the door to the conference room. Katrina was leaning against the wall, visibly shaken. Angus Dove, a dapper, elderly gentleman wearing a tartan bow tie, was making his way slowly down the internal spiral staircase that connected the two floors of the public relations firm.

Time seemed to stop as Dove descended the steps. The crowd parted to let him pass into the conference room. He emerged a moment later.

"Will somebody please call emergency," Dove said, his lightly Scots-accented voice wavering. "And nobody touch him."

Before Isobel could volunteer the information that she'd called already, the hush was broken by another man galumphing down the stairs so heavily it seemed the wrought iron might give way at any moment.

"What the hell is going on?" he bellowed through lupine, nicotine-stained teeth.

"Barnaby," said Dove, "I fear we have a little situation."

"Don't be such a goddamn PR flack, and tell me what the hell is going on!"

"A client, here for a meeting. Seems to have…seems to have…"

"Seems to have what, Angus?"

"Died," Isobel blurted out, her voice projecting several notches higher than she'd intended in both pitch and volume. Angus Dove and Barnaby Flight, the two senior partners of the public relations firm, turned to look at her.

Isobel swallowed. "It's Jason Whiteley. He was here for a meeting with Katrina, Aaron and Liz, and I had just settled him in the conference room with some coffee. I left to get the snacks, and when I came back he was dead."

Behind Dove and Flight, she could see more employees lining the spiral staircase, conveying the news upward from rung to rung in muted whispers.

"Who the hell are you?" roared Barnaby Flight.

Isobel looked around at the sea of suspicious eyes and shrugged meekly.

"Nobody. I'm just the temp."

TWO

James Cooke tried to ignore his cell phone, which was ringing again at the bottom of his gym bag. He was determined to finish two more rounds of bench presses, then shower and have a cup of coffee before talking to anyone about anything. Mondays were always busy at Temp Zone, and today would be worse than usual because his boss, Ginger Wainwright, was on vacation. Knowing that he and the other recruiters would have to pick up the slack and stay into the evening, he'd given himself permission to work out longer and arrive late. He wasn't ready to leave his endorphin high behind and face the world. Besides, he couldn't imagine who could be trying to reach him so urgently.

"Excuse me? Excuse me!"

James set his weights down with a clang and looked up at the skinny white girl standing over him. She'd recently started working out at his Harlem gym and was always lurking in the weight room chatting up guys with the lamest, most transparent conversation-starters. So far he'd been able to avoid her by pretending not to speak English.

"Can you either turn off your phone or answer it? It's kind of annoying."

So are you, thought James, grunting in response.

He sat up and dug around in his bag for his phone. Just as he disentangled it from his spare jock strap, it stopped ringing.

"Oh, well." The girl tossed her long dark hair over her shoulder and pointed at his midriff. "Arms look good, but you want to pay more attention to your abs."

James full out growled at her as she walked away toward the weight machines swinging her thin hips, but she just waved at him over her shoulder. One way or another his workout was over, so he hauled his 250-pound frame off the bench, tucked his bag under his arm, and headed for the locker room. He considered the gym a shrine for private, intense workout, a time to commune with his body. This little squirt was trying to turn it into her personal pick-up joint.

To be fair, she hadn't been trying to strike up a conversation this time; she'd only been suggesting that he answer his phone. Well, he thought sternly, one thing always led to another.

James had just stepped into the shower, when his phone rang again.

"Goddammit!" he cursed at the tile walls.

He took his hand off the hot water knob, which, fortunately, he had not yet turned on, and reached for his bag. This time he managed to grab the phone on the third ring.

"What?" he barked.

There was a pause, and then an all-too-familiar voice launched into an all-too-familiar monologue.

"I'm sorry to keep calling, but it's an emergency and you're not at your office. You were so mad at me last time when I didn't tell you right away, and the police aren't here yet, and I didn't want you to be mad at me again, so I—"

"Isobel! Slow down, slow down!" James grabbed his towel and wrapped it clumsily around his waist. "Where are you?"

"At Dove & Flight. I didn't have anything to do with this—you have to believe me. It's crazy! I mean, what are the odds of me being in an office with a murder two times in three months?"

James felt his chest tighten, and he pulled the phone away from his ear to check the number. Yes, it really was Isobel, and she really was saying what he thought she was saying.

"Isobel."

"What?"

"Are you telling me that someone at Dove & Flight is dead?"

"A client. And I didn't do it. I mean, I did do it—but I didn't mean to, I swear!"

James massaged his brow, trying to make her words mean something else, but he couldn't.

"What do you mean, you *did* do it?" he asked slowly, not wanting to hear the answer.

"I served him coffee right before he died."

"And the coffee killed him?"

Isobel paused. "Well, actually, I don't know. I just sort of assumed it did. But—oh, my God! The pot is still on in the kitchen. I have to go!"

"Wait—WAIT!"

But she was gone. James threw the phone into his bag. So much for his shower.

She was right—it was crazy, he thought, as he pulled on his pants over his slick, sweaty legs. But he had no reason *not* to believe her. In the three months he'd been sending her out on temp jobs, James had learned that Isobel was many things—endearing, annoying, witty, and even, sometimes, if his defenses were down, attractive—but she wasn't a liar. Nor, despite the fact that she was an actress, or a would-be actress, or some sort of actress-in-training, was she unnecessarily dramatic. There had been real panic in her voice. If she said someone was dead, as unlikely as it might seem, someone was dead.

He had to get his ass down to Isobel's office in midtown, that much was certain. He couldn't let her face the cops alone if there was any chance she was responsible, even accidentally. Isobel didn't always know when to cork it, and she didn't always make the best first impression, especially on people who lacked a finely tuned sense of the ridiculous. And cops fell squarely into that category.

James cast his mind back to their first meeting, when Isobel had flounced into his office with her round gray-green eyes, shiny brown ponytail and translucent skin. Against his better judgment, he'd let her steamroll him into sending her out on a temp job, despite the fact that she'd never worked in an office. It was only supposed to be a half-day of phones and light typing at a bank. Nothing in the job description mentioned discovering an obnoxious secretary sitting on the pot with a pair of scissors plunged into her chest, nor the task of cleaning up the mess. Of course, the crime scene folks and the building staff had taken care of the blood, but Isobel had been the one to clear up the confusion by correctly fingering and trapping the killer. She had never been more appealing than at that moment.

But there was nothing appealing about Isobel now, and he groaned in frustration at the garbled message assaulting his ears over the subway loudspeaker. It was just intelligible enough for him to catch the general drift: a suspicious package at 145th Street. Downtown trains delayed until further notice. He pounded up the steps to the street, his breath misting in the frigid January air, just as a bus barreled up to the curb. James shot his MetroCard into the reader and started down the aisle.

"Need the fare," the bus driver called after him.

"What? This is an unlimited card."

"You gotta wait eighteen minutes before you can use it again. You just used it."

James stormed back to the front of the bus. "Damn right I just used it. On the subway, which isn't running."

"They shoulda given you a transfer."

"Well, they didn't," James growled.

Two elderly women exchanged a glance and pulled themselves to their feet. They hobbled toward the rear of the bus, preferring to maneuver their canes down the aisle than be attacked by a raving, fare-deficient madman.

The driver gave an exaggerated sigh, as if he were talking to a five year-old. "You gotta *ask* for one."

"I didn't have time to ask. I'm late, and I've already shelled out the money for an unlimited card, so don't you go goddamn limiting me!"

"Well, this is the Limited bus," joked a wiry Hispanic kid in horn-rimmed glasses. James glared at him and he shrank back into his seat.

"Eighteen minutes or pay the fare," the bus driver said stoically.

James ignored him and plopped down next to the Hispanic kid, who receded even further into the blue plastic.

The bus driver shifted into neutral and turned around in his seat. "Either pay the fare or get off the bus," he said, in a voice that brooked no argument.

"What are you gonna do, throw me off?"

There was a collective intake of breath from the passengers. In response, the bus driver pulled his walkie-talkie from his belt and began to speak.

"This is the 101 Limited, bus number 6650, operator 142. I've got a large, African-American male, won't pay his fare—"

"Son of a bitch! I don't have time for this!" James roared.

He stormed through the open doors, nearly knocking over a gaggle of teenage girls running to catch the stalled bus. A middle-aged woman in a suit stuck her mouth up against an open sliver of window.

"Now you've held up the whole damn bus! You're not the only one who's late, you know!"

"I'm the only one who's late to a murder!" James shouted back, although he realized as soon as the words were out of his mouth that they didn't exactly help his cause.

THREE

ISOBEL CROUCHED EYE-LEVEL WITH the counter and examined the coffee in the pot. Had any of the others helped themselves? She wished she could remember how much was left after she'd poured Jason Whiteley's cup. Then again, if she waited long enough, the answer might manifest itself in the form of another dead body. Horrible thought.

"What are you doing?"

Isobel jumped and turned to see Katrina standing behind her.

"Don't do that!" Isobel held her hand over her pounding heart. She pointed to the half-empty carafe. "I'm checking the coffee. Has anyone else had any?"

"Why?" Katrina looked puzzled. "What does it matter?"

"Because that's obviously what killed him. There was something in the coffee."

Katrina stared at Isobel.

"What?" Isobel said.

"That never even occurred to me," Katrina said, sweeping a coppery curl behind her ear.

"It didn't?" Little warning hairs began to prickle the back of Isobel's neck. "Wasn't he your biggest pain in the ass client?"

Katrina's face flushed the color of her hair. "Are you suggesting that I—"

"Of course not! I just thought that somebody might have…" Isobel shook her head. "I don't know what I thought."

Katrina stepped further into the kitchenette and pulled the door closed. "Look," she said quietly, "I know what happened at that bank job you were on, but even though Jason is…okay, dead…it doesn't mean somebody killed him. I'm sure there's a logical explanation, like he was sick and nobody knew it. But nobody here—and that includes you and me—poisoned his coffee." Katrina allowed herself a little laugh. "You were always such a drama queen."

Isobel bristled. "That's not true!"

Katrina cocked her head at Isobel. "Freshman year? When you had a crush on that guy, what was his name? And you wrote all those love poems and stood outside his dorm and sang them to your own tunes?"

That was the problem with college friends, thought Isobel. They remembered all your stupid behavior and never hesitated to out you at some particularly inopportune moment. At least there was nobody else in the room. Isobel tuned out Katrina as she rattled on. As much as she liked Katrina, right now Isobel was finding her maddening. Even the fact that Katrina's hair should have—but didn't—clash with the pink of her Chanel jacket irked her.

"Okay, okay, I get the point," Isobel said, irritated. "Are the police here yet?"

"Yes. And the medical examiner. That's what I came in here to tell you. They want to talk to you."

"I found him, so I'm automatically the prime suspect. For now."

Katrina threw her head to the ceiling and mouthed "drama queen."

Isobel turned back toward the kitchen counter, but Katrina pulled her around. "And leave the coffee."

Isobel set her hands determinedly on her hips. "What if somebody pours it out? Or, worse, drinks it?"

Katrina pursed her lips, then with long, graceful fingers, reached for the carafe.

"Wait!" Isobel snatched a dishcloth from the counter and handed it to her. "There might be fingerprints."

Katrina rolled her eyes. "Somebody's been watching too much 'SVU'."

"Just do it, okay?"

"Fine. We'll bring it with us and tell them what you suspect." Katrina wrapped the cloth around the handle and looked thoughtfully at the carafe. "I suppose it's not entirely out of the realm of possibility that someone killed him. He was an asshole."

"And I'm not a drama queen," Isobel insisted.

Katrina gave her an annoyingly smug look as they left the kitchen together. "Well, maybe not as much as you were in college."

"Do you have any particular reason to think the coffee was poisoned?" asked Detective O'Connor, a towering blue-eyed blond with a light Irish accent and a refined turn of phrase. He would have been attractive if his head weren't just a bit too small for his body. His partner, Aguilar, was a short, chubby Filipino, with deep-set dark eyes and a crew cut. Together, they were a walking sight gag, although the small empty office they'd commandeered offered little room for pacing.

"Not really," Isobel said. "But it's the last thing he ingested."

O'Connor nodded. "We'll test the remains in the cup and the pot. So, you settled him in the conference room, he asked for coffee, and then?"

"He didn't ask for coffee. I just brought it. I also set out soda and water on the side table."

Aguilar turned his penetrating gaze on Isobel. "He didn't ask for coffee?"

"No, but he looked like he could use a cup."

"What do you mean by that?"

Isobel shrugged. "It just seemed like he wasn't totally awake yet."

"So you brought him the coffee, and then what?" O'Connor asked.

"I set it in front of him, and he said thank you."

"But you don't know if he ingested any."

Isobel hesitated. "I guess not. I just assumed he did."

"Never assume. It makes an 'ass' out of 'u' and 'me'." O'Connor nodded genially at Isobel. "Rule number one of police work. But we'll test the coffee all the same."

Isobel tried to smile, despite the fact that she'd been hearing that tired old adage from her father since she was about eight.

"What happened next?" O'Connor asked.

"I went back to the kitchen and unwrapped the fruit and pastries. When I came back, he was face down on the table."

"So, let me guess, you *assumed* he was dead," said Aguilar.

"I was right, wasn't I?" Isobel retorted.

"What do you know about Jason Whiteley?" O'Connor asked. "It interests me that your first instinct was that his death was a homicide."

"Why should that interest you? It's only an *assumption*." She cast a smile at Aguilar, whose eyes glinted dangerously.

"There's a difference between assumption and instinct," O'Connor instructed. "Rule number two of police work is to follow your instincts."

Thinking back to her experience at the bank, Isobel knew he was right. Her assumptions had gotten her into trouble, while her instincts had led her to the killer. But she felt a demon possess her, and she asked, in her most ingenuous voice, "Could you elaborate on the distinction between the two? I think I was absent from class that day."

Before O'Connor could respond, a commotion erupted in the hall.

"Since when does a temp need a lawyer?" Barnaby Flight's snarl penetrated the standard-issue office door, only to be quashed by a deep, resonant voice that simultaneously calmed and excited Isobel.

"I didn't say I was her lawyer, I said I was her—" The door swung open, and James Cooke stood there, filling the frame. "Representative," he finished.

Aguilar jumped to his feet, as did Isobel.

"James!"

"This is a police matter," Aguilar said sharply, his hand on his gun. "I'll have to ask you to leave."

"I'm Isobel's representative at Temp Zone. As her official employer, I have as much right to be here with her as the employees of Dove & Flight have to be with that fat loudmouth who didn't want to let me in."

Isobel thought she saw a flicker of a smile cross O'Connor's face, but it dissolved so quickly, she couldn't be certain.

"We were just discussing the difference between assumption and instinct," O'Connor said in his most polite voice. James glanced at Isobel, who shrugged innocently.

O'Connor returned his attention to Isobel. "An assumption is a conclusion drawn from bits of information. Instinct is blind gut feeling. The reason assumptions are so often wrong is that the information is incomplete, and therefore misleading, while the subconscious rarely concerns itself with fact." He turned to his partner and sighed. "Sometimes I'm glad I majored in English. But only sometimes."

Aguilar looked momentarily confused, and O'Connor continued to James, "Now, I could assume that your presence here indicates a fear that Ms. Spice was the cause of this young man's death and that you think she is in need of protection, both from us and from herself."

Isobel shot James a deadly look.

"However, my instinct tells me," and here O'Connor stood up, so Isobel could see that although James easily outweighed him, the detective was half a head taller, "that Ms. Spice is not responsible for his death, and that it might prove interesting to let you stay, as long as you sit in that chair and don't say a word."

James shut the door in Barnaby Flight's astonished face and settled in the designated chair.

"ID, please," Aguilar said.

James fished in his wallet for his driver's license and handed it to Aguilar, who wrinkled his nose in distaste.

James cleared his throat. "Sorry. Came straight from the gym."

"I believe we were discussing your relationship with Jason Whiteley," O'Connor said to Isobel.

James was on his feet in a flash. "Jason Whiteley?"

O'Connor, Aguilar and Isobel looked at James in surprise.

"Maybe we should be discussing *your* relationship with Jason Whiteley," O'Connor said, his voice hardening.

"Did you know the deceased?" Aguilar asked, his pen poised hopefully in mid-air.

"Did he work for Schumann, Crowe & Dyer, the consulting firm?" James asked.

"Yes."

James glanced self-consciously at Isobel. "My ex-girlfriend works there. I met him once or twice."

"I see," said O'Connor, as Aguilar scribbled enthusiastically on his pad. "My instinct to let you stay has been rewarded already. We'll come back to you in a moment." He turned to Isobel. "Ms. Spice? What about you?"

"I had never met him before this morning. All I know is that Schumann, Crowe & Dyer is a client, and Jason Whiteley is—I mean, was—their internal communications director. He was here for a meeting with Aaron, Liz and Katrina."

"Last names," prompted Aguilar.

"Aaron Grossman, Liz Stewart and," she paused. Aguilar looked up. "Katrina Campbell. But I'm sure she had nothing to do with it. I've known her since college."

"Old friends," murmured O'Connor thoughtfully. "Had you heard much from any of them, either about Whiteley or his firm?"

Isobel stole a look at James, who had sat down again and was frowning at his hands.

"It was my understanding that they were, um, difficult."

"In what way?"

"Demanding. Expected a lot of press coverage without offering much that was newsworthy. But I've heard them say that about other clients, too," she added quickly.

"What was the purpose of today's meeting?" O'Connor asked.

All Isobel knew was that Katrina was nervous about it, but her instinct told her to protect her friend. As pleasant as Detective O'Connor was, she guessed he could apply the screws if need be, and she decided it would be wise to follow rule number two of police work. Besides, she certainly wouldn't want to lead him to any false assumptions.

"I don't know what the meeting was about. I've only been here two weeks. I'm just answering phones, organizing and helping make press calls."

And serving the occasional poisoned beverage, she added silently.

O'Connor turned to James. "What's your girlfriend's name?"

"Jayla Cummings. And like I said, she's an ex. We broke up about three months ago," James said, as Aguilar scribbled. "I don't see how this is relevant."

"Look at it from our point of view," O'Connor said. "You barge in here, insist on being present for Ms. Spice's questioning, and surprise of surprises, we find that you were better acquainted with the deceased than she was. I think I'm entitled to ask a few questions. Wouldn't you say so, Aguilar?"

Aguilar mumbled an affirmative response and squinted at his notepad as if he were having difficulty deciphering his own handwriting.

"What is your present relationship with Ms. Cummings, and what, to the best of your knowledge, was hers with Mr. Whiteley?"

"I haven't talked to her since we split. She's seeing someone else now, which is fine by me. I think she got along okay with Whiteley. To tell you the truth, she hardly ever mentioned him. I couldn't tell you what kind of work they did together."

"And you, I gather, are a personnel recruiter?"

"Yes. With Temp Zone."

"How long have you known Ms. Spice?"

"Three months."

"And in that time, has anything occurred that would make you overly concerned about her? You see, I'm still trying to account for the vehemence with which you insisted on being admitted."

Definitely an English major, thought Isobel. She glanced at James, and their eyes locked for a moment. She wondered whether he would tell O'Connor about the bank murder.

"I would be concerned about any employee who called to tell me there was a dead body in the conference room," James said evenly.

Aguilar looked up from his pad. "You called him?"

"I didn't know what else to do," Isobel said. "It was such a shock."

There was a sharp knock on the door, and a little bearded man in a white coat and latex gloves stuck his head in.

"No blood, no vomit, no feces, no facial distortion. Likely cardiovascular arrest. We'll conduct an autopsy, of course, but it seems straightforward."

"Well, that's that, then," O'Connor said to Aguilar. "We still need to take statements from everyone else." He waved Isobel away. "Please ask your friend Ms. Campbell to come in."

"I'm finished?"

"Easy come, easy go. We know where to find you if we need you." The detective inclined his undersized blond head shrewdly at James. "And you, too, although it appears your concern for your client was misplaced."

FOUR

"I DON'T CARE WHAT HE SAYS, THERE'S nothing straightforward about a healthy young guy like that having a heart attack," declared Isobel.

There was no possibility of privacy at Isobel's desk, which was in an open area near the foot of the spiral staircase, so she and James had taken refuge in Katrina's office while Katrina talked to the police.

"Healthy-*looking*," James said. "He wouldn't be the first twenty-eight-year-old to drop dead from one thing or another."

"Okay, maybe, but—" Isobel stopped. "That's awfully precise. How do you know how old he was?"

James opened the door, glanced out into the hall, which was now fairly deserted, and shut it again.

"Promise to keep this between us?" Isobel nodded, and he continued. "I didn't know him just through Jayla. We were at Columbia together. We were actually in the same fraternity until they shut it down."

Isobel looked aghast. "Why didn't you tell the police? That's withholding information! What if they find out?"

James thrust a warning finger at her. "You just promised to keep this between us, and dead men don't talk. Besides, I wasn't lying about meeting him through Jayla. Until then, I hadn't seen him in years, so I figure that's enough for the purpose."

Isobel eyed James. "What are you hiding?"

He clenched his fists. "I'm not hiding anything. I just—come on, look at me! Big black man barges in out of nowhere, knows the dead guy. You don't know cops." James shook his head emphatically. "What he was saying about assumptions is bullshit. Cops arrest people like me on assumptions every day."

"So were you and Jason friends?" she asked. "And why did they shut down the fraternity, anyway?"

James paced the small office. "He was a smarmy dickhead preppie. Fraternity was shut down after one too many alcohol poisonings. A Barnard girl died after drinking half a bottle of tequila. It was one of the things that led to… Well, you know I left Columbia, right?"

Isobel nodded. She knew James had struggled with alcoholism since dropping out of college. She thought he'd managed to stay sober for the last three months, but she couldn't be sure.

James looked down at his hands and flexed his fingers. "After that incident, I was given a little nudge by the administration."

"They kicked you out?"

"Yeah, strike three."

"What about Jason? Did he get the boot?"

"Nah. He was a straight-A student, and as far as I know, he never had a problem with alcohol. He was one of those guys who could drink gallons when he felt like it and abstain when he didn't."

Isobel could hear the envy in James's voice and knew he wished he had that kind of control.

"So what happened to Jason after they shut down the fraternity?"

"Couldn't tell you. He probably just moved into a dorm. Or maybe he joined another fraternity. What the hell is this, anyway? An interrogation?"

"Sorry!" Isobel held up her hands. "You know me, I'm just curious. And you have to admit, it's a funny coincidence."

James let his bulk loom over her, and she was suddenly aware of the tangy, not entirely unpleasant odor of his sweat. The back of her neck responded with an unfamiliar tingle.

"Don't think for a minute that I had anything to do with this guy biting it over his morning coffee," warned James. "For one thing, I haven't seen or spoken to him since Jayla's office Christmas party two years ago. For another, it was a heart attack. Accidental death. There's nothing to investigate here, so park your roadster, Nancy Drew."

He moved away from her to give another listen to the hallway, and she felt oddly let down.

"Right. You're right," she said lightly.

He turned around to look at her. "I also want you to promise that you'll accept the medical examiner's evidence and not go snooping around. Okay?"

Isobel could feel a tiny argument forming in the back of her mind, but she squelched it. In her admittedly limited experience, an office death meant a murder, not an accident. She wanted to follow police rule number two and trust her instincts, but she knew James wouldn't leave until she promised not to ask questions. She also knew she wouldn't be able to stop herself.

"Okay, I promise."

She hoped crossing one's legs counted the same as crossing one's fingers, because her hands were on Katrina's desk, and James would almost certainly notice if she suddenly moved them behind her back.

Jason Whiteley, of all people.

James had managed to be polite the few times they'd crossed paths through Jayla, but the truth was there were few people he despised more. Jason Whiteley stood for everything James hated about the Ivy League: entitlement, wealth, and, most significantly, protection from the abuses of a society that wasn't as color-blind as it purported to be. James both loathed and envied the ease with which Whiteley had moved in the world they briefly shared. No matter which fraternity James joined, who his friends were, or how many touchdowns he managed to score for Columbia's pathetic excuse for a football team, he would always be the charity case from down the block. The worst of it was that people like Whiteley forced James to recognize the small, desperate part of himself that felt he, too, was entitled; he, too, should be wealthy; and there was no reason he shouldn't also be protected. Why couldn't he have had a prominent venture capitalist father to stand by his side before the school disciplinary board and talk him out of trouble?

As James made his way up Madison Avenue to Temp Zone, he reminded himself that whatever his failings, he was still alive, and Whiteley was not. For all Whiteley's privilege, James had beaten him in the game of life. Whoever has the most birthdays wins. James Cooke was a survivor. And for that, he suddenly felt guilty. Not for surviving—but for feeling superior that he had.

"Where have you been?" asked Anna Brackett, Ginger Wainwright's second-in-command at Temp Zone. She caught him trying to sneak into his cubbyhole of an office after surreptitiously managing to rinse and towel off his face and underarms in the hall bathroom.

"You wouldn't believe me if I told you," James said. He liked Anna, and if he were inclined to share the morning's events with anyone, it would be her.

"Try me," she said, gently lobbing a steaming mug of coffee from one hand to the other.

"Isobel Spice," he began.

Anna smiled broadly. "Our very own temporary detective."

"Yeah, well, she's at it again. Some guy died of a heart attack at Dove & Flight this morning."

Anna gasped. "You've got to be kidding!"

"She called me at the gym, so I raced over there. I mean, after the last time, I sort of expected the worst."

"Who was it?"

"Some client of theirs. It doesn't seem to be suspicious in any way, but Isobel was freaked out, so I went down there."

Anna sniffed cautiously. "And skipped the shower?"

"Either I stay and stink, or you let me go home."

"I can give you a guest pass for my gym. New York Sports, around the corner," Anna said. "You want to zip over there now?"

"You sure you don't mind?"

"I'd mind more if you didn't."

"That would be great," James said, relieved.

"I was expecting it to be a madhouse today. You know, Monday mornings. But it's been pretty quiet." Anna sighed into her coffee cup and took a sip. "Poor Isobel. First that horrible secretary impaled with scissors, now some geezer keels over."

"He wasn't old," James said, and immediately wished he hadn't.

Anna's eyes narrowed behind her red cat-eye frames. "He wasn't? That's a bit weird, don't you think?"

"Not you, too," James groaned. "Why do you women think a young guy having a heart attack is fishy?"

"Because it is. Call it intuition."

"Well, I'm ignoring it."

"Of course you are. Why should you be any different from the rest of your species?" Anna retorted and returned to her office.

No, no, no, James reassured himself. It was not homicide. It was a heart attack, pure and simple. Just like the medical examiner said.

Except that Jason Whiteley had always had a talent for attracting enemies. There was no reason to think anything had changed.

FIVE

BEFORE ISOBEL COULD TURN HER KEY in the lock, her apartment door was flung open by Delphi Kramer, whose stunning masses of blond curls cascaded around her bare shoulders and into the plunging décolletage of a powder-blue brocaded bustier.

"'Now, what news on the Rialto?'" Delphi demanded.

Isobel took in her roommate's getup with a critical eye. "What happened to the pink one? I liked the pink one better." She indicated the ruffles adorning the dainty three-quarter sleeve. "This is too much froufrou for you." She walked through the open door into the L-shaped studio they shared.

"The pink was nice," Delphi conceded, shutting the door behind Isobel, "but you have to agree, I'm not really a pink person. Something about the blue makes me feel like Helena in *Midsummer*. And it matches my eyes."

Isobel threw off her coat and flopped down on the air mattress that was her haven, tucked under the window across the cramped room from Delphi's perpetually rumpled daybed.

"I never thought I'd say this, but I miss the nose ring and the bangles," said Isobel. "And your singing."

"'The lady doth protest too much, methinks.'"

"I mean it. You've become a real pain in the ass."

"'You hard-hearted adamant!'"

Isobel groaned. "What have you done, memorized the entire collected works?"

Delphi gave a devilish smile. "Just pithy sentences I can bandy about in everyday conversation."

Isobel sighed in resignation. At times like this, she really did find herself longing for the Goth Delphi who had been ill-advisedly pursuing a career in musical theater when they'd first met. Delphi, realizing that Isobel's classically-trained, full-bodied soprano was only one of many such competitive voices, had refocused her attentions on Shakespeare. Having rebelled for years against her natural Botticellian beauty, she had jettisoned the leather and silver jewelry, and immersed herself body, soul, language and wardrobe in the Bard.

"Besides, if you're going to do the thing properly," Isobel said, gesturing at Delphi's lower half, "you should be wearing the bodice with a skirt, not Gap jeans."

"But that would attract attention!"

Isobel snorted. "And this doesn't?"

Delphi set her hands on her hips. "*This* is a synthesis of Elizabethan and modern styles, reflecting my identity as a contemporary Shakespearean actress."

"Who doesn't want to call attention to herself," Isobel said drily.

"'Mend my company. Take away thyself,'" retorted Delphi.

Isobel scowled. "If you don't shut up, I'm going to kick you right in the Coriolanus."

Delphi shook her curls imperiously. "It was *Timon of Athens*."

"No, it was Cole Porter, but never mind," said Isobel. "Can you please just be you again? I've been waiting all day to tell you what happened at work."

Delphi checked her distinctly modern Swatch, whose orange plaid wristband argued angrily with the blue bodice. "Talk quickly. We lost three actors for *King John*, and I'm monitoring the replacement auditions, so I can't be late."

Fine, thought Isobel. You asked for it.

"A client was murdered."

Delphi gasped. "'Hell is empty, and all the devils are here!'"

"Delphi!"

"Sorry, sorry! It was too perfect."

Isobel pulled at a loose string on her pillowcase. "The thing is, it doesn't look like murder, but my gut tells me it is."

Delphi held up a hand. "Just tell me that even though you're the common element here, you don't make people die wherever you go. Because, I swear, if you are, I'm moving out."

"It only happens at work." Isobel reconsidered. "No, that isn't even true. This is my one, two, three, four, five—sixth temp job. Everyone survived in offices two through five."

Delphi peered at her reflection in the diamond-shaped mirror that hung in what passed for a foyer. "Come to the auditions. You can sit behind the desk with me and tell me the rest."

"Under one condition," Isobel said firmly. "That I get to talk to Delphi, not Lady Macbeth, Helena, Beatrice or Viola."

"Deal." Delphi swathed her swan-like neck in a thick woolen scarf and stuffed her puffy sleeves into her coat. "We'll pick up sandwiches along the way, so we can munch rudely while the actors audition. Just like real producers."

"Right." Isobel hauled herself up off her air mattress. "'Lead on, Macduff.'"

"It's 'Lay on, Macduff.'" Delphi gave Isobel a reproachful look over her shoulder. "Everybody always gets that one wrong."

"I HAVE TO SAY, I AGREE WITH JAMES. There isn't any reason to think it was murder," Delphi said, as she took a stapled picture and résumé from a gentleman with a gray beard who wore a white ruffled shirt over jeans. Delphi added his résumé to the pile in front of her, while Isobel silently noted that he and Delphi appeared to share the same tailor. The man retreated to a folding chair down the hall to fill out his audition form.

Delphi continued, "I mean, if we find out the coffee was laced with strychnine, that's a whole different ballgame. But what do you know about this guy that makes you think someone wanted to kill him?"

Isobel had to admit she knew almost nothing about Jason Whiteley. But that didn't mean there was nothing to know. In fact, she did know at least one person who had harbored an intense dislike for him: James.

"There must be something," Isobel said finally.

"Hmmmm." Delphi munched her sandwich thoughtfully. "Was he a popular client?"

"No, he wasn't. That much I do know. But most businesses would go bust if they killed all the clients they didn't like."

"Clearly," Delphi said, somewhat unclearly, as her mouth was full of smoked turkey. "But if you're really convinced someone snuffed him, that's the place to start looking."

"I know that." Isobel was starting to get annoyed. First, Delphi didn't think there was anything suspicious, and now she was stating the obvious. "But what I mean is that there would have to be more to it than the fact that he was difficult."

"If you're determined to nose around—and I know you are, so don't bother denying it—you should start with the people who worked directly with him."

"Thanks, Sherlock. I'd already figured that part out myself."

"Excuse me?"

They paused in their conversation to take in a thin, nervous-looking young man who clutched his picture and résumé to his chest, wrinkling his photo just above the mouth so that it gave him the appearance of a thirteen-year-old with a moustache.

"Are you here to audition?"

"Um, yes. I'm, um, Gary Stinson?" he said, sounding unsure whether or not he actually was.

Delphi consulted her sign-in sheet. "You're at 8:50. Fill out this form and have a seat."

He took the form, his hand trembling. "Um…will they be wanting tights today?"

Isobel looked at the ceiling to keep from laughing. Delphi had taught her that trick to keep from cracking up onstage, but Isobel had found it just as useful in real life. Unfortunately, Delphi had chosen to employ the same tactic, and their eyes met as their glances traveled upwards, forcing them into stifled giggles. Delphi recovered faster, but not by much.

"No," she hiccupped. "Not today."

Gary gave a sigh of relief and shuffled away toward the folding chairs.

"Wait!" Delphi called after him.

He gasped as if he'd been discovered with a hole in his pants and spun around. "What?"

"I need your picture," Delphi said, pointing to his chest.

He crept back to the table and set it in front of her with a reverential pat, and then retreated to the folding chairs, where he took a seat next to the graybeard.

Isobel and Delphi immediately flipped over the picture to examine the list of credits stapled to the back. Contrary to what Isobel expected, Gary's résumé was jam-packed with impressive, if incongruous roles, mostly in college productions.

Delphi pointed to a listing for Hamlet and rolled her eyes.

At that moment, an angular, unattractive young woman emerged from the audition room, shaking her head and muttering to herself, and Delphi gestured to another woman, who appeared to be trying to disguise her advancing age with a girly flowered dress that looked to be Laura Ashley, circa 1992. Delphi disappeared momentarily to lead her into the audition room, and Isobel stared absently across the room at Gary, reviewing what she knew about Jason Whiteley.

He was a demanding client.

He was a heavy social drinker, at least in college.

He worked with James's ex-girlfriend.

James didn't like him.

James had lied to the police.

"Stop!" she said aloud, forgetting herself. Gary looked up, startled, but she ignored him. All her thoughts were leading back to James. He couldn't possibly have had anything to do with this. He wasn't even there! He said he'd been at the gym, and from the way he'd smelled when he burst into Dove & Flight, there was no doubt he was telling the truth.

Delphi returned after a moment and glanced at her watch. She indicated the two men, young and old, who were left in the hallway.

"These are the last two. We can go inside and watch their auditions, if you want. It's really fascinating to sit on the other side. You learn a lot. Mostly what not to do," Delphi added under her breath.

"Okay," Isobel said, grateful for the distraction.

While they waited for the not-so-young woman to finish her audition, Delphi folded the chairs, and Isobel turned her thoughts toward the three people responsible for the Schumann, Crowe & Dyer account.

Aaron Grossman was an Orthodox Jew with five kids and another on the way, although he was only twenty-eight. He left work every Friday at three o'clock (two o'clock in winter) in anticipation of the Sabbath, which prompted barely concealed disapproval on particularly hectic days, although nobody dared lodge an official complaint. He had only recently been made a senior associate, and it was generally known that he didn't like working with women—young women in particular.

Liz Stewart, pregnant with her first child, was an athletic blonde with a wry sense of humor and what she liked to describe as a completely useless philosophy degree from Yale. It was Liz who had proclaimed public relations the burial ground for liberal arts majors. She had also confided to Isobel that she planned to allow her maternity leave to lapse into permanent at-home motherhood, but made Isobel promise not to let on to any of her colleagues. Isobel liked Liz for her straightforwardness and her random references to obscure Gregorian chants.

And then there was Katrina. She and Isobel had been English majors together at the University of Wisconsin, frequently vying for control of seminar discussions. That sense of competition had carried over into their friendship, mostly on Katrina's side, so that Isobel was never entirely sure where she stood with her friend. She was surprised that Katrina had embraced her arrival at Dove & Flight—had even shown her off. It was Katrina who kept finding more work for Isobel to do, which was why she was still there, two weeks after her initial three-day assignment had ended. But the occasional snide comment, like the one about her being a drama queen, seemed designed to keep her off balance. Isobel sensed it was insurance against the possibility, however remote, that she might somehow show Katrina up. Isobel knew that Katrina had briefly considered a modeling career, but she was determined to prove to the world that she had more to offer than long legs and a pretty face. She was an incredibly hard worker, a trait she had inherited from her father, who had hustled his way up from the mailroom to become CEO of a major international communications company. Katrina had told Isobel more than once that she intended to stake her professional claim in the world without help from him or anyone else.

On the face of it, none of them seemed murderous by nature. But rather than let go of the idea of homicide, Isobel resolved to widen her net and take a closer look at the other employees at Dove & Flight when she returned to work the next day.

Laura Ashley emerged triumphantly from the audition room, a wide grin on her face. Delphi turned to gesture to the graybeard, but he had disappeared.

"I think he's in the…um…" stammered Gary.

"Bathroom?" supplied Delphi helpfully. Gary nodded. "Okay, you're on." Delphi tapped Isobel on the shoulder. "Come on. This should be good."

They followed Gary into the large, black-walled studio theater where Graham Davies, the director, was sitting. Isobel fully expected him to be sporting an anachronistic ensemble similar to Delphi's and was disappointed to see that he was clad mundanely in a button-down Oxford shirt and chinos. He did, however, have an impressively long mane of chestnut brown hair that Isobel suspected accounted for a significant portion of his authority. Delphi handed Gary's résumé to Graham, and they took seats behind him. Gary tiptoed to the front of the room, his head receding into his neck as if he were shrinking from a nonexistent spotlight.

"Welcome, Gary," Graham said expansively. "Did you bring two pieces? One contemporary, one classical?"

Gary gave a terrified nod. "I'd like to do Willy Loman from *Death of a Salesman*."

Isobel nudged Delphi. "Isn't he about forty years too young?"

Gary went on, "And for my classical piece, I'd like to do something I wrote myself."

Isobel caught Delphi's eye and their heads immediately inclined toward the ceiling.

"How intriguing," Graham said simply. "Let's start with Willy Loman."

And then a strange thing happened. Gary dropped his voice and let his shoulders sink, and suddenly he appeared, if not forty years older, at least ten. His natural timidity highlighted the salesman's pathetic desperation, and although it wasn't wholly convincing, he was far better than he had any right to be.

"Very nice," Graham said, when Gary finished. "May we hear your, er, classical piece?"

Gary immediately pumped out his concave chest, took an aggressive stance, and began to speak.

"'Thou hast pained me much, but my pain is as nothing to thine,'" he began.

Isobel watched the back of Graham's head for signs of mirth, but he seemed to be concentrating hard on Gary's performance. The self-penned classical piece was riddled with "thees" and "thous," but otherwise made little sense. It did, however, provide Gary with the opportunity to be loud and forceful, quite the opposite of Willy Loman. Still, Isobel found it hard to believe there was nothing in all of Shakespeare's works that would have served the same purpose.

As the last words died in his throat, Gary's quivering mien returned, and Delphi shepherded him back out into the hallway, leaving Isobel alone with Graham. He turned around and smiled warmly at her.

"Educational, isn't it?"

"Definitely! But why do you have them do a contemporary monologue if you're casting a Shakespeare play?"

"It always illuminates some aspect of the actor that doesn't come through in their classical piece. Willy Loman here was a perfect example, wouldn't you agree?"

Isobel nodded. "I'm glad I saw him do that."

Graham gestured to the stage. "Would you like to hop up there and do a piece?"

"No, thanks. Shakespeare is Delphi's thing. I do musicals."

"I always find that singers do well with Shakespeare."

"Thanks, but I don't have a monologue," she demurred.

Graham winked. "When in doubt, just write one yourself!"

Delphi returned with the graybeard. In a stentorian voice, he announced his name, Walter Fox, and his pieces: Willy Loman and Polonius.

Graham made a show of looking at his watch. "It's getting late. Let's just cut to the chase and hear the *Hamlet*, shall we?"

Walter nodded and launched into Polonius's famous litany of advice to the departing Laertes. Walter's voice was resonant and impressive, but, strangely, he was less compelling than timid little Gary. By the time he reached "Neither a borrower, nor a lender be," Isobel's mind was wandering back to Jason Whiteley. She could tell from

Delphi's squirming that she, too, was bored. Graham's long mane was bowed in front of her, and Isobel was glad that he had skipped the contemporary monologue. Despite the fact that Walter was, on the face of it, more appropriate for the part, she doubted his Willy Loman would have been as good as Gary's.

"'This above all: to thine own self—'" Walter paused. Delphi, Isobel and Graham looked up expectantly.

Walter dropped his hands. "I'm sorry," he said, shaking his head in confusion. "Line?"

The words burst from Isobel without thinking. "'—be true!'"

Walter gave her a sheepish but grateful smile, and Delphi giggled under her breath, "Well, that was a real Woody Allen moment!"

"'To thine own self be true,'" Isobel repeated quietly.

She was proud that she had correctly remembered a line of Shakespeare. But more than that, she was proud that she had hewn to that advice once before in a difficult situation, and she knew that, despite her friends' warnings, she would not hesitate to do so again.

SIX

Isobel was surprised and secretly pleased to learn that her presence was requested at the mandatory staff meeting the next morning. The accordion wall separating conference rooms B and C had been opened, forming a space just large enough for the sixty or so employees of Dove & Flight Public Relations to squeeze into. That included everyone from Angus Dove and Barnaby Flight down to the back shop staffers who handled mailings, database services and accounting. For Isobel's private purposes, it couldn't have been better.

Armed with a cup of Starbucks' finest, Isobel arrived at the conference room just before ten. Even though the coffee pot had been replaced, she had decided to ingest only outside food and drink until her suspicions were allayed. Those who were already gathered were buzzing quietly, and, for the first time, she realized how many people at the firm she still didn't know. Just as she was pondering how best to meet them all, a lanky, buff man with closely cropped iron-gray hair blocked her path. He wore a baseball jersey, and, improbably for January, Bermuda shorts.

"My fair lady Isobel, melodious songbird, your reputation precedes you," he said, doffing a faded red baseball cap.

Isobel wasn't sure whether to be alarmed or amused. "Not another Shakespearean, are you?"

"Not I, indeed! Jimmy Rocket, at your service. I merely pine, on a daily basis, for the lost, lissome loveliness of the English language."

"Is that your real name?"

He pulled a face. "Sadly, yes. James Earl Rocket. I briefly considered the possibility of Francophilic pronunciation for the latter portion of that unfortunate moniker, but I think it lacks a certain *quelle heure est-il,* don't you?"

Before Isobel could think how to respond, Katrina joined them. "Hey, Jimmy."

Jimmy tipped his cap again. "The ravishing Ms. Campbell! Och, aye, lassie, there's a moose loose aboot the hoose!"

"Jimmy, you get weirder every day. And I've told you, my family is English. Save your burr for Angus."

"Nay, lassie, he'll only consider my burr a slur!"

"Who is he exactly?" Isobel asked Katrina as they found seats.

"Jimmy Rocket. He's a throwback to an era that never actually existed, but Barnaby loves him. Jimmy's his assistant."

"Seriously?"

"Barnaby won't part with him for anything. Jimmy may be eccentric, but I've never seen anyone type as fast as he does. He also has a practically photographic memory, and he's ridiculously organized. In his dreams, he's Babe Ruth. In reality, he wouldn't make it onto a pro baseball team for the same reason he'd better hope Barnaby never sacks him."

"Which is…?"

Katrina leaned over. "He'd never pass the mandatory drug testing."

"Ah," said Isobel. "So, um, how was your interview with the police yesterday?"

"About what you'd expect. What was my relationship with Jason Whiteley, and where was I just before you found him. But it was pretty half-hearted. They seem to think it was natural causes."

"And what do you think?"

Katrina shrugged. "I just hope we don't lose the account."

She turned to greet Liz Stewart, who had joined them, and as Katrina and Liz added their voices to the chattering chorus, Isobel surveyed the room for other faces she recognized.

There was Dorothy Berman, an attractive woman in her late fifties with the kind of gleaming silver hair that Isobel wouldn't mind having someday. Isobel didn't know much about her except that she handled the healthcare clients, and she had a husband who was a lawyer and a son who was a dentist. Although Isobel had done a bit of file drawer cleanup for Dorothy, most of her time at Dove & Flight had been claimed by Aaron, whose financial services team didn't have a junior associate. Dorothy had her own junior, Penny Warren, the sweet-faced girl whose phone Isobel had used to call 911. Isobel and Penny filled the same role, which amounted to a combination of secretarial and basic client work, since only the senior partners had administrative assistants. Within the working groups, everyone was expected to answer his or her own phone, and any menial tasks that needed doing were assigned to the most junior member of the team. Isobel hardly minded, but she wondered if Penny did.

Penny caught Isobel's eye and flashed an eager smile. Isobel leaned over to Katrina.

"Does Penny always wear headbands that match her outfits?"

Katrina smirked. "Sadly."

"Where did she go to school? Lilly Pulitzer U?"

"Holyoke. She transferred from Barnard. I bet they booted her for wardrobe violations." Katrina nudged Isobel. "Here comes trouble."

Isobel followed her gaze and saw Kit Blanchard, another senior associate, take a seat behind Aaron. Petite and stacked, Kit wore stylish outfits that emphasized her figure, still impressive after three kids. Her long highlighted hair was pushed back with a pair of Prada sunglasses, despite the season. It suddenly struck Isobel that Dove & Flight, notwithstanding the men at the top, was predominantly a female operation. As she looked around, she marked a clear two-to-one ratio.

"Why are there so many more women than men?" she asked.

"PR attracts women," said Katrina. "Probably because it's a 'relationship business,' and we all know how good men are at relationships." Katrina inclined her head knowingly. Next to her, Liz snickered.

Isobel turned again and saw an elderly man with beagle jowls leaning against the wall by the door. From behind large square glasses that had surely gone out of style before she was born, his rheumy eyes roved over the assemblage with the same kind of scrutiny to which Isobel was privately subjecting everyone. He wore a dour expression on his heavily lined face and was dressed far more formally than anyone else, in an expensive suit that had seen better days and a red pocket square.

"Who's that guy?"

"Oh, that's Wilbur Freed," Katrina said with a dismissive gesture.

"I've never seen him before," Isobel remarked.

"You wouldn't. He's a first-class lurker. His job is to keep a tight rein on company subscriptions, but mostly he just sneaks around from office to office distributing news clips."

"Why doesn't he just email them?"

"Wilbur doesn't believe in email," Katrina said. "He barely believes in electricity."

"He's a walking anachronism, but he's an old friend of Angus's," Liz added. "Those Scots are nothing if not loyal."

At that moment, Barnaby Flight clomped to the front of the room, with Angus Dove trailing him stoically.

"They're certainly the odd couple, aren't they?" Isobel whispered.

Katrina nodded. "Seriously. I sometimes think the only reason they joined forces is the bird imagery in their names."

"There are two things I want to address today," Barnaby said without preamble. "I won't keep you long, because I know you're busy. At least, you'd better be." The nervous communal giggle seemed to satisfy him, and he continued.

"First, I want to settle what happened yesterday. It was a terribly unfortunate accident, but the police have confirmed that Jason Whiteley died of a heart attack, and that's the end of that. Now, I don't have to tell you how rumors fly—we're in the rumor business, for God's sake—so I ask that you all be discreet. Please resist the temptation to gossip about this with everyone you know." He surveyed his staff. "I'll be frank. It doesn't matter if Whiteley died because he blew his nose too hard—it doesn't look good. And we're about to be all over the news for another reason. We don't need more slop for the pigs."

At this, a hushed murmur ran through the crowd. Barnaby held up his hand to silence it.

"Which brings me to the main reason for this meeting. Angus and I have been in negotiations for some time now with ICG, International Communications Group. I'm sure you know who they are. They own several distinguished companies in a variety of communications fields, including two other PR shops: Fisher Health Strategies and The Peterson Group. ICG is looking to expand its reach into the niche areas we specialize in, and we will be announcing later today that we have entered into an agreement with them. ICG is buying Dove & Flight."

Everybody began talking at once. Barnaby clapped his meaty hands for attention.

"First off, nothing will change."

"Bullshit," Liz Stewart fake-coughed into her hand.

"We will not be eliminating any jobs, and we will not be relocating our offices. At some point during the year, we will merge with The Peterson Group, which specializes in consumer PR. Not our strong suit, as you well know. Our companies will complement each other nicely, and when that secondary merger is finalized, the combined entity will be known as Peterson, Dove & Flight."

The mutterings grew louder, and Barnaby raised his voice this time, instead of his hand.

"We all know that the financial security that comes with being part of a corporate family means giving up the independence of a privately-owned, self-determining shop. But Angus and I are getting older. Angus faster than me." He glanced at his diminutive partner, who stood next to him, silent and tight-lipped. "We built this business on the strength of our names and reputations, and we want what we've built to outlast us. Our legacy and, to be blunt, your employment depend on this merger. Angus and I are very excited about what this means for us and for you."

Isobel looked at Angus, who looked anything but excited.

Liz leaned across Katrina and said, "I'm just shocked that they bothered to tell us, rather than letting us read about it in the papers. Communications experts are terrible at internal communications. It's like the cobbler's kids going barefoot. Right?"

Katrina was sitting rigidly in her seat between them, staring straight ahead.

Isobel nudged her. "Katrina?"

Katrina shook her head slowly. "I can't believe he didn't tell me. How could he not have told me?"

"Come on, we all know Barnaby has a thing for you, but he wasn't going to tell you before the rest of us," Liz said.

"Not Barnaby. My dad," Katrina said in a hollow voice. "ICG is my dad's company. He's the CEO. I'm going to be working for my father."

"WHAT THE HELL DO *YOU* WANT?"

James didn't have a good answer for that. He had felt compelled to call Jayla, his ex-girlfriend, at her office at Schumann, Crowe & Dyer, but now that she was barking in his ear on the other end of the phone, he wasn't exactly sure why.

"I, um, heard about Jason Whiteley and wanted to make sure you were okay."

"Why wouldn't I be?"

Compassionate as ever, thought James.

"I thought you might be upset."

"I liked Jason," Jayla admitted. "He was an aggressive, horny little bastard, but he was always decent to me."

"They say it was a heart attack," James said.

There was silence on the other end of the phone. Then Jayla asked, "How do you even know about this?"

He paused. "We have a temp at your PR firm."

"It's that little white bitch you're hot for," Jayla snarled.

"How many times do I have to tell you, there is absolutely nothing going on between us!"

"Mmm hmmmm," crowed Jayla.

From the first, Jayla had willfully misinterpreted his interest in Isobel. Besides, he had sworn off women altogether when they broke up, largely because he was still working on being sober.

"I was wondering…was he sick or anything?" James asked.

"Jason? I don't think so. He seemed perfectly healthy to me."

"Did he still drink a lot? Do you know if he did drugs?"

"What is this, a police inquiry?" Jayla snapped. "And why are you calling me, anyway? I thought we weren't speaking."

"How's Michael? You still seeing him?" James asked, trying to keep her on the line.

"None of your goddamn business," she shot back.

James had walked in on one of his best buddies hard at work between Jayla's legs, and that had been the last straw. He hadn't spoken to either of them since. Until now.

"Right. Okay. Forget I called. I just thought maybe somebody killed Jason."

"Yeah. Wait—what?!"

He smiled. That had certainly gotten her attention.

"Like you said, he seemed healthy. Unless it was the booze."

"Oh, I get it. You're worried the same thing might happen to you," Jayla said shrewdly.

James ignored the bait. "Do you know anyone who had it in for him?"

There was silence on the other end of the line.

"Only you, baby," Jayla said finally.

He should never have told her about getting kicked out of Columbia and Jason getting off scot-free. It was just like Jayla to file away a piece of information like that to use against him when the moment presented itself.

"Anyone else? Anyone at work?"

"Not everyone liked Jason. But not everyone likes you either, James."

"We're not talking about me."

"Oh, my mistake," she said sweetly. "I didn't realize there was another topic."

"Come on, Jayla!"

Jayla let out a long, frustrated exhalation, and James could imagine her resting her head in her hands, her beautiful long dreadlocks falling in front of her face and brushing against her luxurious eyelashes.

"I'm sure there were people who had it in for Jason, but it was cardiac arrest, right? So why are you asking me?"

Because Isobel put a bug in my ear, that's why.

"Don't you think it's a little weird for someone our age to have a heart attack?" he pressed.

"Maybe he was born with a heart defect. What do you care, anyway?"

He had no good answer for that. Jayla was feeding him the same arguments he had given Isobel when she had raised these questions.

"You know what's wrong with you, Jayla? You've got no compassion or curiosity."

He could hear her cursing as she slammed down the phone.

James paced to his door and opened it. He contemplated getting another Coke from the office fridge, but decided against it. He'd already polished off two in the past hour.

What a hypocrite, he berated himself. Here I made Isobel promise not to nose around asking questions, and what am I doing? Exactly what I told her not to do.

Then again, he thought as he gave in and made his way down the narrow hall to the kitchenette, knowing Isobel, she had probably found a way around her promise by now.

SEVEN

NOBODY AT DOVE & FLIGHT WAS GETTING any work done. The combination of a death on the premises and a merger announcement had pretty much guaranteed what Katrina usually referred to as a "spa day." The atmosphere put Isobel in mind of a backstage farce, with everybody ducking in and out of each other's offices, spreading rumors, making predictions, and repeating the same conversations over and over, embellishing the details with each retelling.

The only person not participating was Katrina herself. She had taken an early lunch right after the staff meeting, and by two o'clock she still hadn't returned. After bopping past several open doors where she didn't quite feel comfortable dropping in for a chat, Isobel alighted in Liz Stewart's office. Liz had her feet up on her desk and was sipping milk out of a small carton.

"This is my post-lunch lunch," she explained. "I'm trying for the 'six small meals a day thing,' only it's turning into six large meals." She held up a packet of crackers. "I'm attempting to cut meals two and four down to size."

"Do you know what you're having?" Isobel asked.

"Mmmm…girl," Liz mumbled through a mouthful of crackers.

"Do you have a name picked out yet?"

Liz swallowed. "My husband wants Olivia, but we'll have to save that for number two." She touched her belly gently. "She's going to be Eleanor, after my sister."

"That's a lovely name," Isobel said. "What happened to your—"

A sharp knock on the wall behind Liz's chair made Isobel start. "I never noticed there was a door there!"

Liz's lip curled. "Only one person ever uses it. Wanna guess who?" She wheeled her chair to the side and opened it to Jimmy Rocket, who was holding out a blue plastic bin.

"Stick out your can, mama. Here comes yo' back door man!"

Liz laughed and reached under her desk for the wastepaper basket. She dumped the contents into Jimmy's bin.

"For the shredder," Liz explained over her shoulder.

"As you were!" Jimmy saluted with his free hand and pulled the door shut behind him.

Isobel shook her head. "I just can't get over him. Why do you have two doors, anyway?"

Liz rearranged her chair and swung her legs back onto the desk. "Only the group heads get windows. The more junior you are, the farther away you are from any source of natural light. But you're also closer to the bathroom, which for me in my current predicament is eminently preferable. The second door is just a bonus."

"Where does it come out?"

"By the kitchen." Liz winked and held out her crackers.

Isobel accepted the offering. "So what's really behind this merger? Is it what Barnaby said?"

Liz nodded as she crunched. "Probably. I mean, at his age, the thrill of living from retainer check to retainer check has to be long gone. He wants to play with the big boys, and ICG can hand him the kind of Fortune 500 companies he's spent his whole career chasing. This is his last chance to kick it up a level before he retires."

"What about Angus?"

"My guess is Angus would be just as happy to leave his nameplate on the door until it can be buried with him."

Isobel pulled her ponytail tighter and leaned forward. "Can I ask you something?"

"Sure."

"Why were you guys nervous about meeting with Jason Whiteley yesterday?"

Liz frowned. "Who said we were nervous?"

"Katrina."

Liz swung her legs off the desk, knocking her crackers to the floor in the process. She ducked down to collect them, and when she sat up again, Isobel had the distinct impression that Liz had been gathering her thoughts as well as her snack.

"There was a little dust-up a few weeks ago, and this was our first meeting since then. We weren't sure what Jason was going to say." Liz chuckled as if it were all no big deal. "We were half convinced he was going to fire us. Or at the very least, slash our retainer."

"What happened?"

Liz's expression darkened. "It was really Aaron's fault, although he'll never admit it. We pitched an important new exec of theirs named Cal Erskine as a spokesperson on Brazil. You know, consulting in an emerging market. Turns out Erskine has experience in emerging markets, but he's never set foot in Brazil. Not only that, Schumann, Crowe & Dyer doesn't have a single office anywhere in South America."

Isobel grimaced. "That's not good."

"Gets worse. John Fothergill, the São Paulo bureau chief of *The Wall Street Journal*, interviewed Erskine, and the story we were hoping for turned into a slash-and-burn piece on the company for putting themselves forward as experts in Brazil when their guy couldn't even name the capital."

"Ouch! What was the fallout?"

"Well, that's what we were going to find out yesterday. The thing is, it wasn't just that Fothergill made the company look bad—he tore apart Erskine personally."

"Why was it Aaron's fault?"

Liz flourished her milk carton. "Because I asked him point-blank what specific experience the guy had in Brazil. He admitted that he had none, but insisted it didn't matter. He said emerging markets are emerging markets, and it's transferable knowledge. He basically gave me the old, 'the client's signed off on it, so just do your job and don't ask questions, you silly girl' routine."

"I gather Aaron doesn't care much for working women," Isobel observed. "Against his religion?"

"I imagine that's part of it, but he's also ambitious, and his family and religious obligations make it harder to climb the old corporate ladder. They finally made him a senior associate, but how much farther can he reasonably go? He can't be a director if he isn't willing to stay late at the drop of a hat for deal work."

"But what does that have to do with women?"

"He's jealous of anyone who's unencumbered, and if it's a woman, it's adding insult to injury. Someone like Katrina can leave him in the dust. He can tolerate me a little better, because I've got my own automatic glass ceiling."

"How so?"

Liz gestured to her belly. "I don't have a wife at home to take care of Eleanor when she arrives. When I factor in childcare, it doesn't make sense for me to work, since I'll never advance to the salary that would make it worthwhile. The difference is, I'm not bitter about it."

Isobel absorbed all of this. "So Jason Whiteley was going to throw you all under the bus at the meeting yesterday?"

Liz nodded. "In all likelihood. That's why Katrina was dreading it."

"Why Katrina?"

Liz took a deep breath. "She was the one who sent Fothergill the Brazil pitch. Fothergill wrote back something like, 'I think the fact that Schumann, Crowe & Dyer consider themselves experts in Brazil would make a great story.' If you read between the lines, you can tell he'd sniffed out their lack of expertise and wanted to expose them. A more experienced eye would have caught on to what he was planning, but Katrina didn't pick up on it."

"That's pretty subtle. I'm sure anyone would have missed that."

"Maybe yes, maybe no. Point is, she had a chance to nip it in the bud, and she didn't."

"And Jason is dead," Isobel mused. "So now what?"

Liz shrugged. "Who knows? Maybe we'll lose the account, maybe we won't. I suspect we won't."

"Why not?"

"Because Schumann, Crowe & Dyer is also owned by ICG. We're going to be sister companies."

Curiouser and curiouser, thought Isobel, as she left Liz to her milk and crackers and wandered back to her desk to pretend to update a press list. A merger, a heart attack, a little bad publicity…

There was definitely more going on at Dove & Flight than met the eye, and Isobel was more determined than ever to figure out what.

EIGHT

"So, who was it?"

It didn't occur to James that the voice was addressing him, so he ignored it, continuing to grunt and sweat as he heaved the barbell high over his head.

"You don't answer your phone, and you don't answer live people, either!"

James let the barbell drop. It took a moment for his eyes to focus on Weight Girl, who was standing in front of him, her hands on her straight, shapeless hips.

"I thought I heard a mosquito buzzing."

She smiled triumphantly. "So you do speak English. I just wanted to know who kept calling you yesterday."

He wiped his hands on his shorts. "None of your business."

"I know. I was just curious. It seemed important."

"How do you know what it seemed?" he asked, annoyed. "It was a ringing phone."

"Well, you don't have to be an asshole about it."

James started another set of reps, willing her to go away, but she remained by his feet, regarding him with an expression that was either hurt or amused, possibly both.

He hauled himself off the bench and mopped the sweat from his brow. "What are you doing here anyway?"

"Isn't that a little racist?" she asked snidely.

"Look, I grew up in this neighborhood and I'm telling you, you're the minority. I'm not saying there are no white people up here, but if they're here, they're here for a reason." He snapped his towel for emphasis.

"I'm at Barnard."

"So why don't you use their gym?"

Her eyes darted to her feet and she shrugged. "It's never open when I need it. Besides, I'm not really all that comfortable there."

"Why's that?"

She looked up again. "Don't take this the wrong way, okay? But sometimes I feel like a token."

He raised a skeptical eyebrow. "At Barnard? But not here?"

She crossed her arms and her expression changed. "My folks are dead and my aunt raised me on welfare. I got a full scholarship to school. I don't exactly fit in."

So being poor was her sin. Being from the 'hood had been his.

"Aren't you going to ask me what year I'm in, what I'm majoring in, and all that?" she asked, when he didn't respond.

"I figure you'll get to it eventually."

To his surprise, she didn't volunteer the information. "What do you do?" she asked.

"Work out. When people let me."

"I just wanted to make sure you were okay."

James thumped his barrel chest. "Don't I look okay?"

"Like I said the other day, your abs need work." She prodded him in the stomach and he doubled over reflexively at her touch.

Fuming, he watched her stalk off toward a cluster of guys who greeted her far more enthusiastically than she deserved. He reached for his barbell again, but he was suddenly weary. As he passed Weight Girl on his way to the locker room, he overheard her chattering at a studious-looking man with medium-dark skin.

"My girlfriends and I, when we were, like, twelve, we used to sit around and imagine what kind of guys we'd marry, and which of us would marry first, and then the rest of us and in what order."

"This is a gym, not a pick-up joint," James snapped.

His shower failed to relieve his grouchy mood, so he tried to resign himself to feeling unsettled—a new lesson of sobriety—as he headed toward the community center where he attended AA meetings. It was on Broadway and 120th Street, not far from his old stomping ground. Having abandoned his workout early, he had a few minutes to kill, so he headed four blocks south to the Columbia campus. He paused outside the main gate and peered in at College Walk, which was bustling with early evening activity.

Students hurried by in small groups or by themselves, and James was suddenly aware of a deep, gnawing sadness. He had been given a golden opportunity—a top education on a football scholarship—and he'd blown it because of the booze. He had planned to be a lawyer. He'd wanted to go back to his old Harlem neighborhood and hang out a shingle at affordable prices. An alternative to Legal Aid: the personal touch, from a brother who could have gone anywhere, but had chosen to come home. Now he was bouncing from temp agency to temp agency, although he'd held on at Temp Zone for four months, a record for him. He knew it still wasn't too late to go back to college and then on to law school. His dream may have been deferred, but it wasn't an impossible one. He watched a student stumble over a flagstone and drop a stack of books. The thought of racking up student loans as a twenty-eight-year-old sophomore made James feel more like a failure than ever. He pushed aside his fantasy of college and trudged on toward his meeting.

The blue and white linoleum floor of the community center common room was marked with oily black streaks where chairs had been dragged into a circle. James spotted his sponsor, Bill, a slender, wispy-haired man whose sad eyes looked sadder than usual. James sat down next to him and patted him on the back.

"Hey, man. You okay?"

Bill gave a strained smile. "Had the kids this weekend. Tough to let 'em go."

James nodded. There wasn't much to say. Bill was divorced, and his wife had fought visitation until he agreed to go to AA. It was impossible to make up for lost time, although Bill tried hard. Probably too hard. After every visit, he was plunged into fresh despair that tested his sobriety.

"What's up with you?" Bill was always happier to talk about James's problems than his own.

"Too many aggravating females," he said, thinking of Jayla, Isobel and Weight Girl. "Shit! Here comes another."

Felice Edwards, a plump, curvaceous woman who twisted her hair into a different, Escher-like pattern every month, was making a beeline for James. Felice had been the head of Human Resources at Isobel's first temp job—the bank where the secretary was killed. James had taken her out on two disastrous occasions and then coerced her into AA. Despite his protestations, Felice continued to believe he had an ulterior motive in getting her sober.

"James!"

"Hello, Felice," James said, as coolly as possible. "Would you excuse us? We're having a private conversation."

Her smile faded. "I just wanted to tell you I got a new job."

"Good for you."

Felice scowled. "You'd better be nice to me, or I'll use another temp agency when I need help."

It was easy to ignore Felice, but harder to turn his back on the finder's fee that came with reeling in a new client.

He threw up his hands and shot Bill a glance of mock helplessness. "All right, you got me. So where is it you've landed now?"

"I'm working for the city. Office of the—"

Before she could finish, the day's chairperson, a heavy-set Hispanic man in his thirties, stood and called the meeting to order.

"I'll call you," Felice whispered. She crept away and joined the clutch of women she usually sat with.

Great, thought James. Snagged again.

As he listened half-heartedly to the others relate their daily struggles against alcohol, he wondered, not for the first time, what it was about him that attracted these uppity women who thought they knew what was best for him. They were all so goddamn smug and superior, and they didn't know him at all. And yet they somehow managed to get him to do things he didn't want to do. Felice had made it impossible for him to ignore her next phone call, Weight Girl's nosiness had cut his workout short, and Jayla had nearly roped him into a marriage he didn't want.

Then there was Isobel. She got him to do things without even having to ask, which made her far and away the most exasperating of them all.

NINE

ONE OF THE FIRST LESSONS ISOBEL had learned after moving to New York was that if you don't show up three hours before an audition starts, you don't get in, which meant that for an audition scheduled to begin at ten o'clock in the morning, the desired arrival hour became an ungodly one. In the winter, with a reluctant sun and sub-zero temperatures, the ritual became nothing less than torturous, especially when the audition studio was still locked.

Nevertheless, Isobel bounded out of bed at six thirty the next morning primed for adventure. This was no ordinary audition she was heading for today: it was an Equity audition. A Broadway audition.

The notice had appeared in *Backstage* the week before, announcing an open call for replacement principals in *Phantom of the Opera*. With her classically trained soprano and innocent ingénue looks, Isobel knew she was perfect for the role of Christine, the Phantom's paramour. No matter that she wasn't yet a card-carrying member of Actors' Equity, *Phantom* had been running on Broadway for so many years that Isobel was confident most eligible union members had presented themselves and been passed over, leaving room for her to wangle her way in. Even so, she knew she'd have to wait awhile for a break in the traffic. She had planned ahead, arranging with James to send someone to fill in for her at Dove & Flight for the day.

Isobel tried to maintain her excitement and energy as she made her way uptown in the freezing predawn to the Actors'

Equity building on West 46th Street. Sure enough, by the time she arrived, there were fifteen hardy souls ahead of her. She took her place in line, grabbing the last tiny square foot of space inside the vestibule, knowing it wouldn't be long before the line snaked out the door and down the street.

"I'm non-Equity," she whispered confidentially to the woman in front of her. "Do you think I'll get seen?"

The woman stared blearily at her. "Go home."

When the building opened at eight o'clock, the line surged inside and rearranged itself on the stairwell. Isobel spent the next hour trying to fight off fatigue by running through all her audition songs in her head. Finally, at nine o'clock, the Equity lounge on the second floor opened up. One by one, the actors filed past a squat old broad with a shellacked boot-black beehive and rhinestone-studded glasses, who was guarding the entrance to the lounge at a small podium.

She stopped Isobel with a wizened hand dripping with cocktail rings. "Card?"

"I don't have one," Isobel said, "but I was hoping I could get into the *Phantom* audition if it isn't too crowded."

The woman indicated two metal folding chairs at the top of the stairwell. "You can wait there."

"Can't I wait in the lounge?" Isobel looked longingly at the rows of padded chairs and the bulletin boards dripping with casting notices.

"Not without an Equity card." The monitor nodded admittance to several actors who brushed past Isobel disdainfully.

"Do you think I'll get seen?" Isobel asked, for the second time that morning.

"They gotta see every Equity actor who signs up. If that happens before five o'clock, they might see you if they feel like it. But they don't have to."

"But they have to stay until five, don't they?"

"Yeah, but they can sit in the room and pick their noses if they want. This is a union audition. They don't have to see you."

The woman adjusted her gaudy glasses and turned her attention to the next several people, who flashed their colorful ID cards with the identifying masks of comedy and tragedy. Isobel eyed the procession of little cards with envy. Getting into Actors' Equity was a notorious Catch-22: you had to have a union card to get into a union audition, but the only way to get a union card was by getting a union job. Still, there must be some way to go about it. Presumably, the actors walking proudly by her were not born with Equity cards tucked under their umbilical cords.

Realizing she had little choice, Isobel made herself as comfortable as possible on her metal chair and watched the procession continue. After a while, having reassured herself that she knew every verse of every song she'd ever sung for anyone, she settled for people-watching. As eleven o'clock approached, she felt her energy sag. She needed a snack, lunch even. After all, she'd been up since six thirty, and she'd long since finished the one granola bar she'd brought. But she was loath to leave her post, lest her moment come and go. She approached the monitor.

"How are they doing? Do you think I might get seen?"

The woman looked over her shoulder at the lounge, which was mobbed with shiny-faced actors in various states of readiness and repose.

"Nah."

Isobel began to question her chances of success if she couldn't even get into the approved waiting area, but she couldn't bear to give up. She decided a break wouldn't hurt, so she went downstairs to the McDonald's in the building lobby and ate a Big Mac Meal, after which she felt nauseated and even more depleted than before, despite a large Coke.

As the day wore on, it occurred to Isobel that there was probably a good reason why she was the only non-union actor wasting a day in the chilly hallway of the Equity building. But she was different, she reminded herself. She was right for this show, right for this role.

And after all that Coke, she desperately needed a bathroom.

She approached the monitor, who was herself wilting by this point. "I need to use the bathroom."

The woman shook her head.

"Oh, come on!" Isobel protested.

"Use the one in McDonald's."

"It's out of order," Isobel lied as she wiggled back and forth. "Please! I've been sitting here all day."

For no reason that Isobel could explain, the old woman took pity on her. Or maybe she just didn't want to clean up a mess. In any case, she closed her eyes as if hiding her lapse from herself and waved Isobel into the inner sanctum.

Isobel ran straight to the bathroom. Two young women were standing at the sink, refreshing their makeup.

"Jake Lyons won't call me in for anything anymore because I crashed an audition of his once. Didn't matter that I wound up being the director's second choice, he still thinks I'm a pushy bitch," said a pretty, trim redhead.

"You *are* a pushy bitch!" Her friend laughed. "But he's an asshole. He thinks I'm too ethnic for anything that doesn't take place in the shtetl." She glared in the mirror at her long, dark curly hair and prominent nose. "God, I hate casting directors!"

After using the bathroom, Isobel returned to the lounge, trying not to be further discouraged by their talk. Superimposing her brightest smile over her tired features, she approached the supervisor of the *Phantom* auditions, a fey young man who wore his sense of importance as flamboyantly as he did his neon orange sweater vest.

"I'm not Equity, but I was hoping I could sneak in if there's a break in the traffic," she said.

He pursed his lips. "There are one hundred and seventy-four people signed up, including alternates."

"I don't mind waiting," Isobel said airily. "I've been waiting all day."

He leaned forward, his elbows on the desk. "One hundred and seventy-four," he repeated in a nasal whine.

Isobel swallowed. "Can I just wait?"

He looked her up and down and shook his head in disgust. "Suit yourself."

Isobel had no intention of leaving the lounge now that she'd breached the gate, so she made herself comfortable on a seat by the window and watched. Every twenty minutes, the audition supervisor called more people to line up, keeping things moving in a calm, orderly fashion. Every time he called a name that wasn't answered, he put an alternate on the line. A plan began to form in Isobel's mind.

At twenty minutes before five, the audition supervisor rose. "Listen up! Last group of the day."

Isobel darted out of view into the small hallway that led to the women's dressing room and waited. In what appeared to be his last act of authority for the day, the supervisor added three alternates. Then he packed up his belongings and left the lounge past the podium, which the old rhinestoned broad had finally abandoned. Isobel ducked into the dressing room, refreshed her makeup as best she could and hummed a bit to warm up her voice. She couldn't believe she'd been awake since before dawn. There was nothing more enervating than waiting, and she could only hope that her fatigue might have a relaxing effect on her voice.

When she finally emerged from the dressing room, there were only two people left in line outside the audition studio. They both held small white information cards with their résumés. Isobel didn't have a card, and suddenly she was more nervous about whether or not her little trick would work than whether she'd sing well.

At last, the final auditioner, a middle-aged black woman, emerged from the audition studio. She stopped when she saw Isobel hovering in the doorway.

The woman shook her head, confused. "I thought I was last."

"I've been waiting all day to get seen. I'm not Equity," Isobel said.

The woman's features broke into a wide grin and she held the door open. "You go, girl!"

Isobel strode into the room feigning more confidence than she felt, her heart pounding. The casting director and his assistant were packing up, collating stacks of white cards and résumés, and the accompanist, a good-looking, dark-haired young man with wire-rimmed glasses, was closing the piano lid.

"Hi, I'm Isobel Spice!" she said brightly. They all paused in their tasks and looked at her, startled.

"We're done for the day. Come back tomorrow," said the casting director, a gray-haired, pear-shaped man.

"I'm actually non-Equity, and I've been waiting all day to get in," Isobel said, trying to make it sound as if this were a perfectly fine way to pass the time.

"You should be going to non-Equity auditions then," said his assistant, a sharp-featured young woman with straight black hair and a cleft chin.

"I promise you, it's worth your time to hear me. I'm a classically trained soprano, and I'm perfect for Christine." She marched over to the piano and threw her music down. "I'll tell you what," she continued, with false heartiness. "I'll sing while you clean up. Let me entertain you!"

She laughed too loudly, and when she got no response, she looked imploringly at the pianist, who was watching her with a bemused expression on his face. He opened the piano lid, sat down, and played the introduction of her song. Isobel shot him a grateful look, then started on cue. It was hardly her best, but it wasn't as bad as it might have been, given the circumstances. Still singing, she walked over to the casting director and handed him her résumé.

He put it in his briefcase without a glance. "Okay, thanks," he said and left, followed by his assistant.

"*That is the love that's pure,*" Isobel sang to the empty room. "*That is the love—the love that's true.*"

Isobel faced her reflection in the floor-to-ceiling mirror. Her skirt was rumpled, her ponytail askew, and she looked as miserable as she felt. She caught the pianist's eye behind her in the mirror, and he smiled at her. She swallowed hard to keep from bursting into tears.

"You actually got a longer hearing than most, you know," he said. He had a lovely posh British accent.

"Thanks." Shaking with a combination of relief and disappointment, Isobel reached for her music.

"Here, I'll get that." He closed her binder, thick with music, and handed it to her. "Most people, if they think of Gilbert and Sullivan at all, choose from a better-known operetta than *Patience*."

"I was practically weaned on G&S. It suits me. Although that wasn't my best performance," she said ruefully.

"Even if it were, you'd have been casting pearls before swine. I hate to break it to you, but they're not really looking. This is what's known as a required call. Producers must hold them every six months to appear to give every union member a chance."

Isobel stared sullenly at her binder. "I'm not sure if that makes me feel better or worse."

"Well, I think it was cheeky of you to crash the party. I'd like to hear you sometime when you haven't been sitting around wilting all day."

Isobel felt her spirits lift. "You would?"

He pulled a card from his wallet. "Here. May I have yours?"

"I don't have one. But I could write down my name for you."

"Did you bring another résumé? You should always carry extras, you know."

Isobel brightened. "Of course!" She pulled another picture and résumé from her bag and handed it to him.

"Lovely. And the Scottish spelling of Isobel. My mum is Scots." He held out his hand. "Nice to meet you, Isobel Spice. I've got to run, but I'll be in touch." They shook hands, and then he was gone. She glanced down at his card.

Hugh Fremont. Pianist/Conductor/Composer.

She hoped he would call her, although she suspected he was only being polite, like any self-respecting Englishman. Nevertheless, she was enormously grateful to him. His smile and kind gesture were the only things that kept the day from being a total loss.

TEN

"Dove & Flight, this is Mike."

James had no trouble picturing the man on the other end of the phone. Mike Hardy, the short, squat, blond Human Resources director at Dove & Flight reminded James of a rook on a chessboard. Ginger Wainwright had been so eager to win Dove & Flight's business that James had gone out of his way to woo Hardy via several alcohol-avoidant lunches. And what had it yielded? Another dead body on Isobel's hands.

"Mike, it's James Cooke. How's it going?"

"Well, it's been a bit hectic around here, what with the merger and all. Not to mention…well, the merger and all."

"I just wanted to see how Sharon Press made out today in Isobel's place."

"No complaints."

As far as James was concerned, no complaints equaled a thumbs-up. "Glad to hear it. And you're happy with Isobel?"

"From what I hear, she fits right in," Hardy said.

"Good, good. Yeah." James rolled a pencil between his fingers and pondered the pattern of bite marks. "Isobel told me about Jason Whiteley."

"Natural causes," Hardy said briskly. "Nothing to do with us."

"Of course not," James said. "Then again, that's what I'd expect from a PR person." His laugh echoed emptily over the receiver.

"It was accidental," Hardy insisted.

"Of course," said James, backtracking. "I guess I watch too

much crime drama on TV."

"It was a heart attack, pure and simple." Hardy's voice seemed to be growing tenser, and James wondered which of them he was trying to convince.

"Well, I just wanted to check on Sharon. If Isobel has to take any other days off, I'll try to get her to cover."

"Thanks."

"And you still want Isobel coming in?"

"Her group really likes having her, and they can use the help," said Hardy.

"Great," James said. "Assuming she's okay with it, Isobel can stay as long as you need her."

He replaced the receiver and pushed his chair away, irked with himself for continuing to ask questions about Jason. It was ridiculous. He had to stop feigning excuses for these conversations.

"Enough!" he said loudly to his empty office.

Anna poked her head through the open door. "I completely agree! Let's go get some coffee or something."

James smiled. He liked Anna's irreverence. She made no bones about her position at Temp Zone being a stopgap until sales of her artwork reached critical mass. He also admired her disdain for Ginger, which revealed itself whenever their overpowdered, underdressed boss was out of sight.

"We only have a few more days of freedom before Madame Mona comes back from vacation," Anna said.

"Who?"

"The madam in *Best Little Whorehouse in Texas*. It was a movie with Dolly Parton years ago. Okay, I just dated myself."

"Better than dating me," quipped James.

Anna laughed. "You are very silly sometimes, you know that? It's cute."

James had a sudden flash of what it might be like to date a mature woman like Anna. Someone who wasn't a steamroller, who had a good head on her shoulders, and healthy self-esteem.

"I swear, sometimes I feel like Ginger's whore," she said.

Then again, maybe not, James thought, as he pulled on his extra large duffel coat. The phone rang. He glanced down at the caller ID. It wasn't a number he recognized.

"Hang on," he said to Anna. "Temp Zone, James Cooke speaking."

"We never got to finish our little chat the other day," breathed a husky female voice.

James sighed and rolled his eyes at Anna. "Felice. I can't talk right now, I'm just heading out."

"Then call me back," she said and rattled off a number, which he scribbled down. "I'm at the Office of the City Medical Examiner."

"Right," he said absently. Then his brain did a double take. "Hang on—the office of the what?"

"The City Medical Examiner. We need temps over here just like anyone else, so don't blow me off, James, or I'll go to Temporama."

James put his hand over the mouthpiece and said to Anna, "It's a new contract. Give me a few?"

She nodded and left him alone. James shrugged off his coat and sat down again. This was an omen he couldn't ignore.

"No kidding. That must be interesting."

"Nah," said Felice. "Same shit, different office."

"Well, what do you need? Anything immediate?" he asked hopefully.

"That's why I'm calling. I need someone tomorrow. Who've you got?"

"Isobel's free," James said nonchalantly.

Felice didn't respond.

Great, thought James. Another one who's jealous of nothing.

"Come on, you want someone good for your first placement, right?"

Felice sighed. "If she's who you've got, I guess I'll take her."

"She's who I've got," James said firmly.

"All right. I need her all day."

James pulled out a fresh employment application and took down the details.

"So, can we get together for dinner sometime?" Felice asked.

He kept scribbling as he answered, "I've told you. I'm not looking for a relationship right now."

"Um, did I say 'let's get together for a relationship?'"

"Then why do you want to have dinner?"

Her voice took on an extra layer of silk. "Because I like you. And I just gave you a new contract, so you owe me."

James set down his pen and took a deep breath. "Friendship doesn't operate that way. Neither does work. So thanks for the contract, and I'll be in touch."

And before she could protest, he hung up.

That was progress. He had just steamrolled a steamroller.

He glanced down at the employment form. Mike Hardy had given Sharon Press his stamp of approval. She could go back to Dove & Flight tomorrow, and Isobel could go to the Office of the City Medical Examiner, where she could snoop for information about Jason Whiteley to her heart's content. As for him, he was finished making inquiries. He'd done his part. Anything more was up to her.

"Anna?" he called out, grabbing his coat. "Let's go get that coffee!"

ELEVEN

ISOBEL FINISHED THE TALE OF HER wasted day at the *Phantom* auditions and looked expectantly at her friend, Sunil Kapany. They were sitting together at the bar at Vino Rosso where Delphi waited tables, enjoying the best wine they could afford with her employee discount.

"Well, I'm glad I didn't go with you," Sunil said.

"You don't need to. You have an agent now," Isobel reminded him.

Sunil took a sip of pinot noir and brushed his dark, wavy hair off his forehead. "Fat lot of good that's doing me. All he sends me out for are terrorists and deliverymen."

"Since when do terrorists and deliverymen sing?"

Sunil swirled the wine in his glass moodily. "They don't. He seems to have completely forgotten that he discovered me playing the lead in a musical."

Isobel looked down at the pretzels arrayed on her cocktail napkin. She never quite knew what to say when Sunil discussed the difficulty of his ethnicity. He had a gorgeous, rich tenor voice, but he was so obviously of Indian descent that his looks kept him from getting roles that would really showcase his talent. Isobel never felt more oppressively All-American than when she was discussing casting with Sunil.

"When is non-traditional casting going to work for *me*?" Sunil addressed the bottles behind the bar dramatically.

"You did just play Noah in *Two by Two*. That was non-traditional."

Sunil gave her a look. "They cast a Jew to play a Jew. How non-traditional is that?"

"Yes," said Isobel, "but remember, they didn't know you were Jewish when they cast you. They only knew you were Indian."

"Indian Jews: the lost tribe," said Sunil, toasting her. "Can't beat the food."

"Have you told your agent you want to be seen for musicals?"

"He says 'I know, I know,' and continues to send me out for third-world roles." His voice grew pained. "Can you imagine what my mother would say if I played an Arab terrorist? She'd plotz!"

Isobel couldn't help but laugh. "What about opera?" she said, growing serious. "You've got the chops. And they're not as hung up on appearances."

"I wish I liked it better," Sunil said ruefully. "Of course, my dad would love nothing more than for me to follow in his footsteps and be a cantor." He shook his head vigorously. "No way."

Delphi appeared out of nowhere and plopped onto a bar stool next to Isobel.

"'I had rather heat my liver with drinking.'"

"What are you talking about?" asked Sunil. He turned to Isobel. "What is she talking about?"

"*Antony and Cleopatra*, darling," Delphi answered. "So much classier than 'I need a drink.'"

"But not quite to the point," Sunil said. "I have to say, this Shakespeare quoting thing is getting really tiresome."

Delphi sniffed haughtily. "'I wonder that you will still be talking: nobody marks you.'" She turned back to Isobel. "So what did you want to tell me?"

"I'm not going back to Dove & Flight tomorrow."

"Good!"

"James is sending me to the Office of the City Medical Examiner."

Delphi gasped. "What? No! Why?"

"They happen to need someone tomorrow."

"What are you up to?" Sunil asked.

"Nothing." Isobel gave his hand a reassuring pat. "James is just doing this to shut me up. He knows I'm not convinced that Jason Whiteley died of natural causes, and when this came up, he figured it might be a chance for me find out for sure."

"And how exactly are you going to get that information?" Delphi asked.

"I have to check out the lay of the land first. But I'm sure I'll find a way."

"I'm sure you will," said Delphi. "That's what worries me."

"And what will you do when you find out that it was a good, old-fashioned heart attack?" asked Sunil, with a sideways glance at Delphi.

"I'll forget all about it and go back to my job at Dove & Flight until they hire someone permanent to replace me."

"And if you find out something different?"

Isobel shrugged. "I'll go back to my job at Dove & Flight until they hire someone permanent to replace me."

Delphi turned to Sunil. "Notice how she left out the 'I'll forget all about it' part that time?"

He raised an eyebrow at her. "'What, my dear Lady Disdain, are you yet living?'"

"Cute," said Delphi.

"Come on, aren't you impressed?" he cried. "But don't stray further than *Much Ado*. It's the only one I've done."

Delphi turned back to Isobel. "You're still going to forget about it, right?"

"Oh, eventually," said Isobel breezily.

"Isobel!" Delphi smacked the bar with her fist. "You got lucky once, but you might not be so lucky a second time!"

Isobel swiveled her bar stool to face Delphi. "Jason Whiteley wasn't shot, he wasn't knifed, he wasn't bludgeoned. If it turns out to be homicide, it had to have been poison. And if it was, guess who probably served it to him. You have to agree that it's a good idea for me to stay one step ahead of the police. Just in case."

"But why would they tell the PR firm it was accidental if it wasn't?" Delphi asked.

"Maybe to keep people from poking their noses into it."

"Nice to see that's working," Sunil said wryly.

Isobel sipped her wine. "Beyond the inherent improbability of a healthy young man having a heart attack, James says Jason Whiteley wasn't universally liked."

"Why?" Delphi asked.

Isobel thought back to her conversation with James and the unflattering details he had revealed about his own past.

"I can't really go into it, but their paths have crossed a few times. James says the guy was a first-class jerk."

"And you trust James?" Sunil asked.

Without giving it a second thought, Isobel nodded heartily. "Absolutely. I trust James completely."

TWELVE

ISOBEL COULDN'T HELP FEELING THAT Felice Edwards wasn't exactly happy to see her. Then again, Isobel had last seen Felice passed out drunk in the hottest club in town, in front of several of her colleagues and a famous movie director. Or, at least, it *had* been the hottest club in town at the time. Like most establishments of that nature, its fifteen minutes of fame had expired right on time, and Xavier's was now frequented only by the perennially uncool playing catch-up. Although Isobel had successfully unmasked a murderer that night, she doubted Felice remembered their club date with equal fondness. Now that they were face to face again, Felice's unwillingness to look Isobel in the eye made it clear that James had pushed for her to be there.

"It's nice to see you again," Isobel said, trying to inject extra warmth into her voice.

"Yeah, okay. You're in records. Fifth floor." Felice twisted a lock of hair impatiently around a long red fingernail.

"Thanks," said Isobel. "And don't worry, I doubt I'll stumble over a dead body this time."

Felice finally met her eye. "You're in a morgue. Jerome!"

A sturdy-looking security guard lumbered over.

"Show her to records, okay?" Without another word, Felice clacked away down the hall on her precipitous heels.

"How do you like it here?" Isobel asked Jerome as they made their way down the cinderblock-walled hallway toward an elevator. When he didn't answer, Isobel clocked the telltale white buds in his ears. Clearly her conversation was no competition for his playlist.

Seeing the words "Medical Records" engraved on the small plate outside the door brought home what a stroke of luck her placement was. This was exactly where she needed to be. Surely she'd have a spare minute to look up Jason Whiteley.

She passed through the door and turned to thank Jerome, who was already swaggering away down the hall to the beat of his music. The medical records room was vast and dusty, with several desks in the open and what appeared to be a few smaller offices off to the sides. A young woman with full, coral-basted lips was seated behind the central desk, her glossy dark hair swept off her face with tortoise-shell combs.

"Hi, I'm Isobel Spice from Temp Zone."

"Oh, yeah. You're here to help Randy. Randy!" the woman screamed in an impressively piercing, high-pitched voice.

"Do you sing?" Isobel asked.

The woman laughed. "Only in the shower. How come?"

"Um, no reason."

"You're the temp?" asked a male voice from behind her.

Isobel turned to face a thin, pale, middle-aged man with one pair of glasses perched on his nose and another on a chain nestled in the V of his beige cashmere sweater.

She held out her hand. "I'm Isobel Spice."

He grasped her hand and let his eyes roam over her. They lingered on her chest, and he gave a disappointed sigh. "Not much of a 'spice rack.'"

Isobel stifled a gasp. She couldn't have understood him correctly. But the young black-haired woman whispered, "Ignore him. He doesn't get out much."

Great, thought Isobel. A nerdy, perverted wit. What a combo.

"You can type, right?"

"I wouldn't be much of a temp if I couldn't," Isobel said.

Randy gestured for her to follow him. Isobel was stopped by the woman's hand on her arm.

"He's less of a jerk than he seems at first, but I'd take as many bathroom breaks as you can. I'm Eva, by the way."

Isobel smiled gratefully and scurried after Randy, who had disappeared out of sight behind a tall bookshelf. Her pulse quickened at the prospect of unearthing the official reason for Jason Whiteley's death. She'd look up his record as soon as she could ditch Randy.

When she turned the corner, she found him waiting by an empty desk, drumming his fingers impatiently on the dusty surface while a computer whirred into life. Isobel had grown accustomed to the phenomenon of the empty temp desk. Only at Dove & Flight, where she seemed to have settled in for a longer than usual haul, did her workplace look like one that was in active use.

"We need to log the site reports from last year into the system. We're a bit behind." He ogled her posterior. "So are you."

Isobel ignored him and waited for him to continue.

"If you get cracking, you should be able to get through most of them."

"How many are there?" she asked, dreading the answer.

These one-day catch-up jobs were the worst, usually resulting in a finger-numbing, headache-inducing day that was more exhausting than a week of regular office work. In response to her question, Randy ducked around the side of the desk and kicked out a large, heavy cardboard box.

"But wait, there's more!" he announced in game show host tones and proceeded to produce three more boxes.

Isobel tried to calculate how many pieces of paper four boxes could hold. It had to be thousands.

"Did more people than usual die last year?"

Randy extracted a form from the top box and leaned over her, a bit too close for comfort.

"Here you see the name of deceased, time and date of death, cause of death, medical examiner's name—we have a whole staff—and then a short paragraph with illuminating details. If there's no name, just type in Jane or John Doe. If there's no cause of death," he smiled wickedly, "just make one up."

Isobel gasped.

"I'm kidding. Just write in 'natural causes.' That's what a blank means."

He pressed a few keys on the computer and brought up an online form.

"Our tech department created a program to handle all this information, no more, no less. It's pretty straightforward, but I'm over in the far office if you need help." He gave her one last squirm-inducing wink and removed himself, while Isobel silently resolved that if she needed help, she'd ask Eva and not randy Randy.

She needed help almost immediately. Straightforward it was not. The first three questions on the computer form asked for information she either couldn't find or couldn't decipher from the sloppy handwritten sheets that supposedly held all the answers. But Isobel was getting used to this phenomenon, too. The procedural minutiae of any office were second nature to those who worked there and utterly mystifying to the uninitiated.

Regardless, Isobel was relieved to have an excuse to procrastinate so soon, since simply looking at the boxes was making her temples throb. Besides, she didn't care whether or not she did a good job; she was there for one reason and one reason only, and it had nothing to do with bringing the Office of the City Medical Examiner's database up to date.

"If you don't mind, I've got a few questions," Isobel said to Eva a few moments later. "I'd rather limit my interactions with Randy."

Eva turned from her own computer and dipped her head knowingly at Isobel. "Yeah, no joke. What's up?"

Isobel handed Eva a form completed in an illegible scrawl and glanced down at the piece of paper where she'd made some notes.

"The computer screen wants to know the code, record number and status. I don't see anything on this form that corresponds, but the computer won't let me go on to the next screen unless I enter them."

Eva pointed to a box at the bottom of the page. "It doesn't say, but that's the code. It's always a four-digit number starting with O or C. Record number is right here at the top. It's already on the form, preprinted in red. Status you get from the letter in the code. O means a case is still open. C means a case is closed."

"What are the four digits that go with the O and the C?"

"The last four of the social. On a John or Jane Doe, it's 0000 and the letter, usually O, of course."

"Got it. Thanks." She glanced around for Randy, but he was nowhere in sight. "I'm just curious, since the recordkeeping seems so far behind—no offense—where are the current cases?"

"Down in the basement. The morgue office sorts and handles those records. It's supposed to be current, like, within a month, but they're pretty behind too, so they've probably got up to six months' worth of records down there."

Isobel digested this information and began to formulate a plan. She'd wait a bit, maybe until her lunch break, and then head downstairs to the morgue.

It seemed Felice was right: her day was destined to include a dead body or two, after all.

THIRTEEN

INPUTTING DEATH RECORDS WAS TURNING OUT to be one of the absolute worst tasks Isobel had encountered since she started temping. She was no longer a stranger to the monotony of data entry, but the eye strain involved in deciphering the handwriting of the medical examiners made her head feel like it was going to explode. Only one, a Dr. DeAngelis, had neat, meticulous script. After two hours of straining, Isobel finally decided to make her life easier and pull all of Dr. DeAngelis's forms. Since she'd never get through all the boxes, or even part of one, she figured she might as well save her eyesight.

With half an hour left on her lunch break, Isobel made her way to the morgue. As she descended to the basement, it briefly occurred to her that wolfing down a turkey avocado wrap first might not have been the best plan, but it was too late now. The elevator doors opened into what seemed like a cross between an office and a hospital. The floors and walls were white, and the fluorescent lights burned brighter without benefit of natural light peeking in through windows. She followed a sign that pointed to the morgue office. As she walked down the hall, her shoes echoing on the polished linoleum, a door marked "Room 1" opened and two medical examiners emerged, pulling off their masks and gloves, deep in conversation. Isobel shot past, but like a road accident, it proved impossible not to look. An orderly was sliding a table with a cadaver into a vault in the wall. Even though the body was draped in opaque plastic, Isobel gulped back a wave of nausea and hurried down the hall.

She paused outside the morgue office and reviewed what she planned to say. It wasn't one of her better schemes, but it was the best she could come up with under the circumstances. She withdrew from her pocket the death report that she had filled in earlier, in her worst handwriting. She examined the slanting, barely legible loops and scrawls she had made on the page and briefly wondered if she could have been a doctor.

She pushed open the door and approached the receptionist's desk. A plump Hispanic woman welcomed her warmly.

"*Hola, chica*! We don't get many visitors down here. What can I do for you?"

Isobel felt bad about hoodwinking such a friendly face, but she forged ahead nonetheless. She glanced at the woman's nameplate. Wanda Bautista. "You're Wanda?"

Wanda nodded happily.

Isobel smiled. "Nice to meet you. Randy upstairs asked me to check something with you. See this guy who died last year, Jason Whiteley?" She held out her forged form for Wanda to see. "Randy knows someone who knows someone who knows a guy with the exact same name, Jason Whiteley, who died just the other day. Same thing, cardiac arrest, and the same date, only one year later. Freaky, huh?"

Wanda let out a long, slow breath and nodded solemnly. "My great-grandmother died when lightning struck a tree and it fell on top of her on the Fourth of July. Then my great-grandfather married her sister, and a year later to the day, the same thing happened to her!"

Isobel's eyes widened. "No kidding! That's even weirder!" This was going to be a piece of cake. "Anyway, Randy said I should come down here and double-check their socials. Just to make sure nobody's playing a prank and they're not really the same person."

"Who was the medical examiner, do you know?"

Isobel thought back to the other day when the man had poked his head into her interrogation. She didn't know his name, only what he looked like, but she couldn't very well describe him to Wanda without some explanation for having seen him.

She shook her head. "I don't. Can you look it up?"

Wanda nodded, and Isobel gave her the date and the address of Dove & Flight. Wanda consulted a complicated-looking calendar on the computer and pointed to the screen. "That'll be Dr. Daley. You can ask him for the form." She gestured behind her to an inner office, where Isobel caught a glimpse of the little bearded man she had seen at Dove & Flight bustling about the small, white space. What if he recognized her?

"Can you pull the form for me?"

Wanda shook her head. "He has it."

"He looks so busy," said Isobel. "I don't want to bother him."

"It's no bother." Before Isobel could stop her, Wanda called out, "Dr. Daley? I need a form from the other day."

"Just a second!"

Isobel glanced quickly around the room. No place to hide, no possible distraction she could provide. A moment later, Dr. Daley emerged from his office, pulling on an overcoat. Unable to think of anything better, Isobel bent down and pulled off her shoe.

She heard Wanda say, "She's working upstairs in records and needs to see a death report from last week. Jason Whiteley."

Isobel rubbed her foot and waved vaguely upwards with her other hand. "Sorry," she mumbled, "something sticking out on the side…"

She sensed Dr. Daley moving toward the door. "It'll have to wait until I get back. Dead drug dealer on Avenue B."

Isobel heard the outer door slam shut and she straightened up, pretending to test her shoe. "There, I think I fixed it. It was, like, a wire or something."

Wanda was looking at her curiously.

Isobel hurried on, "New shoes. I should probably just return them."

"You'll have to check later when Dr. Daley is back."

Damn, thought Isobel. So close.

"Do you know when that will be?"

Wanda shrugged. "Could be gone all day. You never know. You should just come back tomorrow morning."

Isobel bit her lip. "The thing is, I'm a temp and I'm only hired for today to clean up the files. Randy seemed particularly eager to get this wrapped up. Can you just pull the form for me?"

"I can't give you anything off his desk," Wanda said firmly.

"I only need to look at it. Just to check the socials."

Wanda hesitated. "Well, if that's all you need, I can check it quickly." She snatched the form from Isobel's hand and disappeared into Dr. Daley's office.

Great. Now what?

Isobel glanced into the office and saw Wanda rifling through papers on Dr. Daley's desk. After a moment, she seemed to find what she was looking for. She held an identical form side by side with Isobel's forgery and shook her head.

Without stopping to consider what she was doing, Isobel rushed into Dr. Daley's office, startling Wanda momentarily.

"I just remembered something else I'm supposed to check!" Isobel cried, her face flushed. "Right there!"

Isobel pointed to the bright red, preprinted record number on the top of her forgery, but her eyes darted to the autopsy results on Jason Whiteley's real death form. Dr. Daley's scrawl was among the least legible she had grappled with all morning, but she willed the letters to take sensible shape. It took all her acting training to conceal her reaction from Wanda as she deciphered the words and committed them to memory.

Stomach contents: coffee, eggs, toast.

Blood tested positive for meperidine, digoxin.

Cause of death: poisoning.

FOURTEEN

JAMES WAS SURPRISED TO SEE ISOBEL waiting for him in front of his office building when he emerged at six forty-five. His surprise gave way to suspicion when he saw the feverish look in her eyes.

"What?"

Isobel glanced up and down Madison Avenue. "Not here. Can we get a drink or something?" She put a hand to her mouth. "Oh, sorry!"

He patted her shoulder. "It's okay, I can handle it."

They settled themselves at the lobby bar of a hotel on Madison and 52nd Street, where he used to meet Jayla. As the bartender served his Coke, James realized he hadn't been there since he and Jayla had broken up.

Isobel took a long sip of her wine. Then she set the glass down and looked at him squarely.

"He was poisoned. I saw the autopsy report. There were two things in his blood." She closed her eyes, as if trying to recall the words. "Meperidine and digoxin." She opened her eyes. "And coffee, eggs and toast in his stomach."

James felt his chest tighten, and the dim lights in the bar seemed to flicker. Why should it bother him to know beyond a doubt that Jason Whiteley had been murdered? Hadn't he at one time felt like murdering the guy himself? Maybe that's why it bothered him.

"Shit."

Isobel rubbed her hands together nervously. "What am I going to do? What can I tell them that will make them believe it wasn't me? I served him the coffee!"

James massaged his brow and tried to think. He was, unaccountably, flashing back to the night of the frat party when that Barnard girl had died. She and Jason had been dating, and he had given her a bottle of tequila as both a present and a dare. Jason had been mixing kamikazes California-style, right in her mouth, and when she'd passed out, he'd started making out with her roommate. He had served the girl the alcohol that killed her, and then cheated on her. And James had taken the rap. Jason deserved to have someone serve him poison in return.

"James? James! You're not helping." Isobel snapped her fingers in front of his face, jolting him back to the present.

"Maybe it wasn't in the coffee," he said reflexively. "Maybe it was in the eggs or the toast. Maybe his girlfriend or wife, or his roommate, whoever—maybe one of them poisoned him."

Isobel's brow furrowed. "Do you think? I hadn't thought of that."

"What are those substances? Where do you get them? How do they work?

"No idea. What I really want to know is if the rest of the coffee in the pot tested positive."

"You won't get that from the medical examiner. Only the police will know."

"Okay, so I'll call Detective O'Connor."

James stirred the ice cubes in his empty Coke glass. "Don't do it. Believe me, if you're a suspect, you'll find out soon enough."

"But I want to know beforehand. I want to be prepared. Doesn't it look good for me to be proactive?"

James gave a mordant laugh. She was such a little go-getter. "This isn't like trying to get an acting job. Nothing makes you look guiltier than trying to stay ahead of the cops."

"But O'Connor seemed nice," she insisted. "Well-educated, too."

"Never trust the nice ones," warned James. "They can turn on a dime, and when they do, they're meaner than the mean."

"Then I'll call the surly one. The short one with the beady eyes."

"Isobel!"

"What? I suppose you're going to tell me I'm being racist?"

"No, I'm going to tell you you're being naïve!"

She crossed her arms petulantly. "You also told me I was wrong about Whiteley being poisoned."

"Who got you into the medical examiner's office?"

"Just to prove me wrong, right?"

He threw up his hands. "You got me there."

"When are you going to start believing in me, James? I believe in you, you know! My friend Sunil asked me if I trusted you, and I said absolutely, yes, no question."

He looked into Isobel's lake-colored eyes and found himself saying, in a shakier voice than he intended, "You're just saying that."

She took his hand and he felt a flash of warmth rush up his arm. "I know you think I'm silly and flighty and all that, but I'm not stupid. Can't you trust me like I trust you?"

He felt suddenly as if he existed in a hundred different parts, each with a different possible answer and none of them the response he most wanted to give. He wanted to say that he trusted her, but he didn't. He didn't trust himself, which meant her trust in him was utterly misplaced. Therefore, he didn't—he couldn't—trust her judgment. How could he, when she was so wrong about him?

He shook her off. "Do what you want. I can't stop you. You always just go off and do your own thing anyway."

From the stricken look on her face, he knew he'd picked the worst of all possible responses. Isobel inhaled sharply and paused, half on and half off her barstool, her lips drawn back in a pained smile.

"I only made it through one box of death records. Sharon Press can finish the morgue job. I'm going back to Dove & Flight."

FIFTEEN

"WE MISSED YOU," LIZ STEWART SAID from her perch on Isobel's desk. "The other girl was fine, but kind of serious. You're much more fun." She underscored her point by noisily scraping the bottom of her milk carton with her straw.

"Oh, that's me. Bringing murder and mayhem wherever I go," Isobel said, setting down her coffee.

Liz lobbed the empty milk carton into Isobel's trash can. "Except that it wasn't murder, although it did cause a fair amount of mayhem."

Isobel bit her tongue. She found herself wanting to confide in Liz, but she wasn't even sure she was going to tell Katrina the truth about Jason Whiteley. Delphi knew, but only because she had caught Isobel looking up the two substances online. It turned out that meperidine was the generic name for Demerol, and digoxin was a heart medication derived from the foxglove plant. Delphi had reminded Isobel that while she'd undoubtedly served Jason the coffee, somebody else had dropped the poisons in it, and until she knew who it was, it paid to proceed with caution. And to keep buying her coffee at Starbucks.

"To tell you the truth," Liz went on, "nobody's talking about Jason anymore. The merger has knocked everything else off the table."

Isobel settled herself at her desk and switched on her computer. "So, what's the scuttlebutt?"

Liz leaned forward eagerly, and Isobel realized that she'd been bursting with a nugget of gossip this whole time.

"The big rumble is that it's Barnaby's dream, and Angus is totally against it. Barnaby tricked him into it somehow, and now Angus isn't speaking to him."

Anyone catching Angus Dove's expression at the staff meeting the other day could have seen that he was less than pleased, but before Isobel could point that out, Liz continued, "And Kit Blanchard is fit to be tied. Did you see the look on her face when Barnaby made that comment about consumer PR not being our strong suit?"

"Kit? Why?"

Liz tsked. "Sometimes I forget you don't actually work here, and I mean that as a compliment. Kit essentially *is* our consumer PR department. She gets to do whatever she wants. Has for years. I'm pretty sure she and Barnaby had a thing for a while. It would shock me if they didn't." Liz whispered, "Let's just say Kit's real specialty is acquisitions and mergers, in that order. If you know what I mean."

"Isn't she married with kids?"

Liz sighed. "So young, so innocent." She beckoned Isobel closer. "The current rumor is Aaron."

"What?!"

Liz put a warning finger to her lips. "Unconfirmed, but the signs are there. And, as you may have noticed, he is even more married with even more kids than Kit." Liz leaned back. "Told you she was trouble."

Isobel took this in. "I thought he didn't like working women."

Liz held up her hands. "Far be it from me to try to psychoanalyze Aaron, but I would say his feelings about women—especially forbidden ones—are probably extremely complicated. But I digress." Liz smoothed her blouse over her burgeoning belly. "After ICG buys us and we merge with The Peterson Group, Kit will be absorbed into Peterson's lineup. Even if she keeps her title, she'll have to answer to a higher power. No matter how you slice it, it's a comedown for someone who's accustomed to running the show."

"What do you think she'll do?"

Liz shrugged. "Beats me. I try to steer clear of her. I don't trust her not to sniff out my handsome husband from traces of his aftershave on my sweater."

"What about Dorothy Berman? Doesn't the other PR firm ICG owns do something in healthcare?"

"Yes, Fisher Health Strategies. If ICG ever decides to fold them in and make one, giant, über-PR firm, that'll be the end of her, too." Liz glanced at her watch and slid gingerly off the desk. "Speaking of which, we're about to find out if it's the end of us with Schumann, Crowe & Dyer. One of their senior consultants is coming in this morning. You should probably sit in on the meeting. On the off chance that they don't fire us, we may need your help."

"Sure."

"We'll be in Conference Room F. Nobody wants to go back into the one down here after the other day. Too creepy."

"Which one is F?"

"The one upstairs, across from Harm's Way."

"What's Harm's Way?" Isobel asked, alarmed.

"That's what we call the executive suite," Liz said, making a protective vampire cross with her fingers. "I hope you never find out why. Oh, and can you order pastries and stuff? A spoonful of sugar and all that."

Liz returned to her office, and Isobel picked up the phone.

"U-Like Deli, please hold."

While she was waiting for her order to be taken, Dorothy Berman appeared.

"Penny's out today, and I wondered if you might have time to follow up on a press release for me."

"Sure, although I was just asked to sit in on a meeting. But if it can—oh, wait!" She turned from Dorothy and placed her order with the deli. Then she hung up and returned to the older woman. "Sorry about that. I was on hold."

"That's all right. You can do it this afternoon. It's an executive appointment, nothing earth-shaking. Just call the top trades and make sure they got the release, and then ask if they can give it a brief mention. If they seem interested, see if they'd like a bylined article."

Dorothy handed Isobel the release and a stapled spreadsheet. Her heart sank when she saw it had close to 150 names on it. This, she had learned, was a popular managerial ploy: getting her to agree to a small assignment, only to have it morph within seconds into an all-day behemoth. She was still examining the list, when Aaron sidled up to her desk and cleared his throat.

"I have a press release I'd like you to follow up on," he said, addressing his shoes. "Oswald Insurance. It's a new product."

"I already did that one," Isobel said, relieved that she wasn't about to be hit with more work.

He held out the release and a press list. "This is a different new product."

Isobel glanced at the names. "But I just called all these people the other day."

"Call them again."

As he retreated, Isobel tried to imagine stiff, conventional Aaron with Kit Blanchard, cougar extraordinaire. It seemed impossible. Liz had to be wrong.

Isobel set Aaron's press list next to Dorothy's. There were easily 300 names between them. After her mind-numbing experience at the medical examiner's office, the thought of another daylong, detail-oriented task—not to mention the strain on her voice from all those phone calls—was not appealing.

But she had to do something. Despite Aaron's directive, she couldn't bring herself to bug the same people again so soon, so she picked up Dorothy's list and dialed, determined to take a good long break after every ten calls.

"May I speak to Joel Ri_k·n?"

"Speaking."

"Oh, hi! This is Isobel Spice from Dove & Flight. We sent you a release this morning announcing…"

She trailed off, realizing that she had forgotten to look at the release to see what she was pitching. She shuffled the papers.

"Um, it's a new directors and officers insurance policy for—"

"We're a medical trade," Ripkin snapped and hung up.

Isobel looked down and saw she'd grabbed Aaron's release by mistake. "Brilliant." She slammed down the phone.

"Not going well?" Katrina asked from behind her.

Isobel swiveled her chair around. "How do you do this all day?"

"I don't. I get someone like you to do it. Can I talk to you in my office?"

Isobel, relieved to have an excuse to defer her current tasks, followed Katrina, who shut her office door behind them.

"Do you want to stay here?" Katrina asked.

"What do you mean?"

"I'm leaving Dove & Flight, and I want you to come with me."

"Whoa! What are you talking about?"

"I vowed a long time ago that I wouldn't work for any of my dad's companies. He's making that really difficult, because he keeps buying more."

"Yeah, but it's not like you'd be working for him directly. He'd be more of a figurehead, right?"

"You don't understand." Katrina paced over to her corkboard and began rearranging the colored pushpins into a circle. "I worked really hard in school, but it was never good enough. If it was an A-minus, it should have been an A. God forbid I ever saw a B. And then when I didn't get into Harvard or Yale, my dad decided I was always going to need his help. Which is ridiculous!" She stabbed a pushpin with such force that the bulletin board swung back and forth.

"Of course it is! You're totally capable and very smart," Isobel reassured her, although she couldn't help but enjoy a teeny bit of *schadenfreude* at the discovery that Katrina had been rejected by the Ivies.

Katrina settled the corkboard and began pulling out the pins. "I got this job all by myself. And you know what my dad said?"

"What?"

"He said, 'You should have told me. I could have gotten you in there.' As if I hadn't just done exactly that on my own!" She stalked over the desk and dropped the pushpins into a container. "Do you know he wanted me to be a model?"

"I thought that was your idea."

She shook her head fiercely, and her russet hair swung back and forth like a shampoo commercial. "He suggested it. He thinks my looks will get me farther than my brain. He thinks my looks are unique. My brain…not so much."

"Oh."

"Don't get me wrong—I love my dad. I do," Katrina said, sitting down heavily. "I just don't want him in any position to pull strings I don't need pulled."

"So you're leaving?"

"I called a headhunter this morning. She had something that just came in—corporate communications at a big international bank. They're also looking for someone to fill the assistant position." She looked hopefully at Isobel. "Are you interested?"

Multiple thoughts jockeyed for supremacy in Isobel's mind. The first was that she wasn't about to abandon a hot murder trail. The second was that she didn't dare work for another international bank, because the last time she did that, someone died. The third was that number two was a ridiculous reason, because it had already happened again. The fourth, which she realized fleetingly should have been the first, was the one she finally articulated to Katrina.

"I'm really flattered, but I can't commit to anything full-time. I know I've gotten comfortable here, but it's still a temp job. I have to be free to audition and take an acting job if I get one."

Katrina stared at her as if she had answered in a foreign language. "Are you sure? I mean, a bird in hand and all that. Especially in this economy."

"I know," Isobel said. "But I'm not a bird-hunter by profession."

They regarded each other in perplexed silence. With her father's track record of snapping up communications companies, Katrina was probably always going to be on the run. No matter what she did, people were likely to cry nepotism. It was an occupational hazard of being heir to an international communications conglomerate, which, it occurred to Isobel, Katrina would probably inherit whether she proved herself elsewhere or not. Given that, it was a little hard to feel sorry for her.

Katrina waved Isobel off. "Okay, forget I said anything. It might not even work out, and I don't want word getting out that I'm looking to leave.

Isobel nodded. "Sure. But I'm curious—why do you want to bring me so badly?"

Katrina shrugged. "If I can bring someone, it makes me a more attractive candidate." The phone rang. "Yeah, she's in here. I'll tell her." She hung up. "Your deli order is here."

Isobel returned to her desk to collect her delivery, still smarting from Katrina's admission that she wanted Isobel only to improve her own chances. She should never have gone looking for a compliment. Tray in hand, Isobel carefully navigated the spiral staircase. As she snuck a chunk of melon from under the plastic, she couldn't help wondering whether having her father breathing down her neck was the real reason Katrina suddenly wanted out of Dove & Flight so badly.

SIXTEEN

Isobel knew that James's ex-girlfriend, Jayla, had worked with Jason Whiteley at Schumann, Crowe & Dyer, but she never expected to meet her in person. From Jayla's reaction, Isobel was ready to bet it was a surprise to her, too. Upon hearing Isobel's name, Jayla had withdrawn her hand as if she'd been scalded, and Isobel entertained a fleeting regret that she hadn't poisoned today's coffee. Observing her now across the conference table, Isobel realized that it must have taken Jayla every ounce of self-control not to rake her long crimson nails across Isobel's cheek. Every once in a while, Jayla would shoot a murderous look in Isobel's direction, and Isobel couldn't begin to fathom why James's ex-girlfriend should loathe her so much.

"The bottom line," Jayla said, after another digressive glance at Isobel, "is that we're getting pressure from ICG to keep you on. The partners aren't happy about it, but they have no choice. So you're officially on probation."

Isobel could sense her colleagues' relief. Katrina seemed to be sitting up taller, Liz had audibly begun breathing again, and Aaron was almost grinning.

"Don't get too excited," Jayla continued. "We have a big announcement in the offing and it's a potential minefield. What I'm about to tell you requires complete confidentiality. Everyone in this room will be held accountable." She turned a meaningful eye toward Isobel.

Isobel stood up. "That's all right. I have other things to do."

Liz pulled her back down. "Whatever it is, Isobel will probably be working on it."

It was clear that Jayla didn't relish the idea any more than Isobel, who knew full well that if she were privy to the ensuing conversation, any future disasters would be attributable immediately and exclusively to her.

Jayla set her mouth in a thin line. "We're about to announce a deal with a big publicly traded company, but we're at odds with them about the level of press exposure. They want to keep it under the radar, but it's a big win for us and we want to get some play from it. How would you advise us to proceed?"

Aaron rolled his pen between his fingers thoughtfully. "We should determine which reporters follow this company regularly. If we confine our outreach to that group, it will be hard to argue that we overreached."

Jayla nodded. "I'm fine with that, but you'll have to put together your own list. I don't want to ask the target for theirs."

Aaron eyed her steadily. "You'll have to tell us the name of the company."

Jayla looked around the room and then sighed. "MacBride's."

The name meant nothing to Isobel, but the others immediately perked up. Katrina must have sensed her indifference, because she leaned over and whispered, "Huge investment bank. Right up there with Morgan Stanley and Goldman Sachs."

Jayla stood up. "Timing is ASAP. If you botch this one, that's it, no matter what ICG says." Aaron remained seated while Jayla turned one final malevolent gaze on Isobel and let Liz escort her out.

When they were gone, Aaron rose as well. "Katrina, this one's on you. Pull together a smart list, and then call to confirm that they still cover MacBride's. Nothing in email, no names, use caller ID block. Nothing to trace the query back to us."

He strode out briskly, leaving Isobel and Katrina alone. Katrina leaned back in her chair and folded her arms.

"What on earth is up with you and Jayla Cummings? I had no idea you knew each other, let alone hated each other."

"I don't hate her. I'd never even met her before today." Isobel ripped a sheet of paper from the pad in front of her and started shredding it absent-mindedly. "She used to date my temp agent, though. They had a nasty breakup, and from her attitude this morning, all I can think is that she blames me, though God knows why. It's not like there's anything going on between James and me."

"Do you want there to be?"

Isobel arranged her yellow paper shreds into a small neat pile. "No. Yes. I don't know. He's not my type, and I'm not his. No. What about you?"

"What about me…what?"

Isobel swept the paper shreds into her palm and crunched them. "Aren't you surprised that Aaron put you in charge of this highly sensitive confidential press list?"

"Why wouldn't he? I'm the most junior person on the account. It's the sort of thing I usually do, plus I'm sure they want to keep our billing down right now, and I'm the cheapest, next to you." Katrina brightened. "You can make the calls after I pull the names."

Isobel frowned. "But what about the Brazil pitch?"

Katrina froze. "What about it?"

Isobel struggled to find the least accusatory words. "You didn't notice that the reporter was sniffing around?"

Katrina inhaled sharply. "What? That wasn't me! Liz sent that pitch out. She was the one who didn't pick up on the significance of that email!"

Isobel backtracked immediately. "Sorry! I didn't…I don't know why I thought it was you."

Katrina's blue eyes blazed. "Who needs my dad when I've got you to assume that if somebody did something stupid, it had to be me?"

She stormed out, and Isobel berated herself for shooting off her mouth without thinking. Even if Katrina had sent those emails, she wouldn't have wanted to admit it. But her anger struck Isobel as genuine. Was Liz lying? It's never fun to take the blame, and in a case like this, it might have gotten Liz fired. But she wasn't fired—nobody was. In the end, they didn't even lose the account. So was there some other reason Liz didn't want Isobel to know she was responsible? Or was Katrina putting on a show?

Isobel finished tidying up the conference room and returned to her desk, where Aaron was waiting for her, a stack of stapled glossy sheets in hand.

"I need you to run these up to Barnaby's office. It's slides for a new business presentation and he has to sign off."

Happy to have another reason to put off making follow-up calls, but a little apprehensive about what might await her in Harm's Way, Isobel made her way down the hall. She passed the kitchen and the conference room of death, and chugged up the spiral staircase. She had just reached the top, when somber old Wilbur Freed materialized, seemingly out of nowhere.

"Watch it!"

As they collided, magazines and news clippings flew from his hands and tumbled through the slats to the floor below.

"I'm so sorry!" Isobel clambered back down and knelt on the floor, setting Aaron's slides next to her. She gathered Wilbur's scattered papers, fully expecting him to come down and help her. When he didn't, she piled his papers on top of hers and clumped back up the steps.

His beagle jowls sagged with displeasure. "Who are you, anyway?"

"Isobel Spice. I'm temping."

He accepted his magazines with a dismissive grunt. She waited for him to move aside to let her pass, but he loomed over her like a hovering hawk. She gave up and pressed her body against the railing, and he stomped past her down the stairs.

"Chivalry is clearly on life support," she muttered.

Harm's Way was on the far end of the top floor, and Isobel found it hard to believe it had been furnished by the same people who'd appointed the bland, blond offices below. Original art and sleek chrome coffee tables adorned the upholstered conversation areas, while the hush created by the absorbent plush carpeting hinted at minds too busy publicizing to be disturbed. The partners' assistants, seated behind matching wide mahogany desks, couldn't have been more different. Angus Dove was guarded by Sophie Barker, a quiet middle-aged woman of mousy demeanor and mousier wardrobe. Barnaby, still inexplicably to Isobel, entrusted his secrets and his schedule to Jimmy Rocket, who greeted her effusively.

"Melodious songbird! Come at last to entertain us with a mid-morning tweet?"

"Nothing that distracting. A new business proposal—" Isobel looked down at her empty hands. "Damn! I must have given it to Wilbur. I'll be right back."

"Good luck finding him. Sandburg's cat-footed fog's got nothing on him!" Jimmy called after her.

She scampered back down the stairs, but Wilbur was nowhere in sight. She followed the corridor, glancing into offices as she passed, but he wasn't in any of them. Finally, she rounded the bend to the far corner and found herself facing Kit Blanchard, who sat at her desk polishing her Prada sunglasses.

"Oh! Sorry to bother you. I was looking for Wilbur."

Mindful of Liz's warning, Isobel took a step backwards, as if she were in danger of forfeiting a husband, despite the fact that she didn't even have a boyfriend.

Kit swept the glasses onto her head, her blond hair shimmering as new highlights were revealed.

"You're the temp."

"Isobel."

"Right. Wilbur was here a minute ago. He dropped off a whole pile of stuff for me." She gestured to a stack of magazines on her desk.

"He picked up something of mine by mistake. Do you mind if I take a look?"

"Be my guest."

Isobel easily located Aaron's slides sandwiched in between *Chain Store Age* and *Fortune*. "I bumped into him, and this got mixed up with his papers." Isobel rattled the presentation. "He seemed a bit disgruntled."

Kit waved her arm and her gold bangles jingled. "That's just Wilbur. He's one of those old-timers who hate change. You know the type. He loves to reminisce about the good old days, when press releases were hand-delivered by messenger."

"Surely he's gotten used to it by now."

Kit rolled her eyes. "He even waxes nostalgic for the days when you had to fax breaking news to Dow Jones and Reuters simultaneously, so one wire service wouldn't get the edge over the other. And don't get him started on the internet. He believes that information is too readily available, and collating it is a lost art."

Isobel fanned the pages of the presentation to make sure they were intact. "So, how necessary is what he does here?"

"Not. He doesn't do anything we couldn't all do for ourselves."

"Well, sorry to bother you."

Jimmy was waiting for her when she returned, shifting back and forth on the balls of his feet like an outfielder awaiting a fly ball. "Did you manage to locate the elusive Mr. Freed?"

"No, but I got what I needed." Isobel held out the presentation. "Would you do the honors?"

"I shall waft my way in there now, before the songbird takes flight again before Flight."

He bounced off to a dark wooden door, knocked, and entered. At the next desk, Sophie Barker shook her head in bewilderment. Isobel returned a conspiratorial smile and looked around. Angus and Barnaby had the two large corner offices, and she knew from the day she was hired that Mike Hardy, the Human Resources director, had his office nearby.

There were several other upper management caves to which Isobel couldn't ascribe ownership. Through Flight's open door, she could hear him ranting on the phone. A watch alarm went off, and Sophie stood up.

"Have to remind Angus to take his heart medication," she explained. She took a pill bottle from her desk and disappeared into his office.

Barnaby's second line rang, and Isobel glanced down at the caller ID.

It was the NYPD.

She snatched it up. "Barnaby Flight's office."

"This is Detective Aguilar for Mr. Flight."

"I'm sorry, he isn't in today," Isobel said, her heart racing. "But he asked me to be sure and take a message if you called."

There was a pause, and then Aguilar continued. "This is regarding the death at your office."

"Yes?" Isobel held her breath.

"You can let him know we tested the coffee in the carafe and there was no trace of any foreign substance."

Isobel braced herself against Jimmy's desk. "Really?"

"That's correct."

She didn't need to probe further. She knew Whiteley had been poisoned—she even knew with what. But now she knew she hadn't done it.

"I'll make sure to give Mr. Flight the message right away."

She hung up, both relieved and confused, just as Sophie returned.

"Thanks for grabbing that," Sophie said. "Who was it?"

"One of the detectives from the other day. They tested the coffee in the pot, and it hadn't been tampered with."

Sophie exhaled deeply. "Well, that's a relief! The partners will be very glad to hear that."

Some demon prodded Isobel to improvise. "But he did say Jason Whiteley was poisoned, even if it wasn't in our coffee. With Demerol and digoxin."

Sophie paused, her hand hovering over the back of her

chair. Her face grew a shade paler, which made her look suddenly younger and more vulnerable.

"What is it?" Isobel asked.

Sophie shook her head and sat down. "Nothing." She quickly tossed the pill bottle back in her drawer and started hammering away on her keyboard. "Sorry, I have to get back to this report."

At that moment, Jimmy reappeared and thrust Aaron's new business proposal into Isobel's hand. "Approved with the understanding that you will incorporate the edits noted on pages seven and thirteen." He saluted. "Go forth and pitch!"

But Isobel was barely listening. Sophie hadn't done a particularly good job of concealing her surprise at the mention of the two substances. And Isobel had a pretty fair guess which one had caused her discomfort.

SEVENTEEN

Isobel arrived home to find Delphi kneeling on the floor wearing a long, ruffled rehearsal skirt with her Nine Inch Nails T-shirt. It made a nice change from the jeans and bustier look, although it wasn't, strictly speaking, an improvement. Isobel tried to tiptoe around her, but Delphi, sensing her presence, swung around, clenched her fists and intoned:

> *Grief fills the room up of my absent child,*
> *Lies in his bed, walks up and down with me,*
> *Puts on his pretty looks, repeats his words,*
> *Remembers me of all his gracious parts,*
> *Stuffs out his vacant garments with his form;*
> *Then, have I reason to be fond of grief?*
> *Fare you well: had you such a loss as I,*
> *I could give better comfort than you do.*

Delphi melted to the floor in a heap, and Isobel, recognizing her cue, applauded enthusiastically.

"That was great! What was it?"

Delphi sat up and pushed a nest of blond ringlets out of her eyes. "Constance from *King John*. What else? We open next week."

Isobel threw her bag and phone onto the kitchen counter. "Will you think I'm a philistine if I say they all sound the same?"

"The same might be said of your precious Gilbert and Sullivan," Delphi grumbled. "You are coming opening night, right?"

"Of course! Wouldn't miss it."

In truth, Delphi's monologue was far better than Isobel expected. She really did have a knack for Shakespeare. Delphi's musical instincts stood her in good stead when she didn't have to match pitch.

Isobel opened the fridge and pulled out a can of Diet Coke, which she popped open. She leaned on the counter.

"I'd never even heard of *King John* until you were cast in it."

Delphi hitched up her voluminous skirts to perch with modern abandon on the kitchen stool. "It's not done very often, which is why Graham chose it. We'll have a better chance of getting agents and casting directors in to see it than if we do *Richard III* or something."

"Why not do a comedy? Or at least one of the tragedies?"

"They're overdone." Delphi jumped down from the stool and yanked off her skirt. "This thing is starting to bug me."

"You, too?"

Delphi gave her a dirty look and threw the skirt across the room where it landed on her bed. "Besides, the histories offer dramatic opportunities you can really sink your teeth into, plus the language is more oblique. If we can pull it off, we look that much better."

"Who is Willy Loman playing?" asked Isobel.

"The title role, of course."

"Of course."

"So what's new at the spin shop?"

Isobel filled her in on the highlights of her day, minus the confidential business portion.

"Do you really think Angus poisoned Jason Whiteley with his own heart medication?" Delphi asked, unpiling her hair from its messy topknot.

"Not Angus, necessarily." Isobel, in sympathy, undid her ponytail and wound the rubber band around her wrist. "But if he keeps a supply of digoxin in his office, anyone could know about it. Anyone could have taken it and—"

"And what? Gone to Jason's house that morning and fixed him a digoxin omelet? And what about the Demerol? Where did that come from?"

"So you think it's a coincidence?"

Delphi pulled a pile of takeout menus from behind the cutting board and rifled through them.

"Maybe he had a heart condition that nobody knew about. And maybe he also had a bad back. He was taking both drugs and overdosed accidentally." She held up a menu. "Chinese?"

Isobel nodded and tapped her soda can on the counter. "I suppose that's possible, but stay with me for a moment. Barnaby was pushing for the merger to go through, and he knew Jason was going to give them the old heave-ho. He saw Jason as a threat, so he helped himself to Angus's medication and…"

"You're back where you started. The coffee in the office was clean. Nobody from Dove & Flight killed him."

"Just because the coffee was clean doesn't mean it wasn't somebody from Dove & Flight." Isobel grabbed the menu from Delphi. "Maybe somebody there had a relationship with Jason outside work. Kung pao chicken."

"Okay, but you're still faced with the question of where and when." Delphi shook her phone. "Shit. I'm out of charge."

"Here, use mine." Isobel handed over the menu and her phone.

"I think you're getting hung up on coincidences," Delphi said. "Hello? Yes, that's us. Scallion pancakes, one moo shu beef, one kung pao chicken. Brown rice." Delphi hung up. "Half an hour, but you know it'll be here in ten minutes."

Isobel's phone rang in Delphi's hand, and before Isobel could wrest it from her, Delphi answered.

"'How now, wit? Whither wander you?'"

"Give me that!" Isobel snatched her phone back. "Hello? This is Isobel."

"Not Rosalind?"

Isobel paused, confused by the reference and by the British-accented voice she didn't recognize. "I'm sorry, who is this?"

There was a sigh on the other end of the phone. "How easily one forgets the smile-tapped heart."

Isobel groaned. Not another one. "Is that Shakespeare?"

"No, it's Fremont. I just made it up on the spot."

Isobel felt a delighted flush. Hugh Fremont, the audition pianist from *Phantom*. Surprise of surprises, he had called.

She shot a glance at Delphi who was eyeing her quizzically.

"That was my roommate," Isobel explained. "She's a bit of a Shakespeare nut. Emphasis on the nut."

"No, no, it was refreshing," Hugh said. "It's been a long time since anyone called me a wit."

"It's nice to hear from you."

Isobel turned away, but Delphi stalked her, panther-like, mouthing, "Who is it?"

"I meant it when I said I'd like to hear you sing under better conditions," Hugh said. "I'm putting together a little cabaret of my own songs. I'd like to try you out on a few—if you think that might interest you."

"Definitely! I love singing new music. I'm so flattered that you thought of me."

"Yours was one of the more memorable auditions of the day."

Isobel winced. "For all the wrong reasons."

Hugh chuckled. "I wouldn't say that. Are you free tomorrow evening? I've got studio space uptown. Can you meet me around seven?"

"Sure," Isobel answered, her voice brimming with excitement. Under normal circumstances, she might have tried to check herself, but it was her exuberance that had caught his attention in the first place. She wrote down the address on Claremont Avenue, near Manhattan School of Music.

"I did my Master's there and never left the neighborhood," Hugh explained. "So I'll see you then?"

"Yes, looking forward to it. Thanks so much for calling!"

Delphi downed the rest of Isobel's Diet Coke with a loud sucking noise and slammed the can down on the counter. "Who, pray tell, was that?"

Isobel gazed up at the ceiling to short-circuit an imminent rush of giggles, then contained herself and looked at Delphi.

"I think it was Romeo."

EIGHTEEN

"I don't know what you see in that Spice girl."

Jayla swiveled her barstool to face James, her eyes brimming with challenge. He thought back to the last time he'd been in this bar, when Isobel had told him she believed in him, and then ignored his advice and taken herself back to Dove & Flight.

"It's all in your head," he said gruffly. "Now that you've met her, you can see she's not my type."

He wished Isobel had at least warned him that she and Jayla had met. He might have been better prepared. Better yet, he wouldn't have asked Jayla to meet him for a drink. He'd struggled with the decision to begin with, but he had come to feel a strange sense of responsibility for Isobel.

"Go back to what you were saying before," he continued. "The police say there was nothing in the coffee?"

"Yes. They came back to us, wanting to know if we had any information about where Jason was earlier that morning. They still don't believe it was accidental."

That much James knew from Isobel's foray into the medical examiner's office, but he didn't want to let on to Jayla.

"What did you tell them?"

"There wasn't much to say. Jason didn't come into the office that morning. He went straight to Dove & Flight for his meeting."

"But that doesn't mean he didn't go somewhere else first," James pointed out.

Jayla rolled her eyes. "Obviously. He could have gone anywhere: the gym, a diner, an AA meeting."

James ignored the dig. "Did they check his calendar?"

"The only thing there was his ten o'clock meeting at Dove & Flight and a two o'clock conference call."

They sat in silence for a moment. Jayla stirred her vodka cranberry, and James clinked the ice in his Coke glass.

"I don't know why I'm telling you any of this," she said finally.

"Well, I appreciate it."

She sighed and pushed her glass away. "No, that's not true. I do know why."

James looked at her expectantly. She lowered her eyes and carefully folded a corner of her cocktail napkin.

"Michael and I are getting married."

In spite of himself, James felt a pang at this news. Jayla had once wanted to marry him, though he could never understand why. He had never wanted to marry her. He knew he should be happy for her that what had started as a meaningless affair with his buddy Michael had led to this. Marriage was all-important to Jayla. He should have been relieved, but instead, he just felt sad. Because he knew she didn't love Michael. Not the way she had loved him.

He managed a smile and patted her hand. "Congratulations. It couldn't happen to a nicer guy."

Her eyes flicked up and met his. "Guy?"

"Michael is lucky. You're a great catch, Jayla. For the right person," he added quickly, seeing the flash of accusation in her eyes.

She withdrew her hand and shifted on her barstool. "Anyway, I thought you should know. Will you come to the wedding?"

James smiled. "I'd like that."

"But don't even think about bringing Isobel."

As if he would ever be that suicidal.

"Another round?" For a change, the bartender's intrusion was welcome.

He glanced at Jayla who nodded. "Yeah, thanks." James watched the bartender move away. "You know, I don't know much about what Jason's been up to these last few years. It's not like we stayed in touch. Obviously, he was doing well for himself at your firm. Was he married?"

"No. As far as I know, he was perfectly happy playing the field." Jayla sucked up the last of her drink and released the straw back into the glass. "He went on a few dates with Katrina Campbell from Dove & Flight, but I don't think it went anywhere."

James cocked his head with interest. "Really? First I've heard of that."

Jayla shrugged. "Why would you?"

"Did he ever date anyone else he worked with there?"

Jayla shook her head. "Nah. One's married and preggers, and the other's a dude. No, I take that back. You can't really call an Orthodox Jew a dude."

"Did Jason get along with them?"

"Well enough, until the Brazil thing."

"What was that?"

"They sent out a pitch that exposed us to a reporter in a very damaging way. We were going to fire them until Clark Schumann—he's the head of the firm—told us we couldn't."

"Why?"

"Dove & Flight is being acquired by our parent company. The word came down from on high that we had to give them another chance."

"But except for that, Jason got on with them all right?"

"Well, there was one incident with Aaron Grossman that I know about."

As the bartender set down their drinks, it struck James that Jayla must really feel guilty about marrying Michael to be speaking so freely and for so long.

"You gonna tell me the story?" he asked.

She took a long sip of her new drink, gave a satisfied smile, and leaned forward. "Jason and Aaron were having lunch—this was right after we hired them—and Aaron ordered a salad. When the waiter brought it, Aaron was going on about something and not really paying attention. Jason noticed that the salad had bacon bits on it. Not only did he not warn Aaron, he actually laughed when Aaron ate a few bites before he realized it."

James cringed. "That's not right."

"You know it," Jayla said. "Aaron still had to make nice because we're a client, but he was always very cool toward Jason after that."

"Is that everyone at Dove & Flight?"

"Everyone who counts. Jason met Angus Dove when they pitched us the business, but Aaron, Liz and Katrina were our team." Jayla slapped her hand on the bar. "Wait, I forgot Kit Blanchard. She's his sister-in-law. No, wait, let me get this right. Kit is married to Jason's brother's wife's brother."

"That's not a sister-in-law. That's—I don't know what that is. An out-law." He laughed at his joke, but Jayla didn't so much as curl a lip.

"That's how we found them in the first place," she went on. "We were looking for a PR firm, and Jason recommended them because of Kit. But I don't see why any of this matters. We know he wasn't poisoned at Dove & Flight, so why do you care? Your precious Isobel had nothing do with it."

"How about you?" he shot back. "What was *your* relationship with Jason Whiteley?"

In a swift movement, she grabbed her purse from the bar and slid off her stool, her almond cat-eyes wide with fury.

"You can be a real asshole, you know that?" she hissed. "Thank God I'm marrying Michael. You are so not worth it!"

Lord, save me from my own big mouth, he thought as he watched her brush aside a hapless waiter who was blocking her path to the door. Maybe he and Isobel had more in common than he thought.

NINETEEN

THE RUMBLE STARTED DOWN THE HALL and rolled toward Isobel's desk, gathering additional voices until it finally erupted into loud, creatively turned f-bombs from the small group gathered around her centrally located computer.

Kit Blanchard shook her exquisitely highlighted head. "Five points in ten minutes!"

Dorothy Berman gazed at the screen in wonder. "I've never seen anything like it."

"We are so screwed," Liz said under her breath.

"Who made the calls yesterday?" Aaron asked, looking around. His voice trembled and his face was deathly pale under his black beard. "Who confirmed the reporters covering MacBride's?"

Isobel meekly held up her hand. "I did."

The group pulled away from her as one, eyeing her with a mixture of pity and horror.

"Katrina asked me to take care of it," Isobel added quickly. The others shifted their gaze to Katrina, who seethed in Isobel's direction, but Aaron kept his eyes fixed on Isobel.

"What exactly did you say to the guy at the AP?"

Isobel held up her hands in self-defense. "I—I just asked if he still covered the company. That's it!"

"Did you give your name? Did you say you were from Dove & Flight?"

"No! I used caller ID block, and I didn't say who I was or why I was calling, just that I wanted to confirm his contact information." She looked imploringly at Katrina. "I don't understand what's going on."

"The AP reporter ran a story late yesterday afternoon, saying a call from Dove & Flight confirmed suspicions that MacBride's was preparing to sell off their consulting business," Katrina said in clipped tones.

Isobel felt the color drain from her face. "But Jayla said specifically that MacBride's didn't want any publicity at all!"

"And this is why!" Aaron pointed a quivering finger at Isobel's computer screen. "MacBride's is publicly traded. The stock price is moving. It shot up as soon as the market opened."

"But isn't a higher stock price good for them?" asked Penny Warren, who Isobel suspected had spent her sick day shopping for a new matching outfit.

Aaron gave an exasperated sigh. "Not when they're trying to sell the company! Now it's going to cost more, which might make Schumann, Crowe & Dyer balk. On top of that, it's a phony lift. MacBride's will shoot down the rumor, and the price will crash, but by that point it will be too late to do the deal. It's terrible for them."

"And terrible for us," Liz said, as the air was rent by the groaning complaint of the spiral steps. "Here it comes," she added, unnecessarily.

"What in holy fucking hell happened?" Barnaby's bellow ricocheted off the walls, preceding his appearance, which reminded Isobel of a water buffalo stampeding to an oasis.

"I just got off the phone with Tony Campbell. You all know who that is!" He glared at the group, letting his eyes rest on Katrina. To her credit, she held his gaze, but Isobel saw that her right leg was trembling. "I get it. You don't want Dove & Flight to merge. But who the fuck is trying to sabotage the deal?" He railed on. "First that preppy little twit croaks over his coffee, and now MacBride's stock price is through the roof on a rumor that came from *our* company! The ICG merger is on the skids—unless somebody can twist daddy around her little finger and get him to change his mind!"

There was an audible gasp and every eye was on Katrina. She took a deep breath, opened her mouth to say something, then turned on her heel and marched down the hall. Her office door slammed, and Liz muttered, "That was ten flavors of wrong."

Barnaby's eyes shot over to her. "If we can't sell the firm to ICG, that's it—it's over. We can't afford to stay in business, because you people are crap at your jobs! And did I forget to mention that Schumann, Crowe & Dyer just shit-canned us? No surprise there. It's one thing to kill a client. But there's no worse crime in public relations than killing a deal!"

And with that, he barreled down the hall, his heavy footfalls punctuated with expletive-laden grunts.

Isobel felt like her insides were made of jello. "I swear, I didn't say anything that wasn't in the script." She grabbed her papers from her desk. "Here. This is what I said. 'Hi, my name is Isobel and I just wanted to confirm that you still cover MacBride's.' Then if they said yes, I said, 'Can you just confirm your phone number and email address…'" She shook her head. "Wait a minute. Was the AP reporter Bob Celauro?"

"That's him," Aaron said.

Isobel held out her press list. "Look at my notes. *N/A*. It wasn't me who tipped him off. It couldn't have been." She looked around the group, her eyes shining with relief. "I never reached him."

TWENTY

"This just doesn't make any sense!" Isobel paced the perimeter of Liz's office. "I know Aaron thinks I'm lying, but somebody else must have called the AP."

"It wasn't necessarily someone from Dove & Flight," Liz said.

Isobel paused in her perambulations. "What do you mean?"

Liz swung her booted feet down from her desk and rolled her chair forward. "Who else knew about the deal?"

"Jayla and her team. And the people at MacBride's, of course, but it sounds like this was exactly what they were hoping to avoid."

"Okay, what about Jayla? We know she wanted to be done with us, but she was getting pressure from above. Maybe she didn't know another way to manage it."

Isobel plopped down in Liz's visitor's chair and leaned back. "Personally, I'd love to make Jayla the bad guy, but this will probably cost them a major piece of business. What could possibly justify engineering that kind of hit for your own company?"

"Then who was it?" Liz ticked off the possibilities. "Aaron looked like someone had just groped his mother. Katrina, well, let's just say that if she wants to sabotage the ICG takeover, there are other, more personal avenues open to her. Me? I don't care enough. I'm out of here in a few months anyway."

"I don't know." Isobel sighed and stood up again. "I think I'll take a walk. I still can't bring myself to follow up on those stupid press releases. You want anything from the outside world? More crackers?"

Liz held up a big box of saltines. "I'm good."

As Isobel hustled down Lexington Avenue, welcoming the bursts of cold wind, she contemplated what Liz had said regarding Katrina. Were there really other, more personal avenues open to her? Barnaby certainly seemed to think Katrina had enough influence over her father to steer the merger back on track. But from what Katrina had told her, Isobel doubted she had her father's ear any more than she had his respect. So maybe she had seen her opportunity to derail the merger and seized it. If it was Katrina, she had set it up neatly by assigning the phone calls to Isobel. But she couldn't have known that Isobel would be so meticulous in her note-taking. Sooner or later, the person responsible for the AP leak would be pinpointed.

Isobel detoured over to Third Avenue, pausing to look in the window of a cheap boutique. A green flowered blouse caught her eye and she went inside to try it on.

"But if it wasn't Katrina, who was it?" she asked her reflection.

"You need something in there?" called the clerk.

"No, thanks! Just talking to myself."

She emerged a few moments later and draped the ill-fitting blouse over the counter.

"Sure you don't want that?" the clerk asked. "It's cute."

Isobel shook her head. "No. And right now that's just about the only thing I'm sure of."

The clerk held the blouse under her chin, and then ducked into the fitting room. Isobel left the store and walked back over to Lexington, where she stopped at Starbucks. The fresh air and unsuccessful retail therapy had done little to unfog her brain; it was time for the heavy artillery. Armed with a tall house blend, and unable to think of any more distractions, Isobel gave up and returned to the office. She set her coffee on her desk, and then followed the hall to the coat closet. As she approached, she became aware of raised voices behind Kit Blanchard's half-closed door.

"How could you do this to me?"

Isobel paused to listen.

"This has nothing to do with you," Kit snapped.

"Nothing to do…" Aaron's voice quivered with disbelief. "Do you have any idea what this means?"

"Don't you think you're being a little melodramatic?"

"I'll tell—" Aaron said.

"No, you won't."

"I trusted you," Aaron said, his voice breaking. "I thought you…I thought we were…"

"Done, Aaron. We're done," Kit said.

Isobel heard the door creak open, and she quickly hid in the coat closet. When she dared peek out, Aaron was slinking away, his head bowed, his hands clenched at his sides. Wilbur Freed came out of the office across from Kit's and followed him. Had Wilbur been delivering magazines or eavesdropping? She wondered what he'd made of the argument. There was no question in Isobel's mind what it meant: Kit and Aaron's affair had been more than just rumor, and now it was over. Poor Aaron. One look at Kit, and he should have known how it would end.

Isobel was so preoccupied as she walked back to her desk that she missed her mouth while trying to sip her coffee. She cursed as it trickled down the front of her sweater, and continued straight to the kitchen. She was blotting the spilled coffee with a napkin when she heard Katrina behind her.

"Hey."

"Hey." Isobel gestured to her chest. "Apparently I have a drinking problem."

Katrina ignored the joke, a grave expression on her face. "Tell me exactly what he said."

"Who?"

"The AP reporter. What were his exact words when you called?"

Isobel set her Starbucks cup down and sat at the table, stretching her legs out. "I never reached him. Didn't Aaron and Liz tell you? After you left, I showed them my press list. I never got him on the phone. It wasn't me."

Katrina pulled out a chair and joined her. "I had a feeling it was something like that."

"You did?"

"I know you pretty well. And I know you know how to stick to a script, which is why I gave you one."

Isobel rolled her napkin into a ball and tossed it aside. "What are you getting at?"

"Somebody tipped off the AP guy, right?"

"Right."

"And what was the result?"

"Schumann's deal with MacBride's is off."

"But more importantly…"

"Dove & Flight's merger with ICG is off," Isobel said.

Katrina waggled a hand from side to side. "At best, it's in jeopardy, and at worst, it's off. So who was most upset about selling the company?"

Isobel looked at her squarely. "You."

Katrina waved her off. "It's easy for me. I don't want to work for my father? I get a new job. But who is fully and personally invested in keeping Dove & Flight independent? I'll give you a hint. It's not Barnaby."

"Angus?" Isobel blinked in surprise. "Did he even know about the MacBride's deal?"

"Of course," said Katrina. "Who do you think brought it in? Those Scots stick together. And he was working on it with Jason before he died."

Isobel rotated her coffee cup absently. "I got the impression Angus just sat in his office and…" Took his meds, she filled in silently.

"No, he works. Not a lot, but he's one of the grand old minds of PR, and he still gets brought in on top deals."

Isobel had to admit it made sense. Nobody was more invested in seeing ICG's acquisition of Dove & Flight fail than Angus Dove.

"So you think Angus tipped off the reporter?" Isobel asked.

Katrina shrugged. "Who else could it have been?"

"But how could he have known we'd be making calls yesterday?"

Katrina wound a stray lock of hair around her finger. "I think that was coincidental. All he needed to know was the basic timing of the deal. Either Jason gave him the rollout before he died, or Angus called Jim MacBride to confirm it."

Isobel shook her head emphatically. "No, he must have known. If he had called on a random day, then everyone would be buzzing, wondering who had made the call. Better to wait until someone else could take the fall for it. It couldn't have worked out better. Easy enough to blame the stupid temp."

"Except that you're still here," Katrina said.

"Only because I showed Aaron and Liz my notes. They saw I hadn't reached the AP reporter."

"Do you think one of them went upstairs to defend you?" Katrina scoffed. "I doubt it."

"But Barnaby—"

"Barnaby assumes it's one of us, and he's probably up there right now trying to decide who to sack."

Isobel regarded Katrina for a moment. "How far do you think Angus would be willing to go to protect the company?"

Katrina frowned. "What do you mean?"

Isobel dropped her voice to a whisper. "What if Jason didn't have a heart attack? What if I told you he was poisoned with the same medicine Angus takes for his heart condition?"

Katrina let out a long, deep breath. "How did you find that out?"

"The other day when I wasn't here, I was actually temping at the Office of the City Medical Examiner. I happened to see his file." Isobel's eyes narrowed. "You don't seem all that surprised."

Katrina shook her head slowly. "I just—I never really believed Jason had a heart attack."

Isobel drummed her fingers on the table. "The only thing is, the coffee I served him was clean, so unless they met before work or something—"

Katrina's hand flew to her mouth. "They did! The morning he died, Jason met Angus for coffee at Starbucks before coming here."

Isobel felt her temples tingle. "How do you know?"

"I saw them together. So did Penny and Dorothy, for that matter."

"Which Starbucks?" Isobel asked stupidly.

"The one around the corner on Lex." Katrina stood up and indicated the Starbucks cup in front of Isobel. " So you might want to switch back to the house brew."

TWENTY-ONE

THE BIGGEST PROBLEM ISOBEL HAD WITH Katrina's revelation was not that Angus Dove seemed no more a murderer than her own grandfather, but that she wasn't sure she believed Katrina about not being materially invested in sabotaging the merger. Katrina might be telling the truth about Jason's early morning coffee with Angus—Isobel could easily confirm that with the others who were there—but if Jason was somehow poisoned in Starbucks, which seemed highly problematic to Isobel, Katrina had just put herself at the scene of the crime.

She was still pondering what all this new information meant, when she saw Aaron approaching from the spiral staircase, looking grim.

"Barnaby wants to see you."

Isobel gulped. "About MacBride's?"

Aaron nodded. "Just bring him your notes and explain."

"But how did he know I made the calls?"

"He demanded to know who it was."

"And you told him?"

Aaron folded his arms across his chest. "Of course I did."

"Any advice before I face the firing squad?" she asked. Aaron shook his head. "Yeah, didn't think so."

Isobel took the MacBride's press list and her script and made her way up the spiral staircase to Harm's Way, a nickname she now fully appreciated. When she arrived at the constellation of assistants' desks, Jimmy Rocket jumped to his feet and placed his red baseball cap over his heart.

"Melodious songbird, though your tune be mournful today, the melody may yet transpose."

Isobel gave a wry smile. "You remind me of my Shakespeare-quoting roommate."

Jimmy thumped his chest proudly. "That was 100% unadulterated Rocket, ma'am."

The phone rang, and Jimmy, his eyes still bathing Isobel with pity, grabbed the nearest length of black plastic.

"Hello?"

He frowned at the lack of response and glanced down.

"Stapler," Isobel pointed out.

"Ah." He thrust it at Isobel. "Call for you on the Swingline!"

For a moment, Isobel forgot why she was there and giggled delightedly at his pun as he answered the real phone. Then a voice bellowed, "You! Now!"

Jimmy put his hand over the mouthpiece and whispered, "It's okay, his bark is much worse then his…nah, forget it. His bite is pretty bad."

Even though she was not an actual employee, Isobel felt her heart pounding as she entered Barnaby's office. He slammed it behind her and did not offer her a seat. He prowled around her in a circle, fairly sniffing her. Then he straightened up and looked her in the eye.

"You made the reporter calls on MacBride's."

"I did." Isobel's voice came out in a squeak. She held out her press list. "But I didn't reach the AP reporter. Look. *N/A*. Not available. And I knew enough not to leave messages anywhere."

Barnaby brought the paper close to his nose and squinted at it. After a few minutes, he belched and peered more closely at her.

"Are you sure?"

Isobel gave a sharp genie nod. "Positive. This is the first confidential assignment I've gotten, so I was careful to take very specific notes."

"You don't seem like an idiot. Then again, the rest of them don't either, until they fuck up and show their true colors."

He stomped around his office, scratching his lower back and muttering to himself. Then he swung around to her again. "You think one of the reporters you did reach called this guy and said, 'What do you know about MacBride's?'"

"Don't reporters tend to keep inside information to themselves? I mean, if they do have news, they want to be the ones to break it."

Barnaby stopped in his tracks. "Who the fuck are you, anyway?"

"Isobel—"

He waved a meaty hand at her. "What are you doing temping? What's your deal?"

"I'm an actress."

"Oh, give me a fucking break!"

Isobel couldn't believe her ears. This man ran a successful PR business? Angus Dove should be thrilled that someone would pay him to be rid of this oaf. They said Barnaby was tops and his clients loved him, but Katrina had told her that he'd been known to make colleagues follow him into the men's room to continue a conversation while he took a dump. Once he'd actually left with toilet paper coming out over the top of his trousers and everyone was too embarrassed to tell him, until Jimmy finally took one for the team. Presumably Barnaby was different with clients, but what did she know? Maybe they found it refreshing.

"What is Meryl Streep thinking?" he growled.

If Isobel really cared about her job, she might have perceived this as a test. But since her future ultimately lay far from Dove & Flight, she figured she had nothing to lose—and everything to gain—by speaking her mind.

"Actually, I was wondering if someone else here made the call and tipped off the reporter on purpose."

Barnaby narrowed his eyes. "And why the fuck would anybody want to do that?"

Isobel was sorely tempted to hurl his own expletives back at him, but instead she answered simply, "To sabotage the ICG merger. Of course."

His reaction was so fleeting it might have gone unnoticed, but Isobel, having set him up, was watching him closely. She was rewarded with the quickest, most furtive glance imaginable at a framed wall photograph of the two founders of Dove & Flight. And despite the fact that Barnaby Flight was clearly a raging egomaniac, Isobel knew he wasn't looking at himself.

"I'm going to do whatever it takes to make sure ICG buys us, so everybody around here better fucking get used to it!" His voice rose and he waved both arms furiously. "Now get out of here and shut the goddamn door!"

Isobel didn't need to be told twice. Barnaby's office had obviously been designed for a much smaller person, and his energy was oppressive, not to mention his physical presence. She leaned on Jimmy's desk, exhaling slowly. He came around behind her and put his face close to her neck. At first she thought he might kiss her, but then he pulled away.

"No visible bite marks. That's good," he said.

Isobel picked up a heavy, old-fashioned letter opener with silver scrollwork and turned it over in her hand. She raised it and made a knifing gesture toward Barnaby's door.

"How can you stand working for him?"

"Down, girl!" Jimmy took the letter opener from her and set it down on his desk.

"I'm serious! How do you stand the abuse?"

Jimmy gazed at the acoustical tiles on the ceiling, as if he hoped to find the answer there. "Now, that's a good question. But I'll tell you, there are just as many folks who don't understand why he puts up with me. So I guess we're just made for each other. I like to think of us as Pyramus and Thisbe, rude mechanicals style."

His comment reminded her of something Katrina had told her.

"Jimmy," she said in a sultry voice, "I have to ask you a personal question."

"Be still, my gallivanting heart!" He dropped his voice. "Sing to me, sweet nightingale."

"I've been told that you partake, on occasion, of certain not entirely legal substances."

Jimmy clapped a hand to his chest in mock indignation. "I? Who would circulate such spurious mongerings?" He leaned in close. "Are you in the market?"

"For information." She looked around. Sophie Barker was at the copier, and Wilbur Freed was sliding silently into Angus's office to deliver his news clips. She continued, keeping her voice low. "You know the medicine Angus takes for his heart?"

"Digoxin?"

Isobel nodded. "How hard would it be to slip into somebody's coffee?"

Jimmy's expression altered. "I gathered from Sophie that such an additive sweetened a certain deceased person's morning beverage."

"It seems that way. How hard would it be, in your expert opinion?"

Jimmy bopped the eraser end of a pencil on his desk blotter in a nervous tattoo. "You do realize there's a world of difference between recreational pharmacology and…what you're talking about."

Isobel put her hand gently on his, stopping the pencil mid-bounce. She wasn't quite ready to tell Jimmy about Angus's meeting with Jason in Starbucks. "I'm sorry. I didn't mean to imply anything. I'm just trying to think this through a little, and—"

"And Angus was bitterly opposed to the merger. He could have—" Jimmy clamped his lips over his even white teeth.

"What?"

Jimmy hesitated. "The police said the coffee Jason drank here wasn't poisoned, right?"

"Right. I'm just asking hypothetically."

"Then I guess it doesn't really matter."

Isobel felt her pulse quicken. "What doesn't?"

"Angus takes his daily pill, but Sophie keeps a liquid suspension for injection in case he has a heart attack. I don't know much, but I do know that tablets would be hard to dissolve in coffee without someone noticing. But the suspension? That's a different story."

TWENTY-TWO

Isobel descended the spiral staircase slowly, pondering Jimmy's disclosure about Angus's liquid digoxin. Taken with Katrina's report of seeing Angus and Jason at Starbucks, it was impossible to ignore the medicine's significance. Could Angus actually have slipped it into Jason's coffee at Starbucks?

Isobel debated sharing this new tidbit with Katrina, but something held her back. She passed Liz's office and looked in, eager to run all of this past her, but she was out. With a sigh of resignation, Isobel returned to her desk and picked up Dorothy's list of medical trade publications. There was no putting it off any longer, and considering that Aaron had ratted her out to Barnaby, Isobel felt no compunction about giving Dorothy's project priority. Upon closer inspection, she saw that the trade publications were ranked by circulation, so she highlighted the top fifteen and made her calls.

In the end, she managed to jolly two editors into accepting bylined articles on the future of plastics in the medical devices industry. Pleased with her success, Isobel gathered her notes and knocked on Dorothy's door.

The older woman was on the phone, but she waved Isobel in and gestured for her to sit. Isobel could tell Dorothy was getting pushback on the other end, but her tone remained impressively calm and authoritative. Her answers managed to be placating, without being condescending. Dorothy rolled her clear, cornflower blue eyes at Isobel and made a jabbering gesture with her free hand.

Isobel smiled in return and examined the photos on Dorothy's desk. She recognized Dorothy with her husband and son at a lobster shack somewhere on the Atlantic coast. There was also a young woman with black hair sitting astride a horse, and an elderly couple toasting each other at a restaurant table.

Dorothy slammed the phone down. "What a noxious blowhard! Sorry about that. How did you make out with the release?"

"Pretty well, I think." Isobel set down the photo of the couple and read from her notes. "*Devices Today* will consider an article as long as it doesn't read like a sales pitch. Limit 750 words, and they can use it for the May issue, but they need it by the beginning of February."

Dorothy tilted her head to the side, considering. "That might be pushing it, timing-wise, but I'll ask. What else?"

"*Plastics in Medicine* will take 1,200 words anytime, and they like data tables."

"That's perfect for them. Anyone else?"

"Sorry. I only called the biggies, and I didn't reach everyone. Do you want me to try a few more?"

Dorothy held out her hand. "No, this is fine. Thank you."

Isobel handed over her notes. "To tell you the truth, I was glad to have something else to focus on after the whole MacBride's thing."

Dorothy nodded. "Crazy day. It isn't usually so dramatic around here."

Isobel eyed her curiously. "Where do you stand on this whole ICG acquisition? Do you think it's good?"

Dorothy pursed her lips. "Depends. Angus and Barnaby will be able to retire in style, but for the rest of us, it's a case-by-case thing."

"I imagine you're especially concerned," Isobel ventured.

A surprised laugh escaped Dorothy's lips. "Why me?"

"Isn't one of the new sister PR firms in healthcare?"

"Fisher Health. I left them to work here." Dorothy's eyes crinkled appealingly at the corners as she smiled. "At the risk of sounding immodest, I think they'd jump at the chance to have me back. So I'd say I'm in a pretty secure position."

"You seem to be in the minority," Isobel said.

Dorothy made a modest, noncommittal sound and rattled Isobel's notes. "Anyway, thanks for this. I appreciate it."

Isobel returned to her desk to find Liz struggling to button her coat over her belly.

She gazed down at her midsection and sighed. "I was so hoping to make it through the winter without having to buy a maternity coat."

"You could just wrap yourself in a sleeping bag," suggested Isobel.

"Ah! Success!" Liz cried, securing the last button.

"Do you have a second before you go?"

"Sorry, gotta run." Liz hurried toward the door. "Hubby is taking me out to dinner tonight. I've been saving up all day, so this will count officially as meals four through six!"

Isobel glanced at her watch, surprised to see it was almost five. Time for her to shove off, too. She wanted to decompress at home before her audition for Hugh Fremont. One unexpected benefit of the day's surprises was that Isobel had forgotten to obsess about it. She was careful to refer to it, even to herself, as an audition, although she harbored hopes that it might turn into a date. She retrieved her coat and was shutting down her computer when she heard a heavy tread on the spiral staircase. Two male voices caught her attention, and the lower one sent an involuntary shiver of pleasure down her spine. She canceled her computer shutdown and watched her desktop restore. Then she resettled at her desk, pulled her ponytail tighter and pretended to busy herself.

Mike Hardy, the HR director, came into view with James close behind him.

"Hi, Isobel," Mike said.

"Hi, Mike. James! What brings you here?"

"I was in the neighborhood and I thought I'd poke my head in."

She eyed him dubiously.

"I gather that little kerfluffle with the AP reporter got cleared up?" Mike asked.

Isobel caught James's frown and quickly said, "It had nothing to do with me."

Mike slid his stocky frame sideways to let Penny Warren pass. James had once told her he thought Mike looked like a chess piece. All Isobel could think was pawn to rook four and wondered if James was thinking the same.

"James and I were just discussing the possibility of adding another temp or two," Mike said. "We're not in a position to hire anybody right now, but as you can see, there's plenty of work. We'd also like to officially make your assignment open-ended. James explained that you're an actress, and I'm sure you can work it out to come and go whenever you have to. What do you think?"

That sort of arrangement was actor/temp nirvana. The only thing better was a direct freelance contract without a temp agency as a middleman. She chanced a look at James, but his expression was unreadable.

"I'd like that. Thanks."

Mike beamed. "Great!" He clasped James's hand and gave it a hearty shake. "James. Good to see you."

"Yeah, you, too."

"You look like you're ready to go, Isobel. I'll walk you out," said James.

As soon as Mike was out of earshot, Isobel said, "Walk me out?"

James inclined his head in amusement. "Do you always work with your coat on?"

She felt her face grow warm. "What are you really doing here, James?"

"You don't believe I came by to see Mike?"

"Not for a minute."

"I thought maybe we could grab a bite to eat," he said, with a too-casual shrug.

Isobel peered at him. "What's going on?"

He gave an exasperated sigh. "You're impossible. I just have a few things to tell you, that's all. Some stuff Jayla told me."

"Jayla? You're speaking again?"

"Briefly. Anyway, I thought we might have dinner."

Isobel inclined her head. "Like a date?"

"Like dinner."

Isobel shook her head. "I'd like to, but I have plans tonight. An audition, in fact." She caught his expression and clucked at him. "Don't look so surprised."

"What's it for?"

"Do you really care?" She softened. "It's a revue of original songs. Let's go, and you can fill me in on the way out."

She switched off her computer again and straightened some papers on her desk, while he examined a series of framed press placements on the wall.

"Impressive stuff," he said.

"Recent events aside, I get the feeling they're actually pretty good at what they do around here."

Dorothy emerged from her office, waving a copy of a magazine in Isobel's direction. "For *Plastics in Medicine*—" She paused and looked from her to James. "Oh, sorry, you're leaving. We can talk tomorrow."

"See? It's like I actually work here." Isobel flashed a proud smile as Dorothy retreated.

James turned around. "Who was that?"

"Dorothy in healthcare. I landed her two bylined articles today."

"Aren't you ready yet?"

Isobel slung her bag over her shoulder. "Now I am. Let's go."

But before they reached the door, Mike Hardy came clattering down the spiral steps, waving his arms frantically.

"Wait! Stop!"

Isobel and James whirled around.

Mike looked distinctly less ruddy and cheerful than he had when he'd left them a few moments ago. In fact, he looked utterly panic-stricken.

"You can't leave. Nobody can. The police are on their way. Angus is dead."

TWENTY-THREE

WOULD HE EVER BE ABLE TO VISIT ISOBEL at her place of work without running into the goddamn cops?

James paced back and forth, while Isobel sat at her desk, nervously shuffling papers.

"Will you sit down? You're making me nervous," she said.

"Stop messing with those papers. *You're* making *me* nervous!"

Isobel gave a frustrated sigh and stood up. "Fine! Will you please just tell me whatever it was you wanted to tell me?"

"I don't want to be overheard."

She thought for a moment. "Liz is gone. We can use her office."

"What about the cops?"

"If they can't find us, they're pretty crappy cops."

It was hard to argue with that, so he followed her a few paces down the hall into the vacant office. She shut the door behind them and put her hands on her hips.

"Okay. What's going on?"

He cracked his knuckles. "It's not really that much."

She eyed him. "But it was worth coming by to tell me in person? Or were you just looking for an excuse to buy me dinner?"

He felt the heat rise to his face. "Who said I was buying?"

She laughed. "You're a gentleman at heart, James. I know that about you, even if you don't know it yourself. So what's the scoop?"

He pulled over the visitor's chair and sat down. Isobel perched on the edge of the desk.

"There's a woman who works here, Kit someone."

"Kit Blanchard."

"Did you know she and Jason were related by marriage?"

Her eyebrows rose in surprise. "No kidding! Is that how Dove & Flight got his business?"

"According to Jayla, yes, although Kit didn't work on the account."

"She wouldn't. She does consumer products." Isobel smiled a smile he'd seen before and didn't much like.

"What?"

"Kit was having an affair with Aaron Grossman who did work on the account. It seems to have ended today, and not amicably."

"And you know this how?"

She shrugged. "I overheard them."

He folded his arms. "You mean you eavesdropped."

"No! I honestly happened to be walking past Kit's office to the coat closet and heard them. I can show you where her office is and where the closet is if you don't believe me—"

"Okay, okay!" He held up his hand to stem the flow. "So what do you think it means?"

"Kit and Jason? I don't know. But they had a relationship apart from work, and that's exactly the kind of connection I was looking for. I knew there was something!" Isobel pressed her fingertips together in a pyramid shape and shut her eyes.

"You're thinking. Stop that."

Isobel's eyes popped open. "What if Jason knew she was having an affair with Aaron, and he planned to tell—wait, how are they related?"

"She's married to his brother's wife's brother," he said slowly, working it through. "But if Jason knew about the affair and was threatening to expose Kit, why would she dump Aaron *after* Jason was dead?"

"Guilty conscience?"

James shook his head. "More likely he'd simply outlived his usefulness. Besides, no matter how you slice it, it's a pretty drastic leap from the simple fact that they're related to a motive for murder."

Isobel picked up a snow globe from Liz's desk and turned it upside down. "I guess. Okay, what else you got?"

"Your friend Katrina was dating Jason."

The color drained from Isobel's face, and James couldn't help but feel satisfaction at having caught her off guard.

She shook her head so vigorously her ponytail smacked her cheek. "She was not."

"You sure about that?"

Isobel hesitated. "How do you know?"

"Jayla told me."

Isobel let out a derisive squawk. "And you think she's telling the truth?"

"Why would she lie to me?"

"I don't know!" Isobel huffed. "Maybe because *she* killed Jason?"

He laughed. "You just don't like her. That's what this is about."

She set the snow globe down. "No, *you* don't like her. Katrina and Jason were not dating. I'm sure of it."

But her last words were colored by a tiny tremor that told him she was far from sure. He stood up, pushed the chair back to where he'd found it, and opened the door.

"Where the hell is everyone?" James made a wide, clumsy gesture in an attempt to take in the entire floor. "Why are we the only ones here?"

"Liz left to meet her husband for dinner, and Aaron left in a grouchy mood because his office floozy dumped him."

She brushed past him, leaving him to shut off Liz's light and close the door.

"Isobel!"

"What?"

He followed her back to her desk. "Don't you think you should keep your voice down?"

"Oh, yeah, the floozy left too," she stage-whispered. "I think Katrina and Penny are here somewhere, and as far as I know Dorothy is still in her office. Freaky Wilbur is probably lurking around, too, like the Luddite angel of death."

"Well, they can't keep us here all night!"

At that moment, they heard footsteps on the spiral staircase and Detectives O'Connor and Aguilar appeared. They slowed as they approached James and Isobel.

"Well, well, well. We've got to stop meeting like this," said O'Connor in his lilting voice.

"Top o' the evenin' to you, Officer," James said, before he could stop himself.

O'Connor's face remained a blank, but Aguilar gave a disapproving grunt.

"Just a few questions, and then you can be on your way," O'Connor said. "When did you arrive here, Mr. Cooke, is it?"

As if he didn't know.

"Around five."

"Did you enter on this floor or the one above?"

"The one above. I came to see Mike Hardy, the HR director. From the moment I got here, I was with him or with Isobel. He escorted me downstairs when we were finished with our business."

"And your purpose here?"

Don't lie to the cops, he reminded himself. Ever.

"Mike and I had things to discuss, and I thought if I came by, Isobel might join me for dinner."

He saw her smirk out of the corner of his eye, but he didn't give her the satisfaction of noticing.

O'Connor shrugged in surrender and moved on to Isobel. "Can you tell me about your movements this afternoon?"

"I was mostly down here. I took a break for coffee, and then I went upstairs. Barnaby called me into his office to ask me about some work I did."

O'Connor made a note. "And did anything in the conversation seem to surprise or upset Barnaby?"

"We were talking about Angus." Isobel hesitated. "No, that's not entirely accurate. We were talking about who might have wanted to sabotage the firm's merger with ICG. See, everyone knows Barnaby wanted to sell the firm and Angus didn't. But something happened—a big story was leaked to a reporter—and I got blamed for it."

James shot her a look, but her eyes remained fixed on O'Connor.

"Did you now?" O'Connor asked lightly.

"I was able to prove it wasn't me. But that left Barnaby wondering who else it might have been. I never even said Angus's name, but I saw Barnaby glance at a photo of him."

O'Connor nodded sharply "All right, then. You can both go."

"That's it?" Isobel asked. "What happened to Angus? How did he die?"

"Let's just say it was a gray area between a heart attack and suicide," O'Connor said.

"What does that mean?" James asked.

"Apparently, after Isobel left him, Barnaby went into Angus's office and they argued," O'Connor explained. "Shortly after that, Angus suffered a heart attack. Where it gets tricky is that he seems to have chosen to die."

James and Isobel exchanged a glance. "What do you mean?" he asked.

"There was a brief window of a few minutes when Angus could have called to his secretary for his heart medication, but she swears he didn't," O'Connor said. "Instead, it seems he spent the last moments of his life writing this."

O'Connor gestured to Aguilar, who held up a plastic evidence bag. Inside was a ripped piece of Dove & Flight letterhead with Angus's already irregular handwriting looking even more fragile than usual.

James and Isobel leaned over and read the note:

For the good of the firm.

"He died holding the pen," said Aguilar.

"For what it's worth, the medical examiner doesn't think the medicine would have saved him even if he'd gotten it in time. It was a massive coronary," O'Connor said.

"What did Barnaby say to him? Does anyone know?" asked James.

O'Connor raised an angular, red-haired eyebrow at him. "Have you ever heard that man speak? Even when he isn't shouting, you can hear him in New Jersey."

Aguilar consulted his notes. "His assistant heard him scream, and I quote: 'This was our last chance to cash in, and you fucked it up by calling the AP. I suppose you killed that Whiteley kid, too.'"

"Well, it's possible," Isobel said.

James shot her a warning glance, but as usual, she ignored him and plunged on.

"Angus and Jason met for coffee in Starbucks the morning Jason died. Angus could have had his digoxin with him and slipped it into Jason's coffee there."

James saw O'Connor's posture stiffen, while Aguilar's normally placid expression grew alert.

"What makes you think there was digoxin in his coffee?" asked O'Connor in a steely voice.

"Is this going to take much longer? I have to be somewhere," James broke in.

O'Connor held out a restraining arm. "Let Ms. Spice answer the question, please."

Isobel appealed to James, and he sighed in her direction. "Just tell them the truth."

"A few days after Jason died, James happened to get a temp request from the Office of the City Medical Examiner, and he sent me. I was delivering some records and Jason's death report was sitting right there on the table. His name caught my eye, and I saw it right before the secretary snapped it up.

Digoxin was one of the substances listed as a cause of death by poisoning."

"Aguilar, confirm that Ms. Spice was at the ME's office that day." O'Connor turned back to Isobel. "Whom did you work with there?"

"Randy and Eva. Oh, and Wanda."

O'Connor waved dismissively in Aguilar's direction. "Never mind. I know Wanda. She's Daley's assistant."

"Tell us more about this meeting in Starbucks. I must admit, that's a piece of information we hadn't uncovered," said O'Connor.

Humility in a cop, if you could call it that, thought James. Then again, he hadn't uncovered it either. He felt a flash of annoyance at Isobel for not filling him in first.

"I wasn't there, but Katrina saw them."

"Which Starbucks?"

"The one right around the corner on Lex. Katrina wasn't the only one there. She said Penny and Dorothy stopped in, too."

"You'd think if one of them saw Angus Dove slip something into Jason Whiteley's coffee, they might have thought to mention it," O'Connor said thoughtfully.

"Unless they didn't realize what they saw," Aguilar pointed out. "And we didn't question them about Starbucks."

O'Connor turned to Isobel. "Are those three still here?"

"I'm not sure about Katrina and Penny, but I think Dorothy is still in her office."

"We'll start with her, then. Maybe we'll get some answers." O'Connor snapped his notebook shut. "Then we'll finally be out of your hair."

And not a moment too soon, thought James.

TWENTY-FOUR

IT WAS WELL AFTER SEVEN WHEN ISOBEL finally left the office. As she raced toward the subway, she called Hugh to apologize for being so late. She hadn't wanted to call in front of James, but he hadn't left her alone for a second.

"If you'd rather postpone, I understand," Hugh said, a note of disappointment in his voice. "But I don't have anything else on tonight, so you're still welcome to—"

"Yes! I can still make it, if you don't mind waiting," she huffed as she jogged toward the subway. "I just need to run home for a few minutes first."

"Whenever you get here is fine. I'm looking forward to seeing you again."

Delphi had already left for rehearsal, and Isobel was grateful to have the place to herself. She hurriedly shed her work clothes and threw on her favorite jeans and a clingy cashmere sweater. At the same time, she ran her voice up and down the scale, and sang through a song or two. Satisfied that she was in far better shape than the last time Hugh had heard her, she grabbed her music binder, bundled herself against the elements, and set out uptown.

Isobel was surprised to discover that the 125th Street subway station was above ground, and when she descended the stairs to the street, she was so turned around she walked a block in the wrong direction before she stopped a passerby and reoriented herself properly. A few moments later, she was ringing Hugh's buzzer.

"Come on up!"

He was waiting for her in the doorway when she arrived on the second floor landing. She'd been so caught up in her own personal drama at the *Phantom* auditions, that beyond a basically agreeable physical impression, she hadn't been able to clearly recall what he looked like. He was about six feet tall, with wavy hair so dark it was almost black, high cheekbones, and expressive brown eyes behind wire-rimmed glasses. He wore jeans and a dark green V-neck sweater, and Isobel caught a bracing whiff of citrus from his cologne.

"I made it," she said, trying to disguise the fact that she was out of breath from only two flights of stairs.

"I'm so glad."

He led her past a makeshift kitchen to a soundproofed room with a baby grand piano and bookshelves overflowing with all manner of musical scores. Isobel wandered over and ran her fingers over the spines.

"I guess I didn't need to bring any music of my own. You have everything!"

"I have a lot," he replied modestly.

"So much music. Where do you sleep?"

"This is just my studio. I coach and compose here. My apartment is a few blocks away. I share this with another pianist. Mostly it works out, although sometimes we have to jello wrestle for it."

The thought of Hugh doing any kind of wrestling, jello or otherwise, was pretty incongruous, and she told him so.

He grinned. "You'd be surprised. Take off your coat, stay awhile. Would you like a cup of tea?"

"Thanks. That would be great."

She threw her coat on a small sofa and seated herself at the piano, where the score to *Sweeney Todd* lay open. She thumbed through the pages, pausing at her favorite song, "Green Finch and Linnet Bird." She fanned her fingers out and caressed the page.

"I want this score so badly, but it's so expensive," she said, when Hugh returned.

"I know. But if there were ever a score worth saving up for, this is the one." He pointed to the music. "Sing a bit for me."

He took Isobel's place on the bench and played the introduction. She tried not to listen to herself, concentrating instead on letting her voice soar and trill without effort. When she finished, the teakettle was whistling.

"Lovely! Just a sec."

Hugh darted out of the room, and Isobel felt her entire body relax. The first song was always the hardest. Whatever she sang next would be easier. Hugh returned a few moments later with two steaming mugs of peppermint tea.

"You really do have a beautiful voice," he said, setting the mugs down on a small side table. "I could tell even from the bit I heard the other day."

Isobel flushed with pride. "Thank you. The truth is, I don't remember much about my actual singing. Just the trial of trying to get seen."

"We'll see if we can make that day worth your while. Do you have something else you could do for me? Something quirkier that shows your sense of humor?"

"What makes you think I have one?"

"Another song or a sense of humor?"

"You know," she said as she flipped the pages of her binder, "I went to an audition last year where they insisted on an up-tempo and a ballad. But I had just sung a song that was somewhere in between, so I didn't know what to offer next. And then I realized what they really wanted was character contrast." She opened her binder to "The Secret Service" by Irving Berlin and set it on the piano. "So why don't they just say that, like you did?"

Hugh sat down and smoothed the pages. "There are a lot of people in this business with a cursory understanding of music. You'd be amazed. Great choice, by the way."

Relaxing even more, Isobel sang through her song, and when she finished, Hugh sat back and regarded her.

"I'm always so pleased when my instincts prove correct. You're quite funny, you know. Would you sing in my revue? I'd be honored to have you."

To her surprise, Isobel realized she had been enjoying herself so much that she had temporarily lost sight of the fact that there was a potential gig in the offing.

"I'd love to!"

Hugh clapped his hands together. "Brilliant! It will be you and a tenor, still to be cast, with me at the piano. Probably a total of fourteen or fifteen songs at Don't Tell Mama."

"What's 'Don't Tell Mama,' other than a song from *Cabaret*?"

Hugh laughed. "You really are new in town, aren't you? It's a very popular cabaret space in the theater district. We'll do four performances, and I'll pay you a portion of the door. I'm sorry I can't pay you for rehearsals, but it will be good exposure for you. And a good experience as well, I hope."

"I'm just thrilled to be working with someone as talented as you."

"You may want to reserve judgment until you hear my songs."

"I'll take it on faith. You've already proven you have good taste."

Hugh glanced at his watch. "Listen, I don't suppose you'd like to grab a bite?"

Isobel felt her heart give a tiny leap. "Sure!"

Hugh stood up and closed the piano lid. "I know a wonderful little place a few blocks away. Real soul food."

As Hugh helped Isobel on with her coat, she reflected on the irony that she was going out for soul food in Harlem, not with James, whom she knew lived there, but with a British pianist and composer who had just hired her. Sometimes, things happened in the oddest ways.

TWENTY-FIVE

JAMES KNEW AS SOON AS HE AND ISOBEL parted ways at Dove & Flight that he'd never make it to his AA meeting, which was a real problem. The temptation to stop in at his local dive was more powerful than it had been in a while. It seemed that in spite of her whole song and dance about believing in him, Isobel thought he was lying about Katrina dating Jason. Even though Jayla was the source of the information, it still came down to Isobel not trusting him, despite her protestations to the contrary.

When he emerged from the subway, he closed his eyes, counted to one hundred, and went home to get his gym bag. Working out often defused his desire for a drink. The trick was getting to the gym, because the impulse to drink didn't always coincide with his proximity to barbells. But as he left his apartment, he felt a rush just from holding his gym bag. He would make it this time. He was strong, in control, and free of burdensome females.

Until he turned the corner and ran smack into Weight Girl.

"What are you doing lurking on the street?" he asked sharply.

"I'm not lurking. I'm coming from the gym."

"Good. Maybe I'll get to work out in peace this time."

She shifted awkwardly and tugged at the ends of her red wool scarf. He suddenly had a vision of her pulling too tight and strangling herself.

"You really don't like me, do you? Is it because I'm a girl? I'm white? Or both?"

He shook his head in bewilderment. "Neither. It's because you're a nosy pain in the ass, and I already have plenty of those in my life. Now, if you don't mind." He tried to pass her, but was frustrated to find that her tiny, bird-like body was somehow blocking his way.

She folded her arms. "You don't know me at all."

"I know you enough."

"Then what's my name? I know yours."

"You do?"

"James Cooke. I asked at the front desk. I'm Lily Rubin."

She held out her hand in a formal greeting. He sighed and shook it as quickly as possible.

"Lily. Okay. I appreciate your entirely misplaced interest in me, but I don't have time to talk. I really need to work out."

"Okay. That's all you need to say. I'll let you go. But you got one thing wrong."

"What's that?"

"I'm a writer, so I find you very interesting. Ciao." She gave a quaint little bowing gesture and moved aside to let him pass.

He was certain she noticed his hesitation, but to her credit and his surprise, she didn't pounce. When he reached the gym, he gave in to the impulse to turn around. She was sitting on the stoop of a brownstone, her arms wrapped around her thin frame, staring straight ahead. What if she wasn't really a Barnard student and didn't have any place to sleep? She looked tiny and vulnerable, sitting there on the freezing stoop, and although the neighborhood wasn't as dangerous as it once was, she was still an easy mark. He took a step toward her.

"James!"

He turned at the sound of his name and was astonished to see Isobel coming down the block from the other direction. His first thought was that she, too, had been stalking him, but then he saw that she wasn't alone.

"I thought you had an audition," he said.

Isobel and her friend slowed to meet him. "I did. This is Hugh. I just sang for him."

"Yes, and she was terrific," Hugh said.

"I'll bet," muttered James.

Isobel shot him a look. "I'm going to be in a revue of his original songs. You could congratulate me."

"I could."

"I'm sorry, I didn't catch your name," said Hugh.

"This is James, my temp agent," Isobel said.

Hugh blinked in surprise. "Really? Not sure I'd have guessed that. Well, here you are with your two employers, both in thrall to you."

"It's very chivalrous of you to walk Isobel to the subway," James said.

"Oh, no." Hugh laughed. "We're on our way to Sylvia's. Do you know it?"

"Um, yeah. I've heard of it," James said, dripping sarcasm.

Isobel shifted awkwardly. "I'd invite you to join us, but I'd rather not mix business with business."

"Oh, go ahead and invite me, so this time I can blow *you* off—" James was interrupted by a tug on his sleeve. He looked down and saw Lily at his elbow.

"Aren't you going to introduce me to your friends?"

"What the fuck?" James stared at her, aghast. "No!"

"James!" Isobel shook her head in disbelief.

"This is Isobel and," he gritted his teeth, "I'm sorry, I forgot your name."

"Hugh."

He hadn't, actually, but he wanted to show the guy how little he cared, and he wanted Lily to understand that this wasn't a social gathering.

"I'm Lily." She smiled around at the small group.

"We, uh, work out at the same gym," James said, pointing over his shoulder in a gesture too contorted to be illustrative.

"So, what are we talking about?" Lily asked brightly.

Isobel bristled. "*We* aren't talking about anything."

James felt his mouth working into a smile, but he suppressed it. It was almost worth Lily's intrusion to see Isobel be out-Isobeled.

"We're off to dinner at Sylvia's," Hugh said. The guy was starting to sound like a broken record.

"Oh, all of you?" Lily asked.

James immediately saw where this was going. "No, just Isobel and Hugh. I ran into them, and we should let them be off on their *date*."

"It's not a date!" Isobel said quickly. She turned to Hugh. "Is it?"

Now it was Hugh's turn to squirm. He managed to prolong the ambiguity by shaking his head, while at the same time saying, "Indeed!" in tones that sounded exaggeratedly upper-crust.

James returned his attention to Isobel. "Well, if it isn't a date, then maybe you'll still consider dinner with me some other night."

Lily clapped her hands in delighted amusement. "I know! You should take her to Simpson's-in-the-Strand."

Hugh threw an admiring chuckle in Lily's direction. "Good one! This is topsy-turvy in every way." He nudged Isobel. "Old W.S. Gilbert would appreciate the joke, don't you think? Me taking you out for soul food and James squiring you to London?"

Isobel gave a wan smile, and James suddenly realized he must be reading the situation completely wrong. She couldn't possibly be romantically interested in this twit. Obviously, she was only having dinner with him because he'd given her a job. Of course, James noted, the same might be said for him.

Isobel grabbed Hugh's arm. "Let's go. I'm starving." She burned James with a look of unadulterated fury and dragged Hugh down the street.

James whirled on Lily. "What is wrong with you?"

She shrank back. "I was just being friendly." He let out a strangled groan, but she pressed on. "Is Isobel one of the nosy women you were talking about?"

"Isobel is none of your business. *None* of my business is your business, so just butt out!"

"That was such an interesting conversation," Lily mused. "You and Hugh were having this passive-aggressive cockfight over Isobel, who couldn't figure out what I am to you. You like Isobel, don't you?"

James gaped at her. This was too much.

He allowed a deep breath to inflate him like a balloon, and he brought his full mass to tower over her.

"Let's get a few things straight. Number one, you are nothing to me. You hear that? Nothing. Just a gym gadfly who doesn't know when to shut the fuck up. Number two, I am not discussing Isobel with you or introducing you to any *acquaintances* of mine. And number three, I am going to the gym *right now*, and if you follow me, I'll…"

"You'll what?" she asked, her defiant little nose upturned.

He thrust a forefinger at her. "I'll have your gym membership suspended for harassment. That I can do!"

He powered his way down the block, and this time he didn't look back.

TWENTY-SIX

ISOBEL HAD DIFFICULTY CONCENTRATING at work the next day. Her thoughts and feelings were all jumbled together, and she knew she needed to separate them into navigable piles. First, there was the double whammy of the MacBride's debacle and Angus's death. Then there was the argument she'd overheard between Aaron and Kit, plus James's bizarre contention that Katrina and Jason had been dating. Aside from that, there was her successful audition for Hugh, followed by that little one-act play on the street. In the end, they never made it to Sylvia's—she suspected Hugh felt awkward about it—so they had enjoyed a cozy Italian meal instead. It had taken a few glasses of wine to shake off the weirdness, but they'd finally relaxed, and Hugh had proven to be charming company.

She pushed away from her desk and paced into the office kitchen, where she opened the fridge, scanned the contents absent-mindedly, and slammed it shut again. She sat in one of the orange plastic chairs and spread her hands out on the Formica tabletop. Who was that little snot bugging James? He obviously wanted nothing to do with her. Isobel knew him well enough to read the signs. She had once been on the receiving end of them herself. Thankfully, their relationship had evolved beyond that first encounter.

But evolved, how, exactly? If she didn't know better, she'd have said James was jealous of Hugh. There was no other explanation for his rudeness. But James had made it clear that he wasn't interested in a relationship with anyone, let alone her, while he concentrated on staying sober. Still, the possibility that a potential rival could provoke him into revealing his true feelings was intriguing.

"Is there more coffee?"

Isobel stirred from her reverie to answer Penny, who was peering doubtfully into the empty carafe.

"I don't see any coffee that you don't see."

"I meant is there any more, period," said Penny. "The box is empty." She held up the carton of prepackaged coffee packs sitting empty next to the coffee maker.

"We should switch to single serving cups," Isobel said.

Penny opened the cabinets, looking for another box. "I guess I'll have to go down to supplies and see if they have more." She paused at the door. "By the way, thanks for doing my work for me."

"What work?"

"The plastics release. I was supposed to do it the other day, but I was out." She pulled off her corduroy headband, examined it, and then pushed her hair back again. "Two hits. Not bad. I usually get more than that."

"Really?" Isobel was too amused by the whiff of competitiveness seeping out from behind Penny's saccharine smile to be insulted. "Where'd you go to school again?"

Penny smoothed her skirt. "I started at Barnard, but I transferred to Holyoke after my freshman year."

"Too many tempting boys across the street?" Isobel wheedled. "Holyoke is pretty much a convent."

Penny's eyes glinted. "I grew up in the city. I decided I wanted my college experience to be elsewhere. Boys had nothing to do with it."

Isobel sat up straight, struck by a sudden thought. "Were you at Barnard when Jason Whiteley was at Columbia?"

The question clearly took Penny by surprise, and for a moment she looked like she wasn't sure which of several responses to offer.

"He was three years older." She snatched up the empty Maxwell House box and hurried out.

Interesting. Jason would have been a senior when Penny was a freshman, which meant they were there at the same time, albeit briefly. Was there some connection there?

Before Isobel could pursue this line of thought any further, Katrina strode into the kitchen, with Liz shuffling behind her.

"See what Isobel thinks," Katrina said, waving in her direction.

"See what I think about what?"

"Katrina's decided that Barnaby killed Angus," Liz said.

Isobel looked up in surprise. "What makes you say that?"

"Angus was getting in his way," Katrina said.

Liz passed Katrina and started opening cabinets. "I don't know. I mean, we all know Barnaby's a clod, but that doesn't make him a murderer. Where's the coffee?"

"Penny went down to get more." Isobel angled her chair to make room for Katrina. "Is this officially another spa day?"

"Definitely." Katrina joined her at the table. "Don't you agree that Barnaby could have had a hand in Angus's death?"

"But it was a heart attack," Isobel reminded her. "And what about Angus's note?"

"Maybe Barnaby stood over him, dangling his heart medicine just out of reach, saying, 'I'm not giving this to you unless you take down my words.'" Katrina suggested.

"More likely Angus felt himself going and decided as his last act to use it to his advantage," said Liz, ripping open a package of saltines.

"A PR man until the end?" Isobel asked.

"Exactly," said Liz. "And it worked. The press is eating it up."

"Well, if Angus weren't already dead, Barnaby would certainly have killed him by now," Katrina said. "The ICG merger is officially off, and Barnaby's fit to be tied."

Liz frowned. "Really? The press hasn't gotten wind of that yet."

Katrina's expression was unreadable. "They will. My dad felt it was just a bit too much bad publicity for his taste."

"At least now you can stay," said Isobel.

Liz looked at Katrina, surprised. "You were planning to leave?"

Isobel bit her lip. "Oops! Sorry. I guess I shouldn't have said that."

Katrina gave a dismissive shrug. "It doesn't matter. We're all history one way or another. Dove & Flight is on the way out."

"I got more coffee," Penny announced, returning to the kitchen. "Should I make a full pot?"

"Might as well," Liz said. "Looks like it's going to be that kind of day."

"What did you mean 'on the way out'?" Isobel asked Katrina.

"Don't you remember what Barnaby said when he screamed at us yesterday about MacBride's? 'We can't afford to stay in business.' When people are angry, they tend to tell the truth—even seasoned PR pros."

"And without Angus, half the brand is gone," Liz pointed out.

Katrina pulled at the nubby wool of her pants. "I don't think Angus fully appreciated how bad their financial situation had gotten or he would have been in favor of the merger."

Liz shook her head. "No, I think Angus considered himself too much of an elder statesman to listen to a bunch of corporate bean counters telling him what to do. For Barnaby it was an ego boost, but for Angus it was probably an insult."

They sat silently for a moment, listening to the coffee drip into the pot. It was Penny who spoke up. Isobel had almost forgotten she was there.

"The police are closing the Jason Whiteley case, you know."

Isobel, Liz and Katrina turned to look at her.

"How do you know?" Isobel asked.

"They talked to Dorothy last night. She saw Angus in Starbucks with Jason Whiteley the morning he died. She said Angus bought tea for himself and coffee for Jason. Then he took the cups over to the counter, where he put milk and sugar in both."

"Did Dorothy see him put anything else in?" Isobel asked.

Penny shook her head. "I don't know, but she was very clear that Angus doctored both drinks. I don't suppose there's any way of tracing it now, but it all makes sense. At least, that's what the police think."

Liz threw up her hands. "So Angus killed Jason, himself, the deal and our jobs. I call that a home run."

Katrina was frowning.

"What is it?" Isobel asked.

"I was just thinking…" She shook her head. "No, forget it."

Isobel wanted to press her further, but she knew better. Katrina had also been in Starbucks that morning. Had she been near Jason? More to the point, had she been near Jason's coffee? Was Katrina now wondering whether Dorothy had seen *her* do something and chosen to keep quiet? Isobel had just been starting to feel she could trust Katrina again, but now she felt that invisible protective wall going up again.

"You were there, too," Katrina said suddenly to Penny.

Penny nodded. "Yes, but I didn't stay. I ran into Dorothy on the street and we went in together, but then she reminded me that I had a press release to get out first thing. I don't even remember seeing Angus and Jason." She wagged a finger at Katrina. "But I do remember seeing you."

Liz looked around the table. "Why do I feel like someone is about to shout *j'accuse*?"

Isobel knew what she meant. Something was not adding up about any of this, but she couldn't put her finger on it.

"We still don't know who tipped off the press about MacBride's," Isobel said, as her mind continued to churn.

"I told you all along it had to be Angus," Katrina said, an impatient edge creeping into her voice. "Obviously, he was willing to do whatever it took to sink the deal, and Barnaby found out."

"Yes, but…"

Isobel suddenly grasped the thought that was eluding her. If Angus's goal was to sabotage the merger with ICG, and Jason Whiteley was about to fire Dove & Flight for the Brazil screwup, why would Angus have wanted to kill Jason? Angus had every reason to want him alive. If a major client was about to derail the merger, why would Angus want to stop him? No, it seemed more likely that they were somehow in cahoots, trying to figure out a way to bring down the ICG deal in a way that would benefit both companies. They both wanted the same thing, and Jason was perfectly positioned to do Angus's dirty work for him. So even though Angus had the opportunity to slip something into his coffee, he had absolutely no motive.

Which meant that Jason Whiteley must have been poisoned somewhere else—and by someone else—entirely.

TWENTY-SEVEN

"How am I going to find out where Jason Whiteley was earlier that morning or the night before?" Isobel asked Delphi.

"I hate to break it to you, but that isn't your job," Delphi said, striding ahead of her. "Hurry up! I don't want to be late."

Isobel jogged to keep up, trying to avoid the patches on the sidewalk that had iced over from the sleet the night before. "But the police have dropped the case, and it doesn't make any sense that it was Angus."

By the time she caught up, Delphi was ringing the buzzer for Graham's studio. Isobel was beginning to wish she hadn't committed her Saturday to helping paint set pieces for *King John*, but Delphi had roped in Sunil, too. She and Delphi squeezed into the tiny, old elevator, which creaked upwards with a disconcerting rattle as it passed each floor.

"And the more I think about it, the more I think Jason was acting not just tired, but downright woozy when he showed up at the office," Isobel continued.

"I hate this friggin' thing," muttered Delphi, her eyes closed.

"You okay?"

"Just a little claustrophobic."

They emerged onto the sixth floor, and Delphi relaxed visibly. With renewed energy, she led the way to Graham's studio. It was freezing, despite the space heaters arranged optimistically around the outer edges. There were flats in various stages of decoration, and a few hardy souls were trying to hold onto their needles as they basted hems on skirts that would have paired nicely with Delphi's blouse *du jour*. Sunil was there already, on his knees, painting an arch. He sat back and dipped his brush in turpentine as they came in.

"'When shall we three meet again?'" Sunil quoted in welcome.

Delphi blanched, and Sunil's fellow painters gasped and stared at him in horror.

"What?" He looked around, bewildered. "It's *Macbeth*."

Gary Stinson shrieked and clutched his chest.

"Out!" hollered Delphi, pointing an accusatory finger at Sunil.

He jumped to his feet. "Oh, come on! And I got here before you!"

Delphi put her hands on Sunil's shoulders and steered him out of the room. Isobel followed, while the others murmured frantically behind them.

When they reached the hall, Sunil folded his arms, and gave his annoyance full rein. "You better have a good reason for this."

"How can you not know?" Delphi fairly wheezed. "It's bad luck to quote from the Scottish play unless you're in rehearsal for it. And you're not supposed to say the actual name in a theater. It's terrible luck!"

"Last I checked we were in a studio."

"It doesn't matter! We're performing here, so for all practical purposes it's a theater. Don't you see? You've cursed our play, and we open on Thursday!"

Sunil threw a pleading glance at Isobel. "This is crazy. Tell her this is crazy!"

Isobel shrugged helplessly. "A lot of actors take this stuff seriously."

"You have to turn around three times, spit, curse, and then knock on the door and ask to be allowed back in," Delphi said.

Sunil snorted. "That's the silliest thing I've ever heard."

"Do it!" Delphi demanded.

She pulled Isobel back into the studio and slammed the

door in Sunil's face.

Everyone in the room, including Graham, stared expectantly at the closed door. After a moment, there was a knock.

"What do you want?" asked Delphi.

Sunil's answer was muffled through the thick metal, so Delphi opened the door a crack.

"May I come back in now?"

"Did you do what I asked?"

"Yes."

Delphi looked at the others for approval. Heads nodded solemnly, and she let Sunil back in.

"I thought you'd be impressed," Sunil said dolefully, as they returned to their paints.

"Not with that quote," Delphi said.

Sunil gave an exaggerated sigh. "There's no pleasing some people."

Before the conversation could devolve further, Isobel reintroduced the question of Jason Whiteley's whereabouts the night before his death, filling in Sunil, who grasped the new topic gratefully.

"There's no reason to think Jason was spending time with anyone from Dove & Flight after hours," he said. "Especially if he was going to see them all the next day."

"We already know he was at Starbucks with Angus. The idea in and of itself isn't farfetched," Isobel pointed out.

"Big difference between a cup of coffee before work and a slumber party," Delphi said, reaching across Sunil to add a dash of gold to his arch. "There, that's much better."

"I get what you're saying," Isobel said, "but there are at least two other people I can think of that he had reason to see outside of work. Kit Blanchard was related to Jason by marriage." She swallowed. "And then there's Katrina."

"Kit and Kat. There's a recipe for confusion," Sunil said. "Maybe you'll find a recording of Jason gasping a name while choking on a cocktail, and you'll get the wrong one arrested."

"Isn't Katrina your friend from college?" Delphi asked.

"Fair weather, but yes." Isobel cleared her throat. "James says she and Jason were dating, but I don't know if I believe him."

Sunil gave her a shrewd look. "I thought you trusted James absolutely. I believe those were your exact words. Or is that only when you like what he has to say?"

Isobel's face grew hot. "I'm just saying maybe his information is bad."

"Why would you think that?" Delphi asked.

Isobel dipped her brush in a can of red paint and swirled it around. "Partly because it came from Jayla, but mostly because Katrina never mentioned it to me."

"Why should she? Especially since you're obviously so hot to make a connection to the murder," said Delphi. "If she didn't kill him, it's none of your business. And if she did? Well, then it's really none of your business!"

"I still don't understand why you're so determined to tie Jason's murder back to Dove & Flight," Sunil said.

"Instinct. Detective O'Connor said it's rule number two of police work. Follow your instincts."

"What's rule number one?" Sunil asked.

"I forget."

Delphi shoved her with her booted foot. "You do not."

"It's not relevant," Isobel said curtly. "There's something about the way it all happened, the timing, that makes it seem like whoever did it wanted him to be found in the office for some reason."

"The most likely reason is to mess up the takeover, right?" asked Sunil.

"And the only person who really had a stake in that died of natural causes," Delphi said. "So there's a dead end, pardon the pun."

"But is it?" Isobel raised her brush and let the excess drip back into the can. "What if James is telling the truth about Katrina and Jason? It wouldn't be her first lie. I'm pretty sure she lied to me about some emails she sent about a client in Brazil."

Delphi stood and stretched her legs. "Lying doesn't make a person capable of murder." She rattled her empty paint can. "Be right back."

"She's right," Sunil whispered. "I lied before about cursing outside the door and all that stuff, and I'm no murderer."

Isobel gasped. "If Delphi ever finds out, she'll become one!"

"Come on, you don't really believe that crap, do you?" He gave a sharp laugh, then his dark features grew pensive. "Do you?"

"It's foolish to tempt fate."

"Is that rule number one of police work?"

"No. Rule number one is 'Don't assume.'"

They regarded each other thoughtfully for a moment. Delphi plopped down next to them with a fresh can of gold paint.

"You know," she said, "Katrina does have a couple of good motives packed in there. And she and Jason could have seen each other the night before. Or that morning if they spent the night together."

"There's something else, too," Isobel said, chewing her lip. "I kind of brushed it off at the time, but it's something Liz said. About Barnaby having a 'thing' for Katrina."

"What do you think *that* means?" Delphi asked.

"I don't know, but I'm betting it's more professional than romantic. Maybe Barnaby sees Katrina as his key to future success. If he thinks she's on his side, and he finds out she's actively opposing him…" Isobel looked up. "I don't think Barnaby's the kind of person who deals well with betrayal."

Delphi sat back on her heels. "Wait. Now I'm confused. Are you concerned *about* Katrina or *for* her?"

"Until I find out what she's hiding from me—both."

TWENTY-EIGHT

When Isobel returned to work on Monday morning, she found a pink Post-it from Dorothy stuck to her computer screen. Following the directive to "Come see me," Isobel hung up her coat and gave a perfunctory rap on Dorothy's door.

"You were looking for me?"

"Yes, thanks." Dorothy made a welcoming gesture. "Come on in."

Isobel took a seat in the visitor's chair and leaned forward expectantly.

Dorothy continued, "You did such a good job on the plastics pitch the other day. You seem like a natural."

"Oh! I thought you might be disappointed that I only got two hits."

"No, no." Dorothy dismissed her concern. "That's about as far as the client can stretch, and it looks like they can meet both deadlines. You did very well."

Isobel chalked up a mental point against Penny.

Dorothy continued, "This is crunch time for the Schüssler annual report, and I need all the help I can get this week. Can you work on it? It might involve a late night or two."

Isobel hesitated, thinking of her rehearsals with Hugh and Delphi's opening. "I have some other things going on this week after hours."

"I'll take what I can get. If you really can't stay, I do have Penny," Dorothy said. "You can bill overtime, you know."

Isobel perked up at the thought of time and a half. "I can make it work."

Dorothy handed her two thick stacks of papers. "Great. You can start by proofing the galleys against the Word document."

Isobel glanced down at the top sheet. Schüssler Medizinprodukte. "I don't speak German. I mean, I know a little from singing, but nothing that would apply to…medical products."

Dorothy smiled. "Neither do I, but it doesn't matter. The client signed off on the content already, so we can assume it's correct. Just make sure nothing got garbled when our graphics guy converted it. He can be a little sloppy sometimes."

Isobel returned to her desk and settled down to compare the two documents. It was a tedious business, since many of the words were technical terms created by stringing other words together. She was reminded of Mark Twain's famous observation that some German words are so long they have a perspective. After a particularly daunting onslaught of vowel-free clusters, she tossed the papers aside and rubbed her eyes. The only thing opera German had prepared her for was conversations about the fickleness of men and the flirting capabilities of women. There was nothing in *Der Freischütz* or *Die Fledermaus* about pacemakers or cochlear implants.

Katrina loomed over her. "You look like you need some lunch."

"Yes! But no schnitzel."

They repaired to a nearby coffee shop, where they tiptoed around potentially radioactive topics by chattering about the whereabouts of various college friends. Isobel was dying to ask Katrina about her relationship with Jason, and she realized this was probably her best opportunity to get the truth. They weren't in the office where they could be overheard, and Katrina had made the overture, so presumably she was trying to move beyond their recent disagreements. Isobel was determined not to let their lunch end without gleaning some new bit of information, although she wasn't sure how to proceed.

"Tyler Schmidt!"

"What?" Isobel was jolted from her reverie by Katrina's exclamation.

"That was his name, the guy who shared all his Astronomy 101 homework with me and got me through the science requirement. He didn't go through puberty until sophomore year."

"He must have started college young, like Percival."

"Oh, yeah. Mini-genius. How old is your brother now?"

"He's about to turn sixteen."

"And he's starting Columbia this fall?"

"Yup. He got all the brains, and I got all the..."

Isobel paused, not out of modesty, but because a thought had just occurred to her. When her brother, Percival, had visited Columbia in October and stayed with her, he had helped her pinpoint an important clue in the murder of the bank secretary, simply by rearranging information on a page. It struck her now that rather than having too little information about Jason Whiteley, she had too much. Maybe a little rearranging was in order. But before she could parse this idea any further, Katrina saved Isobel from the awkwardness of introducing the subject she most wanted to discuss by bringing it up herself.

"Look, I haven't been totally honest with you. I have this feeling you're going to find out anyway, and I'd rather you hear it from me than anyone else."

Too late, thought Isobel, but go on.

Katrina took a deep breath. "Jason and I were dating."

It was at times like this that Isobel was glad she was an actress.

"Wow! I had no idea. Was it serious?"

"Not really, no." Katrina looked down at her hands. "But here's the thing. I was at his apartment the night before he died."

This was news. Isobel worked hard to keep her voice steady in response. "What happened?"

"I went over there to end it."

"Why?"

Katrina hesitated. "It's not really important. But I wasn't the only one there that night. Kit Blanchard showed up. You probably don't know this, but Kit is married to Jason's brother's wife's brother. I think I have that right."

You have that right, thought Isobel. And I do know.

"Is it just coincidence that Jason became a client?" she asked.

"I'm not sure. But I'll tell you one thing, I was more surprised to see Kit than she was to see me. I thought we were pretty discreet, but I guess she knew about us."

"And Jason?"

"He was pretty pissed. For that matter, so was she. It seemed to me like they were in the middle of a fight. I had just gotten there, but as soon as Kit arrived, Jason asked me to leave."

"So you never actually ended it?"

Katrina shook her head.

"And you left them alone together…what time was this?"

"Around ten. Strange time of night for her to show up, don't you think? I mean, she's got kids to put to bed. Why didn't she just call?" Katrina wondered.

"Did you catch any hint of what the argument was about?"

Katrina shook her head. "It could have been about whatever's going on between Kit and Aaron, but if she had something to do with Jason hiring us, it might have been work-related."

Isobel frowned. "Somebody barges into your house spitting mad, then thrusts a glass of I don't know what in your hand, and says 'Drink this'? I can believe they were at odds, especially if Jason knew about Aaron, but how do they get from a screaming slugfest to drinking each other's health?"

Katrina sat back, a strange look on her face. "I wasn't suggesting Kit was the one who killed him. I just thought it was weird that she was there. But, now that you mention it, she could have put the poison in something he would eat or drink later."

"That's awfully risky," Isobel observed. "I mean, what if you or someone else had been the one to eat or drink it? It's not a very efficient way of making sure you're killing the right person."

"Well, anyway, I mostly wanted you to know about Jason and me. I felt funny about not telling you."

Recalling Delphi's words, Isobel said, "It really isn't any of my business."

"I know, but still. And I know you've been curious about Jason, asking questions. I didn't want you to find out some other way."

"So why were you ending it?"

Katrina's face reddened to match the color of her hair. "You are dogged, aren't you?" She swallowed and looked away.

Isobel's pulse quickened. As she watched her friend struggle, she knew that whatever Katrina said next would be the truth.

"It's one of the most embarrassing things that has ever happened to me," Katrina said in a small voice. "You have to swear to keep it to yourself."

Isobel nodded solemnly, and Katrina continued, avoiding her eye.

"I did something phenomenally stupid. I texted Jason a picture of me…you know…naked. And then a few days later, we had this big fight, and he—he threatened to forward the text to my father." She looked at Isobel, abashed. "Can you imagine? I'm trying to so hard to get him to take me seriously. That would have been the end of it. The end!" A tiny tear rolled down Katrina's cheek.

Isobel felt her breath catch. She would never have imagined Katrina doing something like that. "Did Jason send it? To your dad?"

Katrina covered her face in her hands, and Isobel had to strain to hear her words.

"Worse. He sent it to Barnaby."

TWENTY-NINE

HUGH CLOSED THE THREE-RING BINDER of music on the piano rack. "You seem preoccupied."

Isobel flopped onto the small sofa in his studio, and a pile of opera scores spilled into her lap. "Sorry. Just some stuff at work," she said, restacking them neatly at the other end.

She couldn't stop thinking about what Katrina had told her. Isobel wondered if she would be more embarrassed if someone sent a naked photo of her to her father or her boss. She didn't really consider Barnaby her boss, nor was she particularly invested in what he thought of her. A director would probably consider it a plus. People were always shedding their clothes in the theater. The only person who corresponded in any way was James, and she had to admit, the thought wasn't entirely upsetting.

"Isobel?"

Or Hugh. That wasn't so upsetting either.

"Right, sorry. Do you want to run the song again?"

Hugh glanced at his watch. "I think we have time before Sunil gets here."

The prospect of Sunil's arrival energized her as she wrapped her mouth around the witty patter lyrics to Hugh's song, "Don't Go Away Mad." Over dinner the other night, Hugh had lamented the lack of talented tenors, and Isobel had immediately proposed Sunil. Hugh had auditioned him over the weekend, and hired him on the spot.

As soon as she finished singing, the buzzer rang.

"Nicely done. You make me sound like a better composer than I am," Hugh said. He let in Sunil, who greeted Isobel with a hug.

"You know, I've only ever heard you sing through a door," Sunil said, releasing her.

"Let's remedy that right now," said Hugh.

Isobel and Sunil sang through a snappy little song called "You're Mine 'til Something Better Comes Along," which featured cleverly crafted interlocking parts.

"Practically perfect on the first go," Hugh enthused. "Do you know what that kind of song is called, when two parts are sung separately and then miraculously, they fit together?"

"Is there a name for it?" Isobel asked. "I always called them two-part songs."

"It's called a quodlibet," said Hugh.

"My brother Percival is a Latin scholar, but I bet even he doesn't know that," Isobel said, pleased.

Hugh gestured to Sunil. "All right, your turn. Isobel, you can relax for a few minutes."

Sunil ran through one of his solos, while Isobel settled back on the sofa and picked up her dropped train of thought. She was beginning to understand why Katrina was more upset about Jason sending the photo to Barnaby. It was hardly an either/or proposition. Barnaby could just as easily forward the photo to Katrina's father, and that would be more damaging to her in every way. It was ultimately worse than Jason having a hold over her. The photo gave Barnaby leverage over Katrina to get her to convince her father not to drop the merger, and Isobel had no doubt that he would use it. Probably he already had. And that would put Katrina in the galling position of having to advocate for something she didn't want.

Sunil finished his solo, and they ran through several more duets. Then Isobel sang through a torchy ballad that allowed her to dip into her sultry, lower register, which she rarely used. Hugh gave her a misty smile when she finished.

"Gorgeous!" He pulled out his iPhone and tapped the screen. "All right, then. When shall we three meet again?"

Isobel and Sunil gasped, and then laughed. Hugh clucked at them. "Don't tell me you believe all that silly *Macbeth* nonsense!"

"Not us, but a friend of ours sure does," Sunil said.

"How is Thursday evening, same time?" asked Hugh.

"Can't. That's our superstitious friend's opening night," Isobel said. "There will definitely be murder most foul if we don't show."

"What's the play?" asked Hugh.

"*King John*."

"Really? You know, I've never seen that one," Hugh remarked.

"Come with us!" Isobel said on impulse. "I'd love for you to meet Delphi. She's very good, even if she is a bit over the top where the Bard is concerned. We could all go out for a drink afterwards."

Isobel saw Hugh steal an inquiring glance at Sunil, who nodded in enthusiastic agreement.

"Thanks! That would be lovely. Now, when shall we three, er, rehearse again?"

They settled on Wednesday, and Isobel and Sunil left together. It had grown unseasonably warm, and a light rain was falling. Sunil repositioned his large umbrella over them, and Isobel unwound her scarf.

"I'm always dressing for yesterday's weather," she said with a sigh.

"What do you think of Hugh?" Sunil asked, as they headed for the subway.

"I like his songs."

"I think he likes you."

Isobel gave him a sideways look. "What makes you say that?"

"You saw him check in with me before he agreed to come to *King John*. He's trying to figure us out."

"Let him try," Isobel said, secretly pleased. "In fact, if you really want to help things along, you could step it up and flirt with me a bit."

"What about James?"

Isobel's eyes darted right, left, and then behind her. She met Sunil's questioning eyes and said, "The first time I went to Hugh's, I ran into him right around here. And there was this annoying girl with him."

"And you were jealous," said Sunil.

"I was not! Although I think James was."

"And Hugh?"

"It was awkward, but I don't think it occurred to him to be jealous."

They arrived at the stairs leading up to the elevated train stop. "But enough about me. When are you going to make your move on Delphi?" she teased.

"As soon as I get the slightest inkling that it might be welcome." Sunil folded his umbrella, shook it out and vaulted up the stairs. Isobel took two steps up and stopped.

"You know what?" she called. "I think I left my phone at Hugh's. Don't wait for me. I might be a minute."

Sunil gave a knowing laugh. "A minute? More like an hour!"

She responded with an innocent shrug. "See you Wednesday!"

He waved to her and continued up to the platform. As soon as he was out of sight, Isobel took a few steps toward Hugh's apartment, and then, pulling her phone from her pocket, headed off in the opposite direction.

THIRTY

JAMES TOOK ANOTHER PHOTO FROM the envelope and another swig from the bottle. There he was with his coach right after he scored his first goal freshman year, grinning like an idiot. And he was an idiot back then. He remembered what he did right after that game: got shit-faced and locked himself out of his dorm. He'd had to spend the night on a bench in Morningside Park.

He ripped the photo in half and then in quarters, tossing the shreds onto his growing pile. He was almost finished destroying these unpleasant reminders of his past, but if memory served, the last photo was the one he was dreading.

He fortified himself with another gulp of the Johnnie Walker Black he had picked up on his way home after finding the envelope in the inside pocket of his old raincoat. He had searched everywhere for his raincoat that morning until it dawned on him that he'd last seen it at Jayla's. Michael had probably claimed it by now. So he'd dug out an old one that he hadn't worn in years. It hung on him without shape or style, but the weird, cold mugginess of the weather made it the only comfortable choice. If he had felt the pictures in his pocket that morning, he might never have gone into work at all. As it was, he'd only realized they were there on the subway home and had made the mistake of pulling out the top one: a picture of him standing in front of the giant gates of Columbia, his mother proudly at his side, her arm around him. It was the look on his face that had sent him reeling: a combination of eagerness, hope and smug self-confidence. If only he could go back and do it all over again. But of course he couldn't.

He'd gotten off the subway one stop before his own, unable to stand the closeness of the car a moment longer, and ducked into a bar. He'd almost forgotten how good vodka tasted. He hadn't remembered it being quite so delicious, but maybe that was the flavorings. His first drink had been Absolut Citron. The second had been raspberry and then, just for kicks, he'd ordered a chocolate martini. By the time he left the bar, he was in the happy buzz phase, feeling more magnanimous toward his freshman self. A tiny voice in his head urged him to stop, but a second voice answered, *You've still got a few drinks left before it gets ugly. Why stop now*?

But he did stop. Into City Liquors on 125th Street.

"Haven't seen you in a while," commented the proprietor, a slightly-built Nigerian with a big gold hoop earring.

James set a bottle of Johnnie Walker Black on the counter.

The Nigerian looked from the bottle to James. "I thought you…"

"What?"

The Nigerian peered closely at James, pulling back just before James could lash out. "Never mind. That'll be thirty-two dollars and seventy-three cents."

James was short on cash, having spent what he had on top-shelf brands at the bar, so he slid his MasterCard forward on the counter.

Leave now, said the first voice. *Prove you can stop. If you can do it, then maybe you'll be able to drink again.*

"I *am* drinking again," James said aloud.

"Yeah, that's what I meant," muttered the Nigerian.

James ignored him, signed the credit card receipt, and left with his purchase. As he trudged home, he congratulated himself for not ripping the Nigerian's head off. Surely that must mean he had learned to control himself under the influence.

Inside his apartment, he kicked off his shoes and stripped down to his undershirt and boxers. Then he poured himself a large glass of scotch and drank a toast.

"You're all wrong!" he shouted. "I'm drinking like a normal person. So fuck that shit!"

He turned his stereo on, but not too loud. More evidence that he was just fine, thank you. Then he settled on the couch, stretched his legs, and gazed up at the cheap chandelier that had been there when he moved in.

In the relative quiet, however, unpleasant images floated across the movie screen in his mind. He flashed back to Isobel's obvious discomfort when they'd met on the street. He couldn't blame her. He'd acted like a complete asshole. Then again, she was full of shit. After all that talk about believing in him, she doubted his story about her friend and Jason. He refilled his glass and tried to think of something else. An image of Lily recoiling when he threatened to bar her from the gym made him squirm, so he turned up the music. That was better.

It was an old song, one he hadn't heard for years. It had been a big party tune in his fraternity, and it occurred to him with a jolt that it was playing the night Nell drank the tequila and died. He had to stop thinking about that. He tried to steer his thoughts elsewhere, but Jason Whiteley's face, with its careless flop of ash blond hair and the superior smile he always wore, swam in front of James's eyes. Shutting them only brought the image more strongly into focus, so he cranked the music higher and poured himself another drink. He was way past the point of experiencing the pleasant shock of warmth as the alcohol slid down his throat. It may as well have been water.

The phone rang, but he ignored it. When it rang a second time, he picked it up and slammed it down again immediately. That struck him as particularly clever, and he started to laugh. He was still laughing when a loud knocking broke through his consciousness.

"Heeeeere we go," he muttered, as he hauled himself off the couch to answer the door.

A tall, buxom woman with a round, corn-fed face and blond hair pulled into pigtails stood in the hall holding an infant in her arms. She looked completely unlike anyone he'd ever seen in his building. Harlem might be changing, but this chick still didn't look like she belonged there. Or anywhere in New York City, for that matter. She looked like she was from Idaho or somewhere.

"Idaho," he slurred.

The woman looked confused for a minute. Then she gave an awkward smile. "Yes, I guess you are."

"Whathafug?"

"Listen, you're really loud, and you keep waking James."

"I ain't sleepin'," he said, trying to process whether or not she was insulting him.

"I know. And you're waking up little Jamie." She held out the baby. He looked down and saw a plump mini-version of the woman.

"He James? I James." He was vaguely aware that he sounded like a caveman.

"You're drunk. You should go to sleep." She nuzzled the baby's head, but kept her eyes on James. "All the Jamesies need their sleepy-sleep. Okay?"

The word sleep triggered his exhaustion. It sounded like a very good idea. But even in his drunken fog, he was aware of a question burning at the edge of his mind.

"Where yo' man?"

"You mean James?"

"Not the baby." That much he'd understood. "How come yo' man send you down here? He afraid I'm gonna kick his ass?"

"He's still at work. And his name is James, too."

"Too many Jameseseses," he muttered darkly.

The woman smiled and covered the baby's ears.

"My James is as big a motherfucker as you are. And he will kick *your* ass if you don't TURN OFF THE FUCKING MUSIC!"

She took her hands off the baby's ears, smiled sweetly, and walked back toward the elevator, leaving James blinking wearily after her.

Another goddamn steamroller, he thought, and slammed the door.

THIRTY-ONE

ISOBEL SCANNED THE APARTMENT BUZZERS until she found the one she wanted, but before she could press it, a woman exiting the building held the door open for her. Isobel smiled a thank you and rode the elevator to the fourth floor.

There was no answer when she knocked. She knew James was there because he'd answered the phone, although he'd hung up without saying anything. That had struck her as odd, and she'd found herself suddenly concerned for his wellbeing. As she stood outside the closed door, she felt certain something was wrong. She pounded on the door with both fists until he finally yanked it open.

The smell of alcohol was so strong that Isobel had to take a step back. James's gaze hovered blearily over her head as if he were expecting someone taller.

"Tol' you goway!"

"James? It's me!"

He squinted down at her, mumbled something she couldn't make out, and then staggered back into the apartment, leaving the door open. Figuring this was as close to an invitation as she was going to get, she followed him in and shut the door quietly behind her. He was sprawled on the couch, his thick, muscular legs dangling over the armrest.

She reluctantly pulled her eyes away from his legs and assessed the situation. It looked like he was starting to crash, and it probably wouldn't be long before he passed out. Even so, he was big and she was small, and she didn't want to risk getting him angry. She decided her best bet was to act, not talk.

She found the bathroom and dampened a washcloth. Then she took his toothbrush glass, filled it with water, and set it aside while she looked in the medicine cabinet for some Advil.

At the subway stop with Sunil, she'd had a sudden desire to find James and apologize for not believing him about Katrina. He had been telling the truth, and if she hadn't been so dismissive when he was trying to help her, maybe he wouldn't have acted like such a jerk on the street. She'd gotten James's address and phone number from information and called ahead to make sure he was home.

Not only was he home, he shouldn't be left alone.

She returned to the living room. James had pulled his legs all the way onto the couch and was curled into a fetal position. She knelt by his side and rattled the pill bottle.

"You should take some Advil," she said softly.

He turned his glassy gaze on her. "Know you."

"Yes, you know me. It's—"

"Yeahgud." He held out his hand for the pills and she helped him wash them down.

"Lie back, and let me put this washcloth on your head."

As she let go of the cloth, his hand came up and grasped hers.

"Stay. Don' wanna belone."

"Um, okay. I'll stay."

He wouldn't let go of her hand, so she rearranged herself on the floor, knowing she wouldn't be able to hold the position for very long without cramping. The awkwardness of the situation began to sink in.

What exactly did he mean by stay? Until he fell asleep? Or did he want her to spend the night? Even if he thought he did, he would probably feel very differently when he woke up the next morning and saw her there. It would be thoroughly embarrassing for both of them. But at the same time, she couldn't leave him alone in this condition. She pulled James's hand over her shoulder and resettled into a slightly more comfortable position with her back against the couch.

A half-empty bottle of scotch sat on the coffee table next to a pile of shredded paper. Upon closer inspection, she saw that the shreds were ripped photos. One was still intact, and she picked it up.

She spotted James instantly in the group of college kids draped drunkenly and happily over a large sectional sofa. He was holding his fingers in a dorky V over Jason Whiteley's head. Sitting in Jason's lap was a cute, dark-haired girl who reminded Isobel of someone she knew. She looked closer and saw that James's other hand held a bottle of Patrón recognizable by its idiosyncratically shaped bottle.

Was this the girl James had told her about who died at the fraternity party that led to him being expelled? And if it was, was the tequila James was holding the liquor that killed her? Isobel dropped the photo back onto the table and disentangled James's hand from her own. She had written him off as an innocent victim, a casualty of the prejudicial system of school governance that sacrificed the student with the least amount of privilege and protection. Now she wondered how innocent he had been, after all. She also wondered if he would ever be able to stop punishing himself, since it was clear that he was still consumed by guilt, whether or not it was warranted.

He was snoring heavily now, so she stood up and stretched her legs. His face had relaxed into a sweet smile. All men turned into the little boys they once were when they slept.

James.

She and James were so different, but there were certain things they had in common. They were both willing to take chances, and they were both insatiably curious about other people, although she suspected James would be hard-pressed to admit the latter. And here she was in his space, free to explore and learn more about him. If she felt any compunction about snooping, she told herself that in her position, he would most likely do the same.

The apartment was a standard one-bedroom with a galley kitchen, a long living room, and a bedroom that mirrored it on the other side of the wall. The Ikea furnishings told her little about his taste, except for a large print of an elongated pair of crossed women's legs with a valentine-shaped doily covering her intimates. She smiled appreciatively. It was an image that both men and women could find sexy. She hesitated at the entrance to his bedroom. This seemed like an invasion of privacy on a different order, and it occurred to her that James might stop short of exploring her bedroom, if she had her own.

He had rolled over so that his face was buried in the back of the couch. She was glad he was no longer facing her, even though his eyes were closed. Telling herself that she might annoy him less if she knew him better, she entered the bedroom, leaving the door ajar so she could hear if he stirred. His bed was neatly made up with chocolate brown Egyptian cotton sheets and a coordinating comforter with turquoise accents. There was a sleek, low dresser and a small desk with a laptop on it. She passed over the dresser and went straight to the desk.

Three books were stacked to one side: *A History of American Law*, *Representing the Race: The Creation of the Civil Rights Lawyer*, and *Why the Law is So Perverse*. A sheet of paper was tucked inside the latter and she pulled it out. It was a partly completed application to John Jay College of Criminal Justice. She tucked it back and restacked the books.

So James was reapplying to college—and for law. What an interesting choice for him. She supposed it made sense, given the feelings he had about his own history with authority. Was he planning to be a full-time student? A few months ago, the thought of his leaving Temp Zone would have sent her into a panic, but now Ginger Wainwright loved to trot her out as one of their stars, albeit more for solving the bank murder than for her typing skills.

The center drawer yielded nothing but office supplies and old electronics chargers. In the top drawer, she found more supplies, a passport, some financial statements, and return address labels from the Paralyzed Veterans of America. She shut the drawer and wandered over to the bed. Next to the phone she spotted a small, wire-bound notebook. It was open to the middle and the page was covered in James's handwriting.

> *Strength is a muscle*
> *Not bicep or delt,*
> *An internal rubber band that only*
> *Proves itself when stretched*
> *Snaps back when released*
> *Ready for the next assault*
> *Flexible and neat*
>
> *Traveling to a place of dread*
> *Unsure about what lies ahead*
> *Seeds of sorrow newly sown*
> *Staunchly I go on alone*
>
> *Chose to let her go*
> *Sparkling eyes look elsewhere now*
> *Still she haunts my dreams*

Isobel replaced the notebook on James's nightstand and backed away, her stomach fluttering with guilt. She surveyed the room. If she stayed, she'd have to sleep in his bed. How could she possibly do that? She knew that despite her whispered promise, it would be better for both of them in the long run if she left.

She pulled the comforter from the bed, returned to the living room, and covered him with it. The washcloth had slipped from his forehead, making a wet spot on the couch. She brought it back to the bathroom. As she returned the Advil to the medicine cabinet, she accidentally knocked two prescription bottles into the sink. The clatter made her jump, and she hastily replaced them.

She refilled his glass with fresh water and set it next to the pile of shredded photos. In the kitchen, she paused at the sink with the scotch. She had intended to pour it down the drain, but she didn't want him to wake up and think he'd drunk the whole bottle. She could dump it and take the bottle with her, but that might be even more confusing. In the end, she left it sitting in the sink, still half-full. She decided against leaving a note and tiptoed out.

With one last glance at his sleeping form, she wondered whether in the morning James would even remember that she'd been there.

THIRTY-TWO

Isobel spent the next morning drowning in separable prefixes. Despite Dorothy's assurances that the copy had been approved, Schüssler Medizinprodukte had delivered a slew of changes to their annual report, after she'd successfully proofed the galleys the day before. From here on in, any mistakes that made it into print would be hers alone, since they wouldn't be proofing it again. Inputting long, unfamiliar compound words was difficult enough, but she hadn't slept well. She couldn't stop thinking about James, but she wasn't sure what to do next. Should she call and make sure he was okay? Should she wait for him to call her and…what? Explain? Apologize? Thank her?

She didn't want to cause him undue embarrassment, and she knew that even those closest to an alcoholic had to tread carefully. Isobel had hoped to get Delphi's take on the situation, but her *King John* rehearsal had gone late. When Delphi finally got home, she had made it clear that she was too exhausted for conversation.

Isobel leaned on her hand, squinted at a row of consonants, and resolved, for the time being, to give James a chance to call her first.

"Melodious one!"

Jimmy was striding toward her, in a red-and-white-striped, long-sleeved, boat-neck T-shirt and his customary Bermudas.

She shook her head in bewilderment. "Aren't you freezing?"

He rubbed his hands together and shivered. "I need a little chill to keep me from dozing and dreaming."

"There's more than a little chill outside. The temperature completely dropped overnight."

"To placate my mother on whatever lofty or lowly plane she now inhabits, I don my snowsuit before venturing forth into the wild weather. And I usually remember to use the little boys' room first, but not always." He came around behind her desk and whispered, "I wondered if we might put our *têtes* together for a little you-know-what."

"Sure," Isobel said, relieved to have a distraction.

"Perhaps we might venture into a vacant office?"

"Is there one on this floor?" Isobel asked.

"Kit Blanchard's."

"Is she out?"

Jimmy put a finger to his lips and beckoned Isobel to follow. She set aside the Schüssler report and trailed him silently.

Kit's office had been returned to its original pristine, anonymous state. All her personal effects were gone, except for a raincoat which hung, forgotten, on the back of the door, visible only after Jimmy closed it behind them.

"Where's Kit?"

Jimmy drew his hand across his throat, and Isobel gasped.

"Dead?"

"No!" Jimmy smacked his left hand with his right. "Bad mime! Bad mime! Sacked. Gone. Permanent vaycay."

Isobel exhaled in relief. "When did that happen? And why?"

"Yesterday. She and Barnaby met behind closed doors, and next thing I knew, she was leaving on a jet plane."

"She certainly cleared out fast. I didn't even see her go."

"It was after hours. Most people were gone."

"Do you know why?"

Jimmy paced back and forth in front of the bookshelves, which were bare except for a few old media directories. "I do not."

Isobel made a mental note to find out what had happened

to Kit. "Okay, what's up, then?"

"Riddle me this, Batgirl. Sophie told me there was digoxin in Jason Whiteley's blood and something else, but she couldn't remember what. Was it, I don't know, a painkiller, maybe?"

Isobel paused. "Any painkiller in particular?"

"You tell me."

She regarded him curiously. "Okay…Demerol."

Jimmy cracked his knuckles. "That's the one."

"Jimmy, what is this about?"

He ran his hands through his short, gray hair until it stood on end, which lent him an aura of craziness, despite the fact that his eyes looked as clear and focused as she'd ever seen them.

"I know I have a reputation for recreational inhalation. The reason I indulge is that I am frequently in pain. I won't lie and say it isn't also for pleasure, but it does take the edge off. It's my lower back—an old baseball injury from the days when I did more than dream about the minor leagues. But there are some days when I need a little something extra."

Isobel nodded, understanding. "Demerol."

"All regulation, I assure you. Prescription up-to-date and valid. But the thing is, mine went missing about a week ago."

"And you think someone took it and used it on Jason? What made you think the other substance was Demerol?"

Jimmy finally stopped pacing and collapsed into an empty chair. "I found the bottle in Barnaby's office, and it was empty."

Isobel felt a tingle of excitement, but she forced herself not to jump to conclusions. "Maybe Barnaby was in pain, and he needed it? He must know you take it."

"Are you ready for the weirdest thing you don't know about Barnaby Flight?"

Isobel held her breath.

"He's a Christian Scientist. They don't take drugs. Not even a Tylenol. Not even a vitamin."

"We have to tell the police!"

Jimmy leaped up and wrapped Kit's forgotten raincoat around himself. "Barnaby's a bear, a boor, a boob—but he's not a murderer. What would be the good of killing to save your business? Even Bernie Madoff can't run his racket from the slammer."

"But he had a reason to want both Angus and Jason dead—"

Jimmy spun around the other way, disentangling and re-entangling himself in the coat. "Nobody killed Angus. That was a heart attack. And besides, Angus's death accomplished exactly what Barnaby didn't want to happen—Tony Campbell called off the merger."

"Jimmy! Stop doing that. You're making me dizzy."

"Sorry." He unwrapped himself and sat down again.

Isobel continued, "Barnaby knew Jason was going to fire us and cause trouble. He had a motive to kill him. If he had access to your Demerol and Angus's digoxin, then he had means, and he had…well, he must have had some opportunity we don't know about. There's still a lot we don't know."

"I know he didn't kill anyone."

Isobel threw up her hands. "Then why are you telling me all this?"

"I just wanted to know about the Demerol."

"You have to give the bottle to the police. There might be fingerprints on it."

"I can't do that."

"You have to."

Jimmy shook his head. "I don't mean I won't, I mean I can't."

A suspicion stole over Isobel. "What do you mean?"

"I figured if I did it before I knew for sure it was important, it wouldn't be destroying evidence, especially since it was my personal property."

Isobel shook her head in disbelief. "Are you telling me…?"

"It's in a dumpster on Third Avenue. Long gone."

THIRTY-THREE

Isobel's conversation with Jimmy left her head spinning. She had no idea what to do with the information he'd given her, especially since it couldn't be proved. It wasn't just that he'd thrown away the bottle; she only had his word for it that the bottle was ever in Barnaby's office. She still couldn't figure out why he felt the need to tell her. It was almost as if he wanted her to suspect Barnaby, but that didn't square with him tossing the bottle, which was clearly intended to protect Barnaby as well as himself.

Unless the whole Barnaby story was a ruse, and Jimmy was trying to find out for an entirely different reason if Isobel knew about the Demerol in Jason's system. She tried to imagine Jimmy, for all his winking charm and poetic flourishes, killing Jason. He certainly knew a lot about drugs—he had admitted as much. And he was fiercely loyal to Barnaby. Was there more to that relationship than met the eye? If Jimmy was the person responsible for Jason's death, he had just incriminated himself. She might not have enough evidence for the police, but she had enough to be a threat to him.

She saw Aaron enter the kitchen and remembered that she still didn't know why Kit was fired. On impulse, she followed him.

"I'm working on an annual report for Dorothy, so I don't have time for anything else," she said, reaching for the fridge. "I know I've mostly been working for you, so I hope that's okay."

Aaron opened a bottle of water and took a sip. "It doesn't matter. Everything's changing around here anyway."

She shut the fridge and opened the cabinet over the microwave. "Are you going to quit, too?"

"What do you mean? Who quit?"

She hadn't really planned to have a snack, but the bag of potato chips on the bottom shelf was calling to her.

"Kit," she said casually, as she tore open the bag.

Aaron stiffened. "No, she didn't. She was fired."

Isobel feigned surprise. "Why? I thought she was all that and one of these." She held up her Ruffles.

Aaron stared pensively at his water bottle. "People who fly too high don't judge distances properly. Call it the Icarus syndrome."

"How did Kit fly too high?"

He looked up. "Why do you care? You're just a temp."

Isobel threw her arms wide. "So tell me what happened. I'm not materially involved in any of this."

He regarded her for a moment, and when he spoke, there was an edge of resentment in his voice. "She thought Barnaby was going to make her a partner in the firm. But that was before the merger. When he made that remark at the staff meeting about us failing at consumer PR, she realized that Barnaby had been stringing her along. She knew there was no place for her in the new company structure—let alone any kind of partnership."

Suddenly Isobel understood. "You told Kit about MacBride's, and she tipped off the AP reporter."

Aaron closed his eyes and began to rock back and forth on his heels. "She broke her promise. She used me!"

"Then you told Barnaby what Kit had done, and he fired her."

"She was a whore!" The words burst from Aaron's mouth with such ferocity that Isobel practically jumped. "She was too married to look at me, but not too married to look at Jason!"

Jason?

Isobel held her breath, hoping Aaron's vitriol would continue to roll forth. It did.

"She's a demon! She tried to seduce her own brother's wife's—whatever he was—but he refused, because he was dating someone else. Kit found a sexy picture of the girl on Jason's phone and sent it to Barnaby. Jason was furious when he found out."

Kit sent the photo. Kit tipped off the AP reporter. Had she also poisoned Jason? It occurred to Isobel that with one fatal dose, Kit had been in a position to get revenge on Jason and sabotage the merger. And if Katrina was to be believed, Kit had been at Jason's house the night before the murder.

Isobel leaned forward eagerly. "How do you know all this?"

Aaron made a prayerful, keening sound. "I let her tell me things," he said, his voice breaking. "I would meet her nearby after work, once, twice a week—never on the Sabbath, of course. And we would talk. I would tell her…things, too." His expression grew stern. "Working with women is a temptation. The only way is to put them in their place."

Which is where—in a bar? wondered Isobel.

Aaron went on, "And if a relationship exists only in conversation, it's not a sin. Nothing ever happened between us. Nothing…physical."

She felt a brief flash of anger at the man's hypocrisy, but she squelched it to ask one last question.

"Do you know who the girl in the photo was?"

He shook his head furiously. "I don't know, and I don't care."

But I do, thought Isobel. Why is it that every time I ask anyone a question about Jason Whiteley, the answer is always Katrina?

THIRTY-FOUR

JAMES KNEW THAT THE BEST WAY to overcome his pounding head was to work out, but he also knew that the best way to ensure he didn't slip again immediately was to go to an AA meeting. He decided to hedge his bets and do a meeting first, then exercise, but that meant clearing his day. He called in sick to work and, moving more slowly than usual, headed out into the frosty morning. His path to the community center would take him past the gym. Fighting a weird premonition that he would run into Lily, he took a detour on 125th Street—where he spotted Lily walking toward him.

He briefly considered ducking into the Korean deli on the corner, but he knew she had seen him, too. In fact, he had the strange feeling that she had somehow engineered the meeting. He stared straight ahead and picked up the pace.

"James! I have to talk to you."

"Can't. In a hurry."

"Wait! It'll just take a minute."

He stopped, too tired to do battle. "What?"

She was shifting from side to side, her hands in her pockets stretching her coat down toward her knees. "I just wanted to say I'm sorry about last...I shouldn't have..." She swallowed. "You know."

A vague memory stirred in his brain of a small, pale female figure kneeling by his side, gently placing a washcloth on his forehead and holding his hand. He peered closely at her. She returned his gaze steadily.

He sighed and put his hand on her arm. "No, it's cool. We're cool."

Her breath caught slightly. "Seriously? Because I was feeling like I'd, you know, gone too far."

"Let's just forget about it, okay?" He shuffled his feet impatiently. "Look, I gotta go."

To his surprise, she stepped aside. "Okay. Take care of yourself. You don't look so good this morning."

"Yeah, well, that should come as no surprise."

She gave him an odd look, and then shrugged. "See you around."

As he continued toward the community center where the AA meeting was, he was struck by the irony that this was the easiest he'd ever gotten rid of her. The more he tried to repel her, the more she stuck, but giving in a little had prompted her to back off. He would think twice before doing it again, but in this case, he figured he owed her one for coming to his aid during his drunken rampage last night.

As he pulled open the door to the community center, his phone rang. It was Isobel. He knew he should apologize for his behavior on the street the other night. Might as well get it over with.

"Hey," he said. "I've been meaning to call you."

"Oh?"

The hopeful tone of her voice worked like a volume control on his headache, and he was suddenly unable to say what he most wanted to.

"Just to find out if there was any fallout from Angus's death," he said.

He switched hands and shrugged off his coat. Between his hangover and the cranked-up heat in the community center, he was sweating.

"Isobel? You there?"

"Um, yeah."

"Have you finally given up?"

"You mean on the murder?"

"What else?"

She paused. "No, I haven't. I don't know what the cops are doing, but I've found out some more stuff. But that isn't why I called. I just wanted to know…"

"What?"

"If you…if you were…um…if you'd like to see Delphi's play with me. It opens on Thursday."

"Yeah? What is it?"

"Shakespeare. *King John*."

"Don't know that one. I can't check my calendar while I'm talking, but if there's a problem, I'll let you know. It's, uh, nice of you to ask."

"Sure."

"Okay, gotta run. See you Thursday."

As he returned his phone to his pocket, he wondered fleetingly why she had tracked him down on his cell phone just to invite him to a play. Now he wished he had apologized, but she hadn't seemed too upset with him. Hell, she'd even invited him out. Something indefinable was nagging at him, but he didn't suppose it mattered. Steeling himself to face his support group, he pushed open the door to the meeting room and went through.

ISOBEL STARED AT THE PHONE. Either it was too painful for James to admit she'd seen him in that condition, or he had no memory at all of her being in his apartment the night before. He was certainly aware of her presence at the time—he had practically begged her to stay. Now she wondered what would have happened if she had. That lame "Oh, I was planning to call you" didn't fool her for a second. That's what she said whenever her mother called. He was avoiding her. Why had he even bothered to accept her invitation to Delphi's play? Maybe because he knew she wouldn't dare mention last night with other people around—

Her stomach lurched. What on earth had she been thinking? She was going with Hugh! She had been so desperate to invent a reason for calling James that she'd completely forgotten. She groaned and put her face in her hands. Now what? She supposed she'd have to tough it out and just hope they didn't get into another dick-swinging competition.

The spiral staircase creaked and Liz rounded the bend, shaking her head in mock despair. "Another month and I'll make more noise coming down those steps than Barnaby on a diet."

"Distract me. I just did something stupid," Isobel said.

"How bad are we talking? I find that the amount of distraction is directly proportional to the degree of stupidity. I want to make sure I can deliver before I promise anything."

"Personal stupid. Guy stupid."

"Follow me," said Liz.

She closed her office door and started to put her feet up on her desk.

"Nope," she grunted. "Can't do that anymore." She sat back and turned her nameplate upside down like a timer. "The doctor is in. What's up?"

"I'm a complete idiot."

"We've established that. Go on."

Isobel bit her lip. "There are these two guys, James and Hugh. I invited Hugh to see a play with me Thursday night. And then I totally forgot I'd done that and invited James, too."

"And you like them both?"

"James is a friend. Actually, he's my temp agent." Liz raised an eyebrow, but Isobel went on. "Hugh is a composer and pianist. And he's English. I'm a sucker for a British accent."

"So you'll make up your mind if and when one of them makes a move on you," Liz said shrewdly.

Isobel flushed. "Yeah, I guess. But they already met once and they didn't exactly take to one another. This could be a disaster."

Liz righted her nameplate. "Take it from me, a little testosterone-fest never hurt anyone. But if you want insulation, invite a few more people. I'll come. What's the play?"

"*King John.*"

Liz made a face. "On second thought, I think I have to mail a letter that night."

"You don't like Shakespeare?"

"Only the comedies." The phone rang. "Hi, Aaron… Yeah, sure, I've got the final. Okay." She hung up and pushed away from the desk. "Hang on. I have to print something." She hit a few keys on her keyboard and hoisted herself up. "I'll be right back."

Isobel slumped in her chair. Liz was probably right. Sunil would be there, too, and Hugh and James were both grownups. Supposedly. The only other option was to uninvite one of them. She picked up Liz's snow globe and shook it. Fake white flakes fell on all the Broadway marquees from the previous year, and she imagined a tiny version of herself standing in front of one of them, pointing proudly at her name.

"Argh!" Liz poked her head in the door. "Printer jammed. Will you cancel out and send it again?"

Isobel set the snow globe down and went around the desk to cancel Liz's print request. She sent the document again and closed it, revealing the email it was attached to. A thought occurred to her. Feeling suddenly light-headed, she clicked on "Sent Mail" and typed the word "Brazil" into the search bar.

A flood of emails filled the column, all with identical subject lines. Isobel clicked on one at random and drew a sharp breath.

"Planning a South American Outpost? Cal Erskine of Schumann, Crowe & Dyer can explain why Brazil is the next hot emerging market."

It was Liz who had sent the emails and jeopardized Jason's account. Katrina had been telling the truth after all.

And if Liz had lied about that, what else was she lying about?

THIRTY-FIVE

"I suppose you think she's faking being pregnant?" asked Delphi.

"Of course not." Isobel tapped the edge of her coaster on the bar at Vino Rosso. "It's just that somewhere along the way, I decided I could trust Liz, which, in this case at least, meant distrusting Katrina. What if I've had it backwards the whole time?"

Delphi looked up from counting the bills in her apron pocket. "Look, just because Liz lied to you about the Brazil thing doesn't necessarily mean she lied about anything else. It certainly doesn't mean she killed anyone. Most people will lie to save face. You would. I would."

Isobel finished her wine and tipped the glass one more time to make sure she'd drained it all. "Lying to save face is one thing, but she pinned it on Katrina. There has to be a reason, and all I can think of is that the emails incriminated her in some way in Jason's death."

"What do you know about Liz?"

"Not that much," Isobel admitted. "Just that I like her. She's funny, and very open, and she's kind of taken me under her wing—"

"And fed you information," Delphi broke in. "Not that you're not adorable and charming to some people—not me, of course—but it does seem like she's gone out of her way to make sure you hear her version of events."

"And Katrina's been the opposite. She hasn't wanted to tell me anything. Which is why it seemed like she was lying."

Delphi folded her money carefully and stuffed it into the pocket of her black pants. "Best thing to do is ignore them both. I think it's time to admit that Jason's death had nothing to do with the office bullshit."

"But what about the personal bullshit? Kit and Jason being related, Kit toying with Aaron, Katrina dating Jason. What about the Demerol in Barnaby's office? Ten minutes ago, you agreed that was significant."

Isobel followed Delphi down a narrow staircase that led past the busy kitchens to a small area with lockers. Delphi hung up her apron in one, removed her coat, and punched her timecard.

"I admit, the Demerol is questionable," Delphi conceded. "But Jimmy tossed the bottle, so it would be hard to prove it ever existed, let alone that he found it Barnaby's office."

"Which in itself is suspicious," Isobel pointed out.

Delphi pulled on her coat and slammed the locker shut with her foot. "The real question is, where are the police in all this? Have they been nosing around the firm?"

"Not since Angus's death. They think Angus did it."

"I don't believe that for a minute. I'll bet you anything they've shifted their focus to Jason's personal life," Delphi said as Isobel followed her back up the stairs. "And if it does turn out to be someone in his personal life who happens to work at Dove & Flight, the clues are elsewhere. Because the one thing we know for sure is that he wasn't poisoned in the office." Delphi turned and called out, "Carlo! I'm leaving."

"*Delphinia bellissima!*" crooned a silky, Italian-accented voice. A raven-haired man with a Roman profile emerged from the depths of the restaurant, his hand over his heart. "I am desolate at your departure!"

"Oh, Carlo, you'll live. Remember, I'm not back until Monday. My play opens this weekend. You are coming, aren't you?"

"How could I miss a chance to gaze upon my favorite *bionda*." He brushed his lips teasingly over the back of Delphi's hand. Isobel rolled her eyes at the maître d's ostentatious adulation.

Delphi rescued her hand. "You would never leave the restaurant for something as frivolous as the theater."

Carlo gave an exaggerated shrug. "You underestimate my devotion, *carina*."

Delphi turned to Isobel. "How do you say 'yeah, right' in Italian?"

"*Buona sera*, Don Giovanni!" Isobel dragged Delphi outside. "I still don't know why you put up with him."

"Because work would be a complete bore otherwise." Delphi wound an iridescent blue scarf around her neck. "Come to my tech rehearsal. We can chat when I'm not on."

Isobel didn't think she could sit through *King John* more than once, even if this was a stop-and-start run-through.

"I'd rather be surprised when I see it on Thursday."

"Oh, come on," Delphi urged. "What else are you doing tonight?"

Without giving her a chance to protest, Delphi looped her arm through Isobel's and steered her down the street.

Graham's studio wasn't far from Vino Rosso. When they arrived, the other actors were in various states of dress, not unlike Delphi's regular attire, with costume pieces over their real clothes. Isobel was surprised at how effective the scenery she and Sunil had helped paint turned out to be.

"What's it about, anyway?" Isobel asked.

"Oh, you know those crazy Plantagenets, it's always something. King John of Magna Carta fame inherits the throne when his brother, Geoffrey, is murdered. I play Geoffrey's widow, Constance, who's pushing her son Arthur to be king. John captures Arthur, who dies trying to escape. Then I die of a broken heart. So, as far as I'm concerned, that's what the play is about."

Isobel smiled. "Bullshit, bullshit, bullshit, my lines..."

Delphi winked. "Exactly."

"Do you get an awesome death scene?"

"Nah. I croak offstage after Act Three, scene four."

They settled in to watch, as Gary Stinson, the wimpy Willy Loman, took the stage and intoned:

> *Here have we war for war and blood for blood,*
> *Controlment for controlment: so answer France.*

"He's really good," Isobel whispered. "Where does all that authority come from?"

"Who knows? And he's got decent legs. I don't know why he was so nervous about auditioning in tights."

"And hold!" Graham's voice echoed in the room.

Delphi sighed. "This is going to be a long night."

Isobel glanced at her watch. "I really should go. I'm beat."

"Oh, just stay and watch my first scene," Delphi pleaded. "It's next. What if you get here late or something on Thursday and miss it?"

"I'm not going to miss it!" Isobel protested. "Besides, I'm coming with a whole bunch of people. Sunil and Hugh. And, um, James."

Delphi put her hand over her heart. "'What warmth is there in your affection towards any of these princely suitors that are already come?'"

Isobel grimaced. "You know, the best thing about your rehearsing *King John* is that you stopped doing that."

"Okay, fine. But seriously, all three of them?" Delphi folded her arms and sulked. "You're trying to upstage me."

Isobel knew that Delphi was only half-joking. "It was an accident. I invited James, forgetting I had already asked Hugh to come with Sunil and me. Actually, I'm hoping to bring a few more people, too, just to defuse the tension."

"Isn't that a little greedy?"

"I mean female friends." She brightened. "Maybe I'll ask Katrina."

Delphi shook a warning finger. "Don't overcompensate. Just because you caught Liz in one fib, doesn't mean you can trust Katrina."

"I'm not talking about trusting her. I'm talking about inviting her to see your play."

Delphi stood up and tied the strings on her bodice together, so that her cleavage increased to hide-and-seek proportions. "You know what I mean. Keep your distance."

Graham's stentorian voice rang out. "Act Two, scene one. Austria, stage right. Philip, Lewis, Arthur, Constance, stage left!"

"Gotta go," Delphi said.

"I'll make sure to laugh at the funny parts," said Isobel.

Delphi scowled. "There are no funny parts."

"Just funny actors?" Isobel called after her. Delphi flipped her the bird over her shoulder and took her place onstage.

THIRTY-SIX

ISOBEL WOUND UP STAYING at Delphi's rehearsal longer than she planned. She was so tired when she got home that she fell into bed with her clothes on and forgot to set her alarm. By the time she arrived at the office the next morning, the place was abuzz with gossip, the locus of which was, as usual, in the kitchen. She poured herself a cup of coffee and tuned in. Apparently, Jayla Cummings had arrived earlier for a meeting with Barnaby, and speculation was rampant.

"Maybe she's going to replace Kit," Penny said.

"Are you kidding?" scoffed Liz. "She must make money hand over fist as a consultant. Why would she take a pay cut to work in PR?"

"She could be angling to be a partner," said Aaron, whose tone reminded Isobel that he considered all professional women ruthless strivers.

"What kind of partner?" Dorothy said. "Everything's going to change the moment the merger is finalized."

"I thought the merger was off," said Penny.

Isobel stole a glance at Katrina, who was staring resolutely at her Ferragamos. When the gathering broke up, she followed her friend down the hall.

"I noticed you didn't say much," Isobel commented. She set her coffee cup next to her computer and pulled out her chair, but Katrina stopped her.

"Not here."

They rounded the bend to Katrina's office, where Katrina shut the door and sank into her chair.

"The merger is back on. That's why Jayla is here. It was one of my father's conditions that they take us back."

"Did you…" Isobel let the question hang.

"Barnaby threatened to send the photo to my father unless I convinced him to give us one more chance." Katrina ran a weary hand over her face. "It was awful, Isobel. My father couldn't figure out why I was being so insistent about the merger going through, when I'd already made it clear that I was pissed about it. I had to make up all kinds of reasons. At one point, I even considered telling him that Barnaby was blackmailing me with something, but I couldn't see how to do that without telling him what. And nothing would make him run from the merger quicker than knowing what Barnaby was up to. And then God knows who Barnaby would have sent that picture to just to get back at me. I'm just so sick of all this." She looked up at Isobel, who saw that her eyes were wet. "All I want is to show my father that I can make it on my own, but I can't shake him. I'll always be a pawn to anyone who knows who he is."

Isobel was tempted to tell Katrina that it was Kit, not Jason, who had sent Barnaby the photo, but she couldn't see how to do that without revealing that Aaron knew about it, which would only make Katrina feel worse.

"Do you trust Barnaby to keep his word?" she asked.

"I made him delete it in front of me. He had it on his phone, and he'd archived it onto his computer. What an asshole."

Isobel was suddenly glad she'd caught Liz in her lie. She felt sorry for Katrina, whose advantages she had always envied, but which had turned out not to be so advantageous after all. She was relieved to be able to be genuinely sympathetic and supportive, without wondering if she was being fed a line.

"How did your father convince Schumann, Crowe & Dyer to take us back? They still had to agree."

Katrina stifled a hiccup. "The retainer is minimal. That's what Barnaby and Jayla are hashing out right now—I was just up there. There's also going to be a personnel shakeup. The financial services group upstairs is going to take it on."

"What about you?"

Katrina gave a sad smile. "Graduate school is sounding pretty good right about now."

There was a knock on the door, and Penny poked her head in. "Can you guys come out? Barnaby is here with Jayla and he wants to talk to everyone."

They returned to the open area in the center of the floor. Jayla stood next to Isobel's desk with Barnaby, Jimmy and Mike Hardy from Human Resources. Jayla's smile slipped a little when she spotted Isobel, but she quickly masked it by picking up her coffee cup and taking an extra-long sip. Katrina and Isobel joined Liz and Aaron. Dorothy and Penny stood next to each other, while grumpy Wilbur Freed remained off by himself, clutching his sheaf of newspapers and magazines to his chest. His gaze shifted momentarily to Isobel, and she had the distinct impression that he was still angry with her for knocking into him on the spiral staircase, even thought that was days ago.

Barnaby rambled on for a while about their new contract with Schumann, Crowe & Dyer and how important it was to work together and keep the lines of communication open, so there were no more "errors in judgment."

Isobel stole a glance at Liz, whose face sobered slightly at this.

"As a show of good faith," Barnaby continued, "I'm giving the account to the group upstairs."

There was a rustle of surprise, as heads turned to Aaron and Liz, who stared fixedly ahead. Oddly enough, nobody looked at Katrina.

"And finally, there's one more important piece of news. The merger is back on."

The murmur swelled, forcing Barnaby to raise his voice.

"And it's definite. Nothing is going to derail it. Not this time."

With that, Jayla collapsed onto the floor, vomit splattering Isobel's desk as she went down.

THIRTY-SEVEN

THERE WAS A MOMENT OF stunned, horrified silence, broken by Barnaby's bellowed command to call 911. Isobel, Liz and Aaron all reached for the phone on Isobel's desk, but Liz was quickest. Mike Hardy knelt by Jayla, positioning her head to the side so she wouldn't choke. Isobel's stomach heaved as Jayla's eyes rolled back into her head. She gripped Katrina's arm and saw that her friend's face was deathly pale against her bright red hair. Dorothy, her face even whiter than Katrina's, knelt on Jayla's other side and pressed her fingers into Jayla's wrist.

"Her pulse isn't regular—I can't count it."

"I think she may be having a seizure," Liz said into the phone. "Late twenties, early thirties... She could have a condition, I don't know. She's a professional acquaintance, not personal..."

Isobel marveled at how calm and matter-of-fact Liz's voice was. She'd certainly be the mom you'd want around in a crisis. Liz gave the address and hung up.

"They said to try to keep her from biting her tongue and choking," Liz said. "They're on their way."

"This doesn't change anything," Barnaby muttered.

Isobel stared at him, aghast. How he could still be thinking of the merger at a time like this was beyond her. She looked down at Jayla, who had started gasping for air.

"Who knows CPR?" Barnaby shouted.

Without answering, Dorothy began chest compressions. Aaron, whom Isobel hadn't noticed disappearing, was suddenly there with paper towels, and began to clean off Isobel's desk.

"This is awful," Penny said under her breath. "What happened?"

"I don't know." Isobel was surprised at how shaky her voice sounded.

Jayla came to with a shudder and vomited some more. Undaunted, Dorothy propped her head up a bit.

"Blurry," Jayla whispered. "Looks funny…"

"You're going to be all right. The paramedics should be here any minute," Mike said. He stood up and gestured for the others to give her some space.

A wet stain darkened the carpet where Mike had been kneeling. Isobel followed the irregular brown pattern until her eyes fell on Jayla's coffee cup, which had come to rest on its side by the filing cabinet. The room suddenly seemed overly bright, and Isobel felt a warning flush. She grabbed one of Aaron's paper towels and sidled over to the filing cabinet. She wrapped the coffee cup in the paper towel and, hoping nobody was looking, retreated to the kitchen to find a plastic bag.

She had just sealed up the cup, when Jimmy's voice startled her.

"What are you doing?"

Isobel jumped and put a hand over her heart. "Oh, my God, Jimmy, you scared the shit out of me!"

He pointed to the bag. "Why do you have Jayla's coffee cup?"

"I'm following my instincts. Think about what happened to Jason. Who's to say somebody didn't try to poison Jayla?"

Jimmy folded his arms and rocked slightly from side to side. "With what?"

"I don't know."

"Not my Demerol, that's long gone."

"Jimmy…"

He narrowed his eyes. "What?"

"Has Angus's office been cleaned out yet?"

"His son came yesterday for his personal effects, and Barnaby took his files."

Isobel frowned. "Well, forget that."

Jimmy took a step toward her. "If you're thinking of the digoxin, remember, Sophie kept it."

She grasped his arm. "Jimmy, can you get back up there and see if she still has it?"

He saluted. "I'm on it."

She followed him out and watched him take the stairs two at a time. When she returned to the group, the paramedics were strapping Jayla to a stretcher.

"What did they say?" Isobel asked Katrina.

"Her heartbeat is all over the place. They're taking her to the hospital."

"Are the police on their way?"

Katrina gave her a look. "Why the police?"

"Um, because we've had two deaths here already?"

"What are you saying?"

"You don't think there's anything odd about this?"

Before Katrina could answer, Isobel saw Jimmy beckoning her from the staircase. Grateful for the escape, she excused herself and met him halfway up.

"It's not there," he whispered.

"Sophie threw it away?"

He shook his head. "No. She said she completely forgot about it, but when we looked in the drawer where she kept it, it was gone. Both the pills and the injectable. And she can't even say for sure when the injectable went missing."

ISOBEL WASN'T SURPRISED WHEN Detectives O'Connor and Aguilar appeared about an hour later. She caught O'Connor's eye and motioned for him to follow her into the kitchen.

"We've got to stop meeting like this," he quipped.

Isobel handed him the plastic bag, and his expression grew somber.

"Jayla was drinking coffee from this cup before she passed out. It may be nothing, but given everything else, I thought it you should have it."

O'Connor nodded. "Good catch. It's time to fingerprint everyone in the office."

Isobel coughed self-consciously. "Just so you know, mine are already on record."

O'Connor regarded her. "And why is that?"

She proceeded to tell him about her experience solving the bank murder.

"Yes, I heard about that incident." O'Connor nodded thoughtfully. "That explains a lot about you. And Mr. Cooke."

He started for the door, but Isobel stopped him.

"Wait! There's one—no, two other things you should know."

He turned toward her, expectantly.

"Angus Dove's digoxin is missing, both the pills and his emergency injectable. It was his secretary, Sophie, who kept it. She said it's gone."

O'Connor jotted the information down in his notebook. "Is she still here?"

"Yes, she's upstairs."

O'Connor nodded. "And?"

Isobel hesitated, and then said, "Jimmy Rocket, Barnaby's assistant, kept Demerol in his office for severe back pain. It went missing just before Jason Whiteley died, and Jimmy found the empty pill bottle in Barnaby's office."

O'Connor gave a dismissive shake of his head. "The Demerol that was in Jason Whiteley's system was also an injectable. The kind you'd get for oral surgery. You could never grind up enough pills to hide in coffee without the person noticing."

A wave of relief washed over Isobel.

"On the other hand," O'Connor continued thoughtfully, "if Rocket had access to pills, he might also have had access to the other. I'll speak to him."

Isobel followed the detectives back out to the group. O'Connor cleared his throat to get everyone's attention.

"Just to make sure we've covered our ground, we'd like to get your fingerprints for elimination purposes. If anybody already has prints on record, there's no need to participate. Please bear with us."

"This is an outrage!" Barnaby roared. "What are you accusing us of?"

"Nothing—yet," O'Connor said pointedly. "But in light of the fact that two people have been found dead in this office, and another has just had a seizure of unaccountable origin, I would say this exercise is overdue." O'Connor took a few steps forward until he towered over Barnaby, who, despite his girth, was not very tall. "Unless you are officially a suspect, offering your fingerprints is voluntary. I'm sure I don't need to point out how ungracious it will look if you refuse."

Barnaby had no answer to that, and as the others took themselves off in groups to discuss this new development, Aguilar unpacked a portable fingerprinting kit. He began to clear a space on Isobel's desk, but O'Connor's hand shot out and stayed his arm.

Isobel's coffee cup, made of the same institutional white china as Jayla's, sat on her desk, undisturbed. O'Connor took a paper towel and, with a glance at Isobel, wrapped his fingers around it. He spoke softly to Aguilar, but Isobel heard him.

"Decant this. And bag the cup."

She wasn't sure what O'Connor was thinking, taking her cup as well as Jayla's, but she knew it couldn't be anything good.

THIRTY-EIGHT

Ginger Wainwright, back from her Jamaica vacation, was prowling the cramped corridors of Temp Zone with renewed vigor. Despite the frigid temperature, she had yet to abandon her island wear. She was flaunting a too-revealing orange tank top that managed to clash with both her tan and her chemically-induced red hair, and she had brought along matching flip flops, which, in a reverse from summer practice, she changed into after she got to the office. James found himself wishing he'd chosen last night for his relapse so he could have postponed having to deal with her for one more day. On the other hand, Ginger never took kindly to unexplained absences, and there was no point in prolonging the inevitable.

After she had poked her head into his office for her obligatory morning reconnaissance and declared herself satisfied with his work during her absence, James shut his door and popped open his first Diet Coke of the day. One benefit of Ginger still being on island time was that she'd come in late, so at least he had enjoyed one last quiet interlude. But now it was time to settle down to work.

He had just started filling out an evaluation form for a potential new recruit when the phone rang. Recognizing the number from Dove & Flight, he picked up.

"Hey, Isobel."

"I have to ask you something about Jayla."

He inhaled sharply. "I told you, that's over, there's nothing—"

"Does she have a seizure condition?"

"A what?"

"She was here for a meeting. Apparently, the merger is back on. Or was—or—actually, I don't know what's going on anymore. But one minute she was fine, and the next minute she had a seizure and passed out."

James stood up and paced toward the window, momentarily forgetting that he was on a corded phone. It tumbled off his desk with a clatter, and he scrambled to pick it up.

He sat down again. "Are you still there?"

"I'm here. Can you think of any reason that would happen to her?"

"She's strong as an ox. A crappy cook, but a healthy eater. And she's a workout fiend." He reflected briefly on Jayla's taut abs and molded upper arms, then pulled his focus back to Isobel. "She didn't take medication for anything that I know of. Just some herbal shit."

"Could she have had a bad reaction to that?" Isobel asked.

"I don't know. Is she okay?"

"The paramedics took her to the ER. And then the cops showed up. It was the same two again, O'Connor and Aguilar. And I showed them—"

James felt his throat tighten. "Showed them what?"

"Jayla had been drinking coffee. The cup went flying when she fell. I saved it and gave it to them."

He didn't know what he'd been afraid Isobel might say, but he was relieved it had nothing to do with her.

"And then they bagged my coffee cup," she continued.

So much for that.

"Why did they take yours?"

"I don't know, but they were identical. Maybe they're thinking that Jayla accidentally picked up my cup, and that was the one she was holding when she passed out. So if her coffee had been poisoned, it was still sitting on my desk."

James picked up the nameplate from his desk and ran his sleeve over it nervously. "It's time we got you out of there."

"Why?"

"Are you serious? What if you're right and Jayla's coffee was poisoned? You could have picked up her cup by mistake!"

There was silence for a moment at the other end. "I like it when you worry about me. It's sweet."

"Dammit, Isobel, I'm serious!"

"I worry about you, too, you know."

That brought him up short. "Worry about me how?"

There was another moment of silence, and when Isobel spoke again, she sounded hurt.

"I didn't expect you to thank me, but I hoped you might have the decency to let me know you were okay."

"I have no idea what you're talking about," he said, exasperated.

"You know, the other night."

A little warning bell went off in his brain, and he felt his mouth go dry. "What other night?"

"Were you so far gone that you don't remember me force-feeding you Advil and putting a washcloth on your forehead?"

He swallowed. "That was you?"

"For God's sake, James, who else would it be?"

As she said it, he realized his mistake. He also sensed, from her sharp intake of breath, that she'd just answered her own question.

"I'm sorry," he whispered. "I thought it was…"

"Lily. I get it. It's fine. I don't know why you don't just admit there's something going on between you two."

"That's not it! I saw her the next day, and my memory was so vague—"

"Vague?" she spat. "You grabbed my hand and begged me not to leave you."

He didn't dare admit that he had no memory of that at all. "When I saw Lily on the street the next morning, something she said led me to believe it was her."

"Forget it. It doesn't matter."

He rubbed his eyes, trying to work it through. "You came all the way up to Harlem to see me? How did you know where I lived?"

"I looked you up. And I was already up there, rehearsing with Hugh."

James felt an unaccountable flash of irritation. "So you thought you'd just check up on me?"

"No! I tried to call you to apologize for not believing you about Katrina and Jason, okay? And when you didn't answer, I got worried. With good reason, as it turns out!"

No wonder Lily had looked at him oddly. But she had apologized. For what, then? She must have been talking about the night she intruded on his conversation with Isobel and Hugh. What had he said to her? He tried to remember. That it was fine. They were cool. Great. He'd essentially given Lily permission to continue stalking him. And on top of that, he was now doubly indebted to Isobel. It was bad enough that he owed her for helping him. Now he had to find a way to soothe her ego for not remembering, or at least not being smart enough to figure it out.

"I should have known it was you. I'm sorry," he said finally. "But one of the reasons I broke up with Jayla is that she couldn't resist jumping in and saving me all the time. I have to work this stuff out for myself."

"And what happens when you wind up in the hospital because you're too far gone to save yourself? You don't get points for doing this alone, James. You get points for staying alive."

"Okay, we're done with this topic," he snapped.

"Fine. I have to get back to work anyway," she said. "You know, considering that Jayla looked after you so well, you might find it in your heart to make sure she's okay."

"Jesus! You really don't know when to stop, do you?"

"Oh, you think?"

The line went dead.

James threw down the receiver and pushed away from his desk. Pacing his tiny office, he threw a few boxing punches, punctuating them with grunts of fury. Then he grabbed his empty soda can, angry that it was Coke and not beer, crumpled it, and threw it at his computer. It ricocheted off and landed on a stack of papers, where it dripped sugary syrup onto a form he would now have to reprint. With a cry of frustration, he swept the papers to the floor. There was a tentative rap on his door.

"You okay in here?" Anna looked in. "No, don't answer that. I can tell you're not. What's up?"

He tried to answer without taking her head off. "Nothing. A personal matter."

"Why don't you take a walk? Get some air."

"Yeah, that's a good idea. Thanks."

She withdrew, and James sank back into his chair. In fact, he didn't want to leave the office. Here, he was safe. He didn't have any alcohol stashed away, and with any luck, he could find something to distract him from this ridiculous situation with Isobel and Lily. He was always most vulnerable to relapse when he was upset, so the trick was to push through it. The only things that ever helped were working out and working. He wiped his forehead, straightened his nameplate, and picked up the stack of papers from the floor. Isobel's interim assessment form for Dove & Flight had landed on top. He shuffled the tangible evidence of her existence to the bottom of the pile and pushed her image firmly from his mind.

THIRTY-NINE

THE ONLY THING MORE INFURIATING than James not remembering she'd been at his apartment was his mistaking her for somebody else. And that obnoxious little gym rat, of all people! Isobel plunged her fists into her eyes to keep from crying, but succeeded only in smearing her eye shadow.

She had gone over there on impulse, and now she regretted it. While there had been nothing attractive about James in the state in which she'd found him, she had to admit that when he'd asked her to stay, she had felt a rush of affection. But it appeared he thought he was asking Lily to stay. She took a tissue from the box on the desk in Kit's empty office, where she'd taken refuge, and blew her nose with enough force to stop up her ears. She tried to lob the tissue into the garbage can by the door and missed. With a self-pitying sigh, she got up from behind the desk and went to retrieve it. Kit's raincoat was still hanging on the door. It was a nice-looking coat.

Finders, keepers, thought Isobel. I could use a decent raincoat.

She pulled the black and tan coat off the hook and tried it on. There was no mirror, but it certainly felt like it fit, though it was a little on the long side. She stuck her hands in the pockets and whirled around. The left pocket was empty, but the right held several pieces of paper. Isobel pulled them out. There were several business cards, a grocery list, a letter on school stationery folded in quarters, and a piece of crumpled blue notepaper. Isobel uncrumpled it.

Craig asked me point-blank, so I told him. I think this evens the score, don't you?
Jason

Isobel perched on the edge of the desk and unfolded the school letter. It was addressed to Kit and Craig Blanchard, thanking them for their donation of $1,000 to the PTA. So Craig was her husband. Jason must have told him that she was hitting on him. Maybe he'd also told Craig about her flirtation with Aaron. No wonder Kit was furious when she showed up at his apartment. But what had Kit done to Jason that had required score-settling? Was it simply that she'd made a pass at him, or was there something else?

One question answered, another raised, thought Isobel, as she changed her mind and hung the coat back up. It would be difficult to pursue any avenue of inquiry regarding Kit now that she was gone. Unless someone else could be convinced to pursue it for her. She pocketed the blue notepaper and returned to her desk.

Aguilar was packing up his fingerprint kit.

"Just out of curiosity, did anyone refuse?" she asked.

He gave a noncommittal grunt in response and joined O'Connor, who was standing by the exit door. O'Connor caught Isobel's eye and waved her over.

"As an outsider in the firm, and an observant one at that, you've probably picked up on some tensions regarding this merger I've been hearing about," he said in a quiet voice. "Is there anything you've noticed that you might want to pass along?"

Isobel regarded him warily. "Are you actually soliciting my opinion?"

He allowed himself a small smile. "What does your instinct tell you?"

"My instinct tells me that someone tried to poison Jayla with whatever was left of Angus's digoxin."

"Go on."

Isobel took a deep breath. "The person who most vehemently opposed the merger is dead. So unless Angus is reaching out from beyond the grave, or somehow left instructions for an accomplice to see it through, there's got to be someone else who is willing to go to any length to make sure the merger doesn't happen. Someone who has something big to gain or lose, which may or may not be directly connected to the business end of it."

"Sounds to me like you're thinking of someone in particular," O'Connor said.

"There is someone, although it doesn't quite square with what happened to Jayla today."

She told them about Kit's attempt to sabotage the merger and her nocturnal visit to Jason's. O'Connor read the crumpled blue paper with interest and pocketed it.

"You're right, it doesn't allow for what happened today. Could she have had an accomplice?"

Isobel hesitated. "There's Aaron, but he was so furious with her for betraying his confidence that I just don't see him helping her again. I think it's fair to say that he's, um, exorcised her."

O'Connor glanced at Aguilar. "We'll follow up on it all the same. Now, is there anyone else you can think of who wanted this merger stopped to that degree?"

Katrina. It was time to tell them about Katrina.

"No one."

O'Connor nodded. "Thank you. You've been very helpful."

She watched them leave and wondered if she'd made a mistake in not sharing her suspicions. She had a flash of standing on an island beach, watching the last ferry of the day depart for the mainland, but she shook off the image and trudged upstairs to find Jimmy.

His brow puckered as she approached his desk.

"You told them about the Demerol," he said in a voice that was more sad than accusatory.

She held out her hands in a helpless gesture. "I had to."

"They won't find anything on me. I gave them the name of my doctor. He'll tell them I've never had an injectable. I don't even think that's something you prescribe."

She drew closer to him. "Jimmy, I need to know what's going to happen to every single person here when the ICG merger goes through."

A flicker of concern crossed his face and he shook his head. "Barnaby hasn't said anything to me about that. I'm not sure he knows yet. It's something that would be hammered out afterwards by the bigwigs. And it might not necessarily happen right away."

"But certain jobs would be eliminated, right? Certain functions would be made redundant?"

"Yes, definitely."

"Is there any way you can find out what Barnaby's thinking in that direction?"

"Short of asking him point-blank? No."

"Can't you ask him?"

Jimmy clenched his fist under his chin in full "Thinker" position. Isobel couldn't help but notice his well-defined biceps stretching the unseasonably thin material of his T-shirt.

"For you, madam, I will endeavor to adopt a ruse so impenetrable that he will ne'er discover my true intent."

It was a relief to have the old, anachronistically bantering Jimmy back, if just for a moment. She dropped a curtsy to show her appreciation.

"Thank you, good knight."

He pointed to the clock on the wall. "You might well say good night!"

Barnaby's door burst open and the big man's head appeared in it.

"Jimmy!"

With a wink at Isobel, he vanished into Barnaby's office.

It was almost five o'clock and she was due at Hugh's studio at seven to rehearse. She took care going down the spiral staircase, which always gave her a touch of vertigo. Aaron was coming out of the kitchen as she passed by.

"Dorothy is looking for you," he said.

"Thanks."

She knocked gently on Dorothy's door. She was at her desk, and Katrina and Penny were standing in front of one of the bookcases.

"Oh, Isobel! I was afraid you'd left." A look of relief washed over Dorothy's face. "We've had a disaster. Schüssler wants a complete redo of the annual report and they go to press with it tomorrow."

"What? But why? It was all fine yesterday!"

Dorothy shook her head impatiently. "I thought so, too. But while all that craziness with Jayla was going on this morning, they emailed me. I didn't see it until just now. Apparently, somebody over there messed up royally. They accidentally sent us the Word file from last year's report. We have to do the whole thing over."

"You have got to be kidding!" Isobel glanced at Katrina, whose mouth was set in a humorless line. "And nobody noticed?"

"We didn't have the account last year," Katrina said. "There's no way we could have known."

"Not to mention the fact that we don't speak German," Penny said.

"If it was their screwup, they should move the deadline," Isobel said.

Dorothy's eyebrows shot up. "If you want to run that one past Barnaby, go right ahead."

Isobel sighed. "So what do we do?"

"We pull a rabbit out of a hat, that's what. Can you stay tonight until we can get it done?"

Isobel held out her hands helplessly. "I can't. I have a rehearsal at seven."

Dorothy rapped a pen on her blotter. "What time will you be done?"

"Probably around nine."

"Would you be willing to come back when you're finished?" Dorothy asked. "You'll get paid overtime."

Ka-ching, thought Isobel.

"Sure, I can do that."

"Great." Dorothy handed Penny some papers. "Can you get started on the charts at the back of the book? Make sure the numbers match up." She handed Katrina a second batch. "You can work on inputting the text in German. We'll have to be doubly careful not to make any mistakes, since at this point, we have to do all the data entry ourselves. If we can assure them it's all correct, they'll deal with the layout tomorrow morning, Frankfurt time." Dorothy leaned back and surveyed her team. "This is how we earn our PR stripes. It'll be fun, in a trench-warfare kind of way."

Isobel groaned inwardly and followed Penny and Katrina out.

"How often does this kind of thing happen?" Isobel asked.

"More often than it should. Damn, I was really hoping to get out of here," said Katrina. "I've had just about enough of this place."

"Me, too," Penny said. "I can't get that image of Jayla writhing on the floor out of my head." She gave a little shiver and left them.

"Here." Isobel held out her hand to Katrina. "I can help you out before I leave."

"Thanks." Katrina peeled off a few pages and passed them over.

Isobel glanced down at the endless, multi-syllabic German words. "This is going to take all night."

"At least you get overtime," Katrina said and stomped off.

And for once, Isobel had to admit she had the advantage over her friend.

FORTY

By the time Isobel arrived at Hugh's, Sunil was already there. He answered the door singing, and she waved a hello to Hugh before settling on the couch to listen. As Sunil finished the last, yearning phrase of his love ballad, she wondered if his mind was turning to Delphi. He held Isobel's gaze an extra moment, then broke the mood and flashed an impish smile as if to dispel any fear that he might be pining in real life.

"That was perfect," said Hugh. "Hello, Isobel."

"Hi, guys. Listen, I know I'm a little late, but I can only stay until nine. I have to go back to my office to work on a last-minute project."

"Given everything that's happened there recently, do you think it's a good idea?" Sunil asked.

Hugh looked from Sunil to Isobel. "What's happened there recently?"

Isobel waved him off. "Nothing, really."

"Only a few mysterious deaths," said Sunil.

"What?" Hugh exclaimed.

"Sunil is exaggerating," she said lightly. "A senior partner died of a heart attack, and the other turned out to be...nothing. It'll be fine. There will be hardly anyone there."

Sunil's dark eyes widened. "And that doesn't strike you as a problem?" He turned to Hugh. "Will you talk some sense into her?"

"I'm not sure I really understand." Hugh glanced at his watch. "But if our time is limited, we'd better get started."

Before Sunil could protest, Hugh started the introduction

to "Don't Go Away Mad." Isobel directed the song to Sunil's stormy countenance, and by the time she finished, they were all laughing. They ran through their duets, and then Hugh turned to Sunil.

"I think you're done for now. I'll just finish up with Isobel, and we'll reconvene…when did we say…Saturday, right?"

Hugh's phone rang. While he took the call, Sunil finished stuffing his music into his bag and pulled Isobel with him to the door. "I still don't feel right about you going back there at night."

She shook him off. "Four women proofreading German? Our greatest danger is drowning in consonants."

"I'm serious. If you feel uncomfortable for any reason, get out of there."

"Of course."

"I'm going to call you later, just to make sure you're okay." He leaned forward and gave her a peck on the cheek. "Sing pretty."

She closed the door behind Sunil and returned to the studio. To her surprise, Hugh was sitting on the couch.

"Just thought I'd relax for a sec," he said.

Isobel frowned. "Okay, but I do have to leave in fifteen minutes."

"No rest for the weary," he said, pulling himself up. But instead of sitting down at the piano, he paused at her side and entwined his fingers in hers. She felt a flutter in her stomach as he caressed her face and then kissed her. His touch was gentle, his lips soft and sweet with the lingering mint of his tea. She reached up and encircled her arms around his neck, and with this encouragement, he grew more passionate. After a moment, she pulled away.

"I've been longing to do that from the moment you came rushing into that audition room," he said breathlessly.

The fifteen minutes passed quickly, and it was another hour before Isobel finally pulled away, setting her blouse to rights and returning stray wisps of hair to her ponytail.

"I really have to go," she said huskily.

"Must you?"

"I promised I would go back tonight. And I like to keep my promises."

Hugh sat up from the couch, knocking over the ever-present stack of music books in the process. "Then promise me you'll come back tomorrow evening."

"Tomorrow we're going to see Delphi in *King John*, remember?"

"Can we have our own private first-night party back here?"

To Isobel's annoyance, she thought suddenly of James, but she quickly closed her mind against him. "I promise." She brushed a lock of hair off Hugh's forehead with her lips. "Now aren't you glad I'm a person who keeps her promises?"

DESPITE HER BRAVADO, ISOBEL had to admit there was something distinctly creepy about entering the Dove & Flight building at night, alone. For once, she didn't mind flashing her photo ID at the security guard and signing in, although she wished he had at least bothered to look up before waving her through to the elevators.

When she arrived on the floor, she buzzed and waited. A few moments later Penny answered the main door, bedraggled and bleary-eyed.

"Am I glad to see you," Penny said. "Come on in. We're in the small conference room."

The fluorescent lights shone harsher than usual against the blackness of the night sky, and Isobel's eyes took a moment to adjust to the halo that seemed to shimmer over every surface. As Penny led her down the hall, Isobel glanced out the window at the office building across the street, where a few other put-upon junior staffers were also working late. She found their presence, distant though it was, vaguely reassuring.

"Dorothy said I could leave when you got here once we bring you up to speed," Penny said.

She pushed open the door to the conference room, where Dorothy and Katrina were seated at the table. Empty chip bags and sandwich wrappers littered the credenza next to a collection of soda cans and a half-melted bucket of ice. With a start, Isobel realized that not only hadn't she set foot in this conference room since the day she'd discovered Jason Whiteley dead, but Katrina was sitting in his chair. If the others hadn't registered the coincidence, she wasn't going to call attention to it, so she pushed the image of Jason's dead body from her mind and dumped her stuff on an empty chair.

"Where do we stand?" she asked cheerily.

Katrina glowered at her. "Why do you sound so happy?"

Isobel suppressed the urge to giggle. "Rehearsal went great."

"Yeah, well, you're like an hour late."

Dorothy looked up from her work. "It should go faster now that you're here. Some of it will be familiar to you from the other draft."

Katrina was leaning her head on one hand, absent-mindedly stuffing soy crisps into her mouth and circling words with a red pencil. "You know, I actually took German freshman year. Too bad I never studied," she mumbled through crumbs.

"Is anyone else here?" Isobel asked, with a vague gesture meant to encompass the entire office.

"I was in Harm's Way earlier, and it looked like everyone had gone," said Dorothy. "Nobody's down here but us."

"Can I go now?" Penny asked.

"Sure, that's fine." Dorothy waved her off. "You've been a big help, but it's really a three-person job."

Katrina pushed her papers aside. "I need a break." She reached for her Diet Coke, gulped down the rest of it, and set the can on the table. "I'll walk you out," she said to Penny.

Dorothy gave Isobel a wan smile. "I really appreciate your schlepping back down here."

Mustering all her willpower not to indulge in a sensory recall of Hugh's curly brown hair and sinewy back, Isobel nodded. She didn't trust herself to speak.

Content at having given lip service to inconveniencing Isobel, Dorothy immediately became all business, with the renewed vigor of a general outlining the battle plan to a fresh recruit.

"We've inputted all the new information, and Penny laid out the photographs they want to use. Katrina is proofreading our document against their data sheets. You can help her by starting at the end and going backwards until you meet in the middle."

"Okay." Isobel pulled forward the stack of papers Dorothy indicated and looked around.

"What do you need?"

"A red pencil."

Dorothy shoved aside some papers. "Katrina must have taken hers."

"That's okay. I've got a few. Be right back."

Isobel returned to her desk. As she reached over her computer keyboard for the pencils, she saw a business envelope tucked under it. She opened it and slid out the contents.

It was a list of the entire Dove & Flight staff. There were 'X's next to many of the names, and a handwritten note from Jimmy at the bottom. One name was circled twice.

'X' means they're out. I circled Wilbur, because not only is he out of a job, he's going to lose his home. Angus set him up in a company apartment in the building and was funneling something extra into his pension. All gone now. Buh-bye.

Wilbur Freed.

Isobel glanced up sharply, half expecting him to materialize suddenly from around the corner. When he didn't, she exhaled slowly and considered this provocative tidbit.

Nobody noticed Wilbur. He was as invisible as his job, unnecessary and redundant, taken for granted. Slinking stealthily from office to office, Wilbur was perfectly positioned to eavesdrop on private discussions about the merger. He must have been better informed than anyone about the twists and turns of the process.

He likely also knew who took which medications, and where he could find them.

Wilbur's identity was tied up in the old world of public relations—Angus's world—Barnaby's world until he'd turned traitor. When Angus had succumbed to his heart attack, Wilbur must have been crushed. What if they had been working together? Perhaps Angus had poisoned Jason's coffee at Starbucks. When Barnaby met with Jayla and revived the merger, Wilbur must have realized that Angus's efforts to preserve his legacy were for naught. It would have been easy for him to swipe the digoxin from Sophie's desk and doctor Jayla's coffee.

"Isobel!"

She jumped and flung a hand over her pounding heart. It was Katrina.

"Don't creep up on me like that!"

"Sorry." Katrina yawned. "Will you duck into Dorothy's office and grab the FedEx envelope on her desk?"

"Sure."

Isobel watched Katrina weave sleepily down the hall. As she stuffed Jimmy's paper into her pocket, her cell phone rang. It was Delphi.

"Hey, what's up? How'd your dress rehearsal go?"

There was no answer, just heavy breathing.

"Delphi? Are you butt-dialing me?"

"Here," rasped a voice.

Panic gripped Isobel. "What's wrong? Are you okay?"

"Stuck...in...elevator. Oh, my God...gonna die..."

"What elevator? The one at the studio?"

"Crappy...piece of...shit..."

Isobel glanced at her watch. It was eleven o'clock. Delphi must have gotten trapped leaving the rehearsal.

"Okay, listen to me," Isobel said in measured tones. "Is there an emergency button?"

"Pressed."

"That's good. That was smart. Do you know if anyone heard it?"

"Graham. Getting…help…"

"Great! I'm sure they'll get you out of there in no time."

Delphi gave a strangled groan. Isobel racked her brain for a way to calm her friend.

"Do you have any water with you? If you do, take a sip."

There was silence on the other end, and then Delphi said in a clearer voice, "Okay."

"Good." Isobel continued to the other end of the hall to Dorothy's office. "Just keep talking to me, okay? How was the dress?"

"F-f-fine."

"Do you want to hear about my night? Hugh and I hooked up. I had to cut it short, because I had to come back to the office. I'm working late on that annual report."

Delphi didn't answer.

Really? Not even interested in Hugh? Isobel thought. This is serious.

"How about this?" She spotted the FedEx envelope on Dorothy's desk. "Why don't you recite some of your lines to me? Maybe that will calm you down."

Delphi whimpered a response. Isobel wasn't sure whether it was affirmative or not, until Delphi began to speak, haltingly, and quietly.

"'Grief fills the room up of my absent child, lies in his bed, walks up and down with me, puts on his pretty looks…'"

"That's great! Keep going."

Isobel reached for the FedEx envelope, and then stopped abruptly, her hand in midair.

"'Repeats his words, remembers me of all his gracious parts,'" Delphi continued.

Ignoring the envelope, Isobel picked up the photograph of the dark-haired girl on the horse.

"'Then, have I reason to be fond of grief? Fare you well: had you such a loss as I—' Holy shit! They're here. Oh, thank God. Isobel, you're the best!"

But Isobel was only barely paying attention. As Constance's lament to her dead child echoed in her ear, she examined the photo and knew she had seen the girl somewhere else.

More importantly, she knew where.

FORTY-ONE

JAMES TOOK HIS EYES OFF JAYLA'S still form just long enough to look at his phone, which was vibrating in his hand. Isobel. After the way she had hung up on him last time, how could she be calling him again?

He had been sitting next to Jayla's gurney for the last three hours, and now Isobel was checking up on him. He didn't want to admit he'd done what she'd demanded he do, so he set the phone on his knee and let the call go to voice mail.

Jayla looked so frail and beautiful, her chocolate skin and tangled dreadlocks set in relief against the stark white sheets. There was something both touching and disappointing about seeing her so...unempowered was the only word he could think of. She looked like a storybook princess—or would have without the tubes snaking out from her nose and arm. It was strange to see her forcefulness squelched. It depressed him to think that if it could happen to her, it could happen to anyone.

His phone gave a little buzz, and the message icon lit up. He'd deal with Isobel later. He hated when she was right, and she had been this time. Say what he would about Jayla, she had gotten him to AA, and she had cleaned him up more than once, both before and after. Except for the last time, when Isobel had stepped in.

He felt a surge of self-loathing, as he recalled his idiotic assumption that it had been Lily in his apartment that night. He shifted the kaleidoscope in his mind and looked back on that night through the rearranged crystals. Isobel, not Lily. He doubted she'd kept the kind of unwavering vigil he was now keeping over Jayla. If he knew Isobel at all, she'd have taken the opportunity to snoop. And what would she have found?

Any number of things. His pre-law books, his college application, his anti-depressants—if she'd been in the bathroom, which of course she must have been. This was just as bad as sleeping with someone drunk and not remembering what barriers of intimacy had been crossed.

Which brought him back to Jayla. If she woke up and saw him there, she would jump feet first into the assumption that his presence meant more than it did. He'd done what was right. He'd checked up on her, he'd sat with her, he would leave her a note, so she'd know he'd been there, but the time had come to do what he really should have done hours ago.

"Michael? It's James. No, wait, don't hang up—it's about Jayla." He proceeded to tell her fiancé what had happened.

"I was so worried! She didn't come home, and she wasn't answering her phone," Michael said. "I'm on my way. Will you stay until I get there?"

He glanced at Jayla. She was as motionless as a statue, her breathing finally even.

"Yeah, sure."

"You're the best, bro. I owe you."

"Yeah, you already owed me," James muttered.

As he disconnected, the phone vibrated again in his hand, and he read Isobel's text as it flashed across the tiny screen.

At office. Need backup immed. Need YOU.

James didn't hesitate. Whispering a good-bye to Jayla and an apology to Michael that he knew neither of them could hear, he grabbed his coat and ran out the door.

FORTY-TWO

Isobel walked slowly back to the conference room, clutching Dorothy's FedEx envelope and turning over her discovery in her mind. What was it Delphi had said at the bar the other night? If it was someone in Jason's personal life who happened to work at Dove & Flight, the clues were elsewhere.

She pulled out her phone. Still no word from James. She detoured to the main office entrance and propped the door open, just in case. Then she returned to the conference room.

Dorothy was alone, resting her chin on her fist, staring into space.

"Where's Katrina?"

"Kitchen." Dorothy looked at Isobel. "Did you get the FedEx envelope?"

Isobel held it out, but the older woman shook her head.

"It's for you."

Isobel tried to steady her trembling hands as she set her phone next to Katrina's empty Diet Coke can. She slid the papers out from the envelope. They were copies of newspaper articles. Isobel skimmed the first one and caught her breath. It was just as she thought.

Barnard Student Dies of Alcohol Poisoning

Isobel looked up. "I—I didn't know you had a daughter."

"It's hard for me to talk about, as you can imagine. She was diabetic." Dorothy held Isobel's gaze. "And it wasn't alcohol poisoning. It was murder."

"But if she drank too much—"

"She did not drink too much! She didn't drink at all. Ever.

She knew what it meant for her. What she didn't know was what a sneaky son of a bitch her boyfriend was."

"Jason Whiteley."

"One weekend when she was home, I overheard her telling a friend that he was always trying to get her to drink. Said it would loosen her up. No matter how many times she told him, how many times she explained, he persisted. The irony is that the amount of alcohol that killed her would hardly have had any effect on a normal person. She couldn't tolerate it at all."

Isobel returned her glance to the article.

Nell Berman, 18, daughter of Dorothy and Daniel Berman, was found unconscious in a fraternity on the Columbia campus. Efforts to revive her were unsuccessful, and she was pronounced dead at St. Luke's Hospital.

Isobel flipped through the other articles. They outlined the fallout, highlighting James's expulsion. Her quick perusal revealed only one brief mention of Jason.

"Your friend took the rap," Dorothy said.

Isobel looked up. "My friend? How do you know about—"

"I saw him here with you. The day Angus died."

Isobel cast her mind back to the day James had come by to invite her to dinner. She vaguely remembered an exchange with Dorothy. Either James didn't see her or didn't recognize her. But clearly, she had recognized him.

Dorothy broke in, as if reading her thoughts. "That's when I realized that you knew."

Isobel started to protest that she didn't know a thing until about ten minutes ago, but thought better of it.

"So you decided to punish Jason yourself?"

Dorothy buried her hands in her face for a moment, but when she looked up again, her bright blue eyes were clear. "I was finally starting to get past it all, when he showed up one day here as a client. Fortunately, I didn't have to deal with him directly. He probably wasn't paying any attention to the rest of us. He may not even have realized who I was. I look different now. My hair is gray. But I took the steps. I was prepared. I visited my son at his dental office and took the Demerol from there. It wasn't hard to sneak Angus's digoxin from Sophie's desk." Her face contorted with regret. "I guess I killed Angus, too. He didn't have the medicine that would have saved him."

Isobel didn't bother to remind her that Angus had chosen not to call for help. Instead, she asked, "Why did you need Jimmy's Demerol?"

"In the end, I didn't, but I saw him taking it one day, and that gave me the idea. I took it from his desk when nobody was looking. When I realized I needed something more potent than pills, I emptied the bottle and left it in Barnaby's office. I hoped the police might suspect him."

"So your plan was always to poison Jason here?"

Dorothy nodded. "I waited until I knew he would be coming here for a meeting. But I got lucky."

"Starbucks," Isobel said.

Dorothy nodded. "There he was, with Angus. Angus brought the cups over to the counter where I was standing. I had already added the digoxin and Demerol to my coffee, and while Angus was adding milk and sugar to his tea, I knocked his wallet to the floor. I switched my coffee with Jason's, and Angus took it back to him."

Isobel exhaled slowly. "You made Angus an unwitting accomplice."

"It was too good a chance to pass up. And once Angus was dead, it was even better. Without him alive to contradict me, I could pin the whole thing on him. When the police asked me what I had seen, I told them I'd seen Angus doctor Jason's coffee." She paused thoughtfully. "It's strange that in the end, Jason died here, where I'd always intended it to happen. It all worked out better than I could have hoped—until you figured it out. Then I tried to silence you, but that didn't go as planned, either, did it? That poor black girl. I hope she'll be okay."

Isobel felt her body grow damp with sudden sweat. The poisoned coffee was meant for her, not Jayla.

"She's James's girlfriend," Isobel blurted out.

Dorothy's body heaved with a strange half laugh. "Poor guy. He can't catch a break."

"Ex-girlfriend, actually. He'd probably have been more upset if it *had* been me," Isobel said.

"I guess we'll find out."

The tone of Dorothy's voice chilled Isobel, and the truth of her present situation suddenly struck her full force. She was alone in a deserted office with someone who had reason to want her dead. But she wasn't alone—and she wasn't the only one Dorothy might want dead.

Isobel ran to the kitchen, her heart racing. Katrina was sprawled on the floor, unconscious, her russet hair splayed across her face and her arms flung out at an unnatural angle.

Isobel threw herself to the floor and immediately felt for a pulse. Katrina's breathing was shallow, and she hadn't vomited. Isobel reached for her cell phone, but she didn't have it. She quickly surveyed the small kitchen. No extension. She didn't want to leave Katrina, but she knew she had to get help. She bolted down the corridor and into the conference room.

It was empty. Without stopping to wonder where Dorothy had gone, Isobel ran to the credenza and snatched up the phone, but there was no dial tone. She grabbed the base and saw the unplugged wire. As she bent down to reconnect it, she heard the door slam shut.

Dorothy was standing in front of it, clutching Jimmy's antique letter opener in one hand and Isobel's cell phone in the other.

"Looks like you already called for help," she said, flashing the phone at Isobel. "We'll just wait, then, shall we?"

FORTY-THREE

JAMES HUSTLED AWAY FROM THE HOSPITAL as quickly as he could. At this hour there weren't many pedestrians, but there weren't many cabs, either. The few he tried to hail accelerated past him, exercising one of the few tacitly acceptable excuses for discrimination by refusing to pick up a lone, large black man, late at night.

He bent his head against the cold wind blowing off the East River and tried not to panic. But there was panic in Isobel's text. And he knew she must really be in danger if she'd forgotten her anger and reached out to him. One thing was clear: she was depending on his presence and nobody else's.

As another available cab left him in the dust, he wondered briefly if she needed him only for his muscle. That skinny British twerp wouldn't be much help in a fight. But if she were in that kind of trouble, wouldn't she call 911? Then again, maybe she had.

He stopped short and pulled out his phone. What was he thinking? She had left a voice mail he had never listened to! He dialed in to retrieve the message and started walking downtown. As her words relayed the short but stunning message, he picked up his pace to match Isobel's rapid-fire patter.

Oh, shit, James, where are you? Okay, listen. I know you hate me, but please listen. Dorothy who works in the healthcare group is Dorothy Berman. Ring a bell? She has a picture on her desk of the girl from Barnard. I need to know what that means. If it's her daughter, and she killed Jason... I'm here alone with her—no, not totally alone—Katrina's here, too. But we're the only ones in the office, so please, if you get this, you have to come down here.

Every muscle in James's body went into overdrive. A flood of emotions overtook him at the mention of the name he'd tried so hard to forget, and he was forced to pause and bend over to catch his breath. Dorothy in healthcare? Last names. From now on, he was going to insist that Isobel use last names! And Isobel was alone with her. If Dorothy had killed Jason—an urge James could certainly relate to—she might kill Isobel. For that matter, she might kill him too when he got there. What was he walking into?

Come on, he told himself. You weigh two hundred and fifty—okay, two hundred and sixty—pounds. Why are you scared of a middle-aged woman?

He leaned against a building, panting. He was wasting time, but there was more at stake in this meeting than Isobel could possibly know. He would be forced to face Dorothy, to talk to her. To say all the things he didn't—couldn't—confess at the time about what really happened. He knew the official version, he knew the unofficial version, and he knew the truth. He was pretty sure Dorothy knew versions one and two. Version three was going to come as a shock.

But he had no choice. If Isobel was right about Dorothy, her life was in danger. He inhaled the cold air with such force that it stung his lungs. Then, with a burst of energy, he took off at a run toward the confrontation he had postponed for too long.

FORTY-FOUR

"KATRINA MIGHT DIE," ISOBEL SAID. "Are you prepared to have her death on your hands, too?"

"She won't die. It's straight Demerol. When she wakes up, she'll be groggy, and she won't remember what she did."

Isobel gave a dismissive snort. "Which is what? Proofreading German?"

Dorothy shook her head slowly. "No. Killing you."

In spite of herself, Isobel took a step backward. "Why would anybody believe Katrina would kill me? We're old friends!"

Dorothy hadn't moved from her position in front of the door, but now she shifted to the side just a bit. It still wasn't enough for Isobel to make a run for it. Not with that nasty-looking letter opener pointed at her.

"Maybe it was Katrina who killed Jason to keep the merger from happening so she wouldn't have to work for her father. Maybe you figured it out and confronted her, and she killed you."

Dorothy's made-up version of events was so close to what Isobel had suspected for so long that it took her breath away. The thought of her disloyalty made her stomach roil with guilt. Not only had she doubted Katrina, now her friend was in danger because of her.

"You're forgetting James," she said, pointing to her phone, which was still in Dorothy's hand. "He's on his way. And he'll know exactly what happened—and why."

Dorothy's almost robotic composure slipped for just an instant. Isobel knew that if she could only hold on until James arrived, there was a chance that Dorothy might fall apart completely. Then again, so might James. It was even odds at this point.

But would he come? Even beyond the very real possibility that he hadn't gotten her message or her text, there were more reasons why he wouldn't come than reasons why he would. But she couldn't let on to Dorothy that there was any doubt in her mind that he would show up. She had to stall for time. She held her hands out in front of her, walked very slowly back to the table, and picked up the papers she had been working on.

"We may as well finish the annual report."

Dorothy froze, and for a moment, Isobel feared she had somehow said the worst possible thing imaginable. Then Dorothy threw back her head and howled with laughter. It was a hysterical sound, truly crazed. Tears ran down her face, and as she wiped them away with her forearm, Isobel heard her ringtone between Dorothy's gasps.

"We'll just...ignore this..." Dorothy panted, pressing a button.

Damn, thought Isobel. If it was James, it meant he wasn't on his way. He intended to question her first before deciding whether or not to come.

Dorothy was clutching at the neckline of her blouse as if she were trying to let in more air. "Did you really...think...we needed to redo the annual report?" she finally spluttered.

Isobel blinked. "What do you mean?"

Dorothy let out a mad cackle. "The real report went to print yesterday, right on time. This was a lure, a distraction. And you came back! When you said you had to be somewhere else tonight, I panicked. That was why I made Penny stay until you got here. I had to keep up the pretense that we were on a deadline. But think about it! Germany is six hours ahead. If they needed it first thing tomorrow morning, it's too late already!"

Isobel's mouth went dry. She had been free, and she had come back of her own accord, tempted by time and a half. She'd walked right into Dorothy's trap. Penny would do whatever was expected of her without questioning the flimsiness of Dorothy's excuse. Katrina might have guessed if she'd worked on the account to begin with, but she was pinch-hitting. No, if anyone should have seen through the pretense, it was Isobel.

"But by all means," Dorothy continued, "if you want to spend your last hours on earth separating prefixes, you go right ahead!"

Dorothy took a small step toward her, raising the silver letter opener, which flashed in the fluorescent light. Isobel made an instinctive dive under the table. At the same time, she heard an enormous smacking sound and a cry. When she opened her eyes, she saw James standing in the open doorway, looking down, horrified, at Dorothy's form, crumpled on the floor.

FORTY-FIVE

"Oh, my God, James!"

"Are you all right?" He made a move toward Isobel and slammed into the conference table. Pain rocketed through his thigh. "Shit!"

"I'm fine. But Dorothy!"

Rubbing his leg, he sank to his knees next to the older woman and checked her. "She's breathing."

"Quick, give me your phone."

He grabbed it from his coat pocket and thrust it at Isobel.

"Stay with her while I call the police," she said. "I have to check on Katrina. She's knocked out in the kitchen."

"What the—?"

But Isobel was gone. He shifted into a sitting position, his stomach clenched in knots. Even though Dorothy was alive, he was afraid she might still cross to the other side just to spite him. He wouldn't have blamed her.

Her eyelids fluttered and drooped again. "You," she moaned.

Isobel returned a few moments later, still speaking into the phone. "Yes, Detective O'Connor. This is his case... And an ambulance!" She handed the phone back to him. "Katrina's still out. Dorothy drugged her."

Their eyes locked for a moment, and then moved together toward the woman on the floor.

"Do you think we need to restrain her?" he asked.

Isobel shook her head. "I don't think there's anything she can do now that you wouldn't be able to put a stop to."

Isobel disappeared under the table for a moment, then emerged with an old-fashioned letter opener wrapped in a paper towel, which she deposited into a plastic bag. "I need that soda can, too." She reached across the table. "I don't know what I would have done if you hadn't come. Next time I'll make sure we're back on speaking terms before I send out an S.O.S."

"Don't worry about it." He cleared his throat. "I don't seem to be able to stay mad at you very long."

Dorothy whimpered and shifted her position on the floor. Isobel took a step backward, and James took the hint. He turned his attention back to Dorothy.

"Are you all right? I didn't mean to knock you down. It was an accident," he said.

"No it wasn't. Just like Nell's death wasn't," she said in a hoarse voice.

James swallowed. Here it comes.

"You're right. Nell's death wasn't an accident. At least, not entirely."

Dorothy pushed herself up against the wall as if she were trying to propel herself through it, as far away from him as possible.

She gazed at him woozily. "I always knew it wasn't you, but it was too easy for the administration to make you the scapegoat. The publicity for the school was bad enough as it was, but it would have been so much worse for them if they'd accused Jason. His father was too prominent, too powerful. There would have been a long, dragged-out, very public case, and he'd have gotten off in the end. At least this way, there was justice for some. For me, but not for you."

James cleared his throat. "Mrs. Berman, there's something you need to know about what happened that night. Something only those of us who were there know."

He sensed Isobel positioning herself behind him, and was glad of the support it suggested, although he knew that when she heard what he was about to say, she might try to disappear through the opposite wall.

"I know what happened," Dorothy said wearily. "He knew she couldn't tolerate alcohol. She told him over and over. He tricked her into drinking somehow, and it killed her."

James took a deep breath and plunged on. "We were drinking Kamikazes California-style. That's when you lean your head back and someone else mixes the drink in your mouth. That's what we were doing that night. And Nell…" He shut his eyes, knowing even as he did so, that he couldn't protect either of them from what he was about to say. "Nell turned to me and said, 'What the hell? One won't kill me.'"

"She did not!" Dorothy hissed.

James continued, rasping on through the squeeze in his throat.

"I knew she shouldn't risk it, but I was too far gone to care. There are things I could have done. I could have grabbed her and taken her away. Hell, I could have knocked the bottle out of Jason's hand. But she didn't want me to. That's what I thought, anyway. Who knows what she really wanted in that moment? You should have seen the triumph in Jason's eyes. Yes, for that, you can blame him. But it wasn't an accident, and it wasn't murder. It was—I don't know what it was. But she asked for the drink. And then she asked for another, and then two more. And I let her."

Dorothy's eyes were closed, and for a moment he thought she'd passed out again. But her mouth began a series of twisting movements and her face flushed dangerously purple against her silver hair.

"That is A LIE!"

The force of her words sent James backward, knocking Isobel into the table. For a moment, they both flailed, but then he felt her hand on his shoulder, steadying them both. Dorothy's eyes were open now, lasering hatred at him.

"She would never have done that. NEVER!"

"James, let it go." Isobel's voice was soft in his ear.

He shook her off, his eyes never leaving Dorothy's. "We have to face the truth. Both of us. We're the only ones left."

"Sometimes the truth is better left avoided," Isobel said quietly.

James whirled on her, rising to his feet in a move so sudden it surprised them both.

"I've been running from this for years! They were right to kick me out. There—I said it! But they should have kicked Jason out, too. They should have kicked him out first." He gestured wildly at Dorothy. "And she needs to know that Nell wasn't an innocent victim. She was a victim, yes, but of her own desire to fit in. To be loved."

"She was loved, you big, fucking animal!" Dorothy's voice sirened into the room. "I loved her, we all loved her!" She bent forward on all fours and pulled herself to her feet. "Don't you dare—don't you DARE blame her!"

"I don't!" James screamed back. They were nose to nose now, but instead of fear or shame, he felt relief uttering the words he had held back for so long. "We were all responsible! We are all—all of us—responsible for our own actions. For God's sake, if I've learned anything in AA, it's that! Nell was playing with fire. She was the only one who really understood what she was doing. She gambled, and she lost! She lost…"

He felt his knees give way under him, and he crumpled into a chair, awash with racking sobs that shook his sturdy frame. He felt Isobel behind him, her arms on his shoulders, as guilt, anguish and relief flooded out of him. He was dimly aware of Dorothy wailing as she sank to the floor.

They were still like that when the police found them.

FORTY-SIX

"WE WERE ON OUR WAY BACK from Kit Blanchard's when we got confirmation of the fingerprints on the coffee cup," Detective O'Connor said.

Isobel glanced over to the other side of the room, where Aguilar was locking handcuffs around Dorothy's wrists. She seemed to have aged decades in the last half-hour. Her pale face drooped, and a dazed deadness had replaced her usually bright, scrutinizing gaze.

"And Dorothy's were on it," Isobel said.

O'Connor nodded. "We were on our way to bring her in for questioning, so we just diverted here."

"I guess I was just one small step ahead of you, wasn't I?" Isobel said.

O'Connor regarded her seriously. "You're lucky that step wasn't any bigger."

There was a bustle in the hall, and Isobel saw Katrina being wheeled past the open doorway on a stretcher.

James returned a moment later. "The paramedics will pump her stomach just in case, but she'll be fine."

Isobel let out a deep breath. "Oh, thank God."

O'Connor turned to James. "You do have a habit of turning up, don't you?"

"Isn't that what you do when someone calls you for help? I'm not so different from the police that way."

O'Connor inclined his too-small head. "Touché."

Aguilar and a policewoman led Dorothy to her feet. She left the room without a backward glance.

"What happens now?" Isobel asked.

"They'll take her first to the hospital for tests, to make sure she didn't sustain a concussion, and then proceed accordingly. I need a word with Aguilar, and then I'll be back to take your statements. I won't be long."

Isobel followed him to the door, as if she were a hostess bidding a guest good night. She stayed staring after him several moments longer than necessary.

James cleared his throat. "Isobel. I'm so sorry. I should have put it all together."

She turned around to face him. He looked drained and vulnerable.

"How could you have known that Dorothy in healthcare was Nell's mother?"

"If I'd known her last name. Or if I'd gotten a good look at her the other day…"

"But you didn't." She walked over and reached for his hand. "You have to let go of that part of your life. You've punished yourself enough. And if what you said tonight is true—"

"Of course it's true!"

"You know what I mean. The point is, what you said to Dorothy was right. You were all responsible, each in your own way, but truly your guilt was the least of it. And at the end of the day, it really was an accident. An error of judgment. Dorothy believed it to be murder, so she took a page out of old W.S. Gilbert's book and made the punishment fit what she thought was the crime. But you've already grown beyond those days. You've learned not to sit silently by when someone needs help. You said it just now, to Detective O'Connor."

James gave her a wry smile. "I really hate it when you're right."

She smiled demurely. "I think it's one of my more endearing qualities."

"You were wrong about one thing, though. In your message, when you said you knew I hated you. You couldn't be more wrong about anything if you tried."

Before she knew it, he had pulled her close, and his mouth, full and bold, was on hers. She didn't resist, not for a moment, and if the flash of desire that shot through her body surprised her, it quickly melted into acceptance of what suddenly seemed the most natural thing in the world.

"Isobel!"

They broke apart, and Isobel whirled around to see Hugh and Sunil standing in the doorway. Sunil's eyebrows were raised in delight, but Hugh, who had been the one to call her name, looked like he'd been punched in the gut.

"What—what are you doing here?" Isobel gasped.

"I heard the whole thing when you answered your phone," said Sunil.

She shook her head in confusion. "I didn't answer my phone."

"Well, somebody did. I heard a woman saying she had lured you here alone and something about how you wanted to spend your last hours."

"Oh, my God, that was Dorothy! She must have pressed the wrong button."

"I called Hugh and we got down here as fast as we could."

"Obviously not fast enough," said Hugh flatly.

"Hugh, I can explain—" she began.

"There's nothing to explain." James put a protective arm around Isobel. "She's with me now."

"Well, she was with me about three hours ago," said Hugh.

James dropped his arm, and Isobel felt her throat go dry.

"It's not—I don't—" She threw a pleading glance at Sunil. "Can you…?"

He threw up his hands in mock dismay. "To tell you the truth, I'm feeling a little left out."

It was Detective O'Connor who unwittingly came to her rescue. He strode into the conference room and addressed Sunil and Hugh.

"Ah! I see you've found your friends. Now that you know they're all right, would you give us a moment? I need to finish taking their statements. You can wait in the kitchen." He ushered them out and pulled up a chair. "Right. Isobel, we'll start with you."

She tried to stay focused on her narrative, but she was achingly, painfully aware of James's eyes boring into her. In the end, she didn't have to connect too many dots. As soon as the police had discovered Dorothy's fingerprints on the coffee cup, they had turned up the story of Nell's death and the single mention of Jason Whiteley, and put most of it together. When they learned her son was a dentist, they realized she had access to professional-strength Demerol, and that sealed it. After Isobel signed her statement, she excused herself to go to the bathroom while James gave his. She hid out for as long as she could, splashing water on her face and trying not to think. When she finally emerged, she found Sunil sitting at her desk.

"You're still here?"

"Of course."

"Where's Hugh?"

"He left."

"Did he say anything?" she asked, dreading the answer.

"Just to tell you that he'll see you at rehearsal on Saturday."

She shook her head in despair. "What should I do? Now they both hate me."

Sunil took her hands. "When you don't know what to do, do nothing. The answer will reveal itself."

"That's annoyingly Zen," she sniffed.

"Listen, I'm starving. Did you ever eat?" Sunil said.

Isobel shook her head.

"I'm ordering us some food. We can pick it up on our way out." Sunil pulled a Post-it with the deli number from her computer monitor, pressed the speaker button on her phone, and dialed.

"U-Like Deli, please hold."

"You've got to be fucking kidding me!" he cried. "It's two o'clock in the morning!"

Isobel left Sunil cursing at the phone and returned to the conference room to retrieve her things. O'Connor had gone, but James was waiting for her.

Before she could speak, he held up a hand. "I crossed a line, personally and professionally. It won't happen again."

"But what if I want it to?" Isobel said, before she could stop herself.

"You don't. Piano Man is more your speed. You don't really want me, and I…" he paused. "I made a mistake."

She took a step toward him, but he skirted around her in a deft move she imagined was a holdover from his days on the football field.

"You said it earlier. We all have to take responsibility for our actions. I shouldn't have kissed you. As for whatever happened between you and *Hugh*," he practically coughed up a hairball pronouncing his name, "whatever mess you left there is for you to clean up."

She felt her face grow hot. "Mess? The mess isn't there, it's right here! Are you so uncertain about your feelings for me that you'll give up that easily? I'll be honest with you. I like you both! I'm completely confused and torn, and I didn't expect to have to come to any kind of decision so quickly. But Jesus Christ, James, if you care anything for me at all, fight for me! Or at least give me some sign that you think I might be worth fighting for."

James shook his head. "I can't fight anymore tonight. I just need—"

"Not a drink," she broke in, her concern pushing everything else aside.

"Sleep. I need to sleep."

"But you're not going to drink, are you? I mean, you shouldn't be alone right now."

To her surprise, he came over to her and put his hands on her shoulders. It seemed to her that he was steadying himself, not her.

"Alone is exactly what I should be." He dropped his hands and moved to the door. "Are your friends still here?"

"Sunil is."

"Get him to see you home. He seems like a good guy," he said and left.

Her eyes flooded with unexpected tears. "So are you, James," she whispered to his retreating form. "So are you."

FORTY-SEVEN

"I'M NOT WALKING DOWN SIX FLIGHTS," Sunil complained.

"It's my opening night, so you have to do whatever I say," Delphi insisted. "Besides, it's your fault I got stuck in that damn elevator in the first place!"

"How is it my fault?" he asked indignantly.

Delphi prodded his chest with her long, filed fingernail. "You brought me bad luck when you uttered the name of the Scottish play. You cursed me!"

Sunil threw an imploring glance at Isobel, who put her finger over her lips and gave her head the tiniest shake.

Delphi, taking his silence as an admission of guilt, spun him around and frog-marched him triumphantly down the stairs in front of her. Isobel found Delphi's sudden possessiveness of Sunil highly amusing. Maybe Delphi knew she only had a few hours before the magic of being seen onstage wore off, but Isobel thought it was more likely a direct result of her own romantic trials of the night before, which she had faithfully recounted to Delphi when she'd finally crawled out of bed at two o'clock that afternoon.

"Man!" Delphi had exclaimed. "Ever hear of too much of a good thing?"

"Yeah, well, now I got plenty of nothin'," Isobel had said, bundling up against the snow. "No, I take that back. I've got two wounded male egos. And I refuse to suck up to either of them."

"That's the spirit," Delphi had said. "See if either of them tries to contact you. That'll tell you everything you need to know. You know how sometimes you aren't sure whether or not you want an acting job, and then when you get it, you're either immediately elated or your heart sinks?"

"Yeah."

"It's the same with men."

Isobel wasn't sure she agreed, since she had been some version of elated while kissing both Hugh and James. Still, she had to admit that despite having spent more time tangling with Hugh, her brief encounter with James was somehow more memorable.

"On the other hand, sometimes you don't get that feeling of elation or despair until you find out you *didn't* get the job. Or the guy," Isobel had said, meaningfully.

She'd left Delphi pondering this as she wended her way back to Dove & Flight to clear out her stuff and say good-bye to the few people she cared about. She'd decided that after everything, she didn't want to stay there long-term. Besides, with Aaron taking over Dorothy's accounts, there was no real need for a second junior associate beyond Penny. Even so, Isobel found herself a little sorry to leave Dove & Flight. She had felt appreciated there in way she hadn't at any other temp job, and there was no knowing what James might have in store for her next. The way they'd left things, she wouldn't be surprised if he sent her to the morgue on an open-ended assignment. From Dove & Flight, it was on to visit Katrina in the hospital to explain, apologize, atone—whatever was necessary to make up for the fact that she had been so quick to assume the worst of her old friend, who had only ever assumed the best of her.

At the office, she'd thanked Jimmy for being so helpful, and confided her misguided final suspicion of Wilbur.

Jimmy had brayed with delight at the thought. "*American Gothic* meets *American Psycho*! Ladies and gentleman, stick a pitchfork in him, he's done!"

Isobel couldn't help but laugh. "Jimmy, you are an original. There is nobody else out there whose mind works the way yours does."

He pulled a face. "Which is why I'm alone." Then he brightened and took her hand, which he kissed with real tenderness. "I shall miss you, melodious songbird."

"And I you."

Liz had given her as big a hug as her expanding belly would allow. "You're out a week ahead of me," she confided. "I handed in my resignation. I'll go to Angus's memorial, and then I'm done with this place."

Isobel hesitated. "I have to ask you something."

Liz met her gaze for a moment, and then looked away. "About the Brazil emails."

Isobel nodded. "Why did you try to pin it on Katrina?"

For the first time, Liz's strong, confident voice faltered. "I got fired from my last job for something similar, which also wasn't my fault, strictly speaking. Aaron never told Barnaby which of us sent the emails. He stressed the fact that they'd been approved by the client. I don't know why I lied to you. I guess I didn't want you to think badly of me, and now of course, you think worse." She gave a sad chuckle.

"No, I don't. Getting to know you has been one of my favorite things about working here. I wish I'd known you in college."

Liz laughed. "Are you kidding? We'd never have gotten any work done!"

The metal staircase began to creak and groan, as Barnaby's bellow echoed, "Is there anyone left in this place to actually do some fucking PR? We could use a little after the shitpile we've landed in!"

Isobel had recognized her cue and bolted, and as she'd left Dove & Flight for the last time, she'd resolved to enjoy Delphi's opening night and not worry about securing another temp job until after the weekend. Now, as she, Delphi and Sunil emerged onto the snowy sidewalk, Isobel found she was glad to savor Delphi's triumph without either James or Hugh in tow, let alone both. They started down the street toward the bar where Graham and the rest of the cast were assembling.

Isobel gave Delphi's gloved hand a squeeze. "You were really, really good."

"Thank you." Delphi's eyes shone with pleasure. "That means a lot coming from you."

"Because I'm such a knowledgeable Shakespearean?"

Delphi elbowed her. "No, stupid. Because you're my best friend."

Sunil turned to face them, continuing to walk backward. "And what, pray tell, am I?"

Delphi gave her head a haughty shake. "'Not so deep as a well, nor so wide as a church-door, but 'tis enough. 'Twill serve.'"

"You just compared me to a deadly wound!" he cried. "'Have at thee, boy!'"

He lunged at Delphi, who grabbed him around the waist, and sent him flying back in the other direction. He skidded on a patch of ice and caught himself, laughing and spluttering, on a fire hydrant.

"That wasn't very nice," Isobel admonished her. "But after last night, I will never, ever fault you for quoting Shakespeare again."

Sunil righted himself and brushed snow off his jacket. "Hey, you know who else was really good?"

"Gary Stinson," Isobel said. "He was terrific."

"No. The girl who played Blanche. Hey, Delphi, you think you could get me her number?"

Sunil grinned mischievously and ran ahead to open the door.

Delphi's mouth dropped open.

"Come on!" Isobel grabbed Delphi's arm and ushered her into the warmth of the bar. "'The course of true love never did run smooth.'"

"You're telling me," Delphi said, and she let the door slam shut behind them.

ACKNOWLEDGMENTS

In the "don't try this at home" category, I would like to thank my friend and pharmacist Ivan Jourdain, who gamely answered potentially awkward questions about poisons in front of curious customers. Pharmacologist James Jones (via Tom Groves) helped refine my fatal cocktail, while Marzena Jablonska cleared up a few outstanding medical questions. My trusted advisors Helen Lessner, Helen Faye Rosenblum, Cornelia Iredell and Elaine Greenblatt were on hand with insightful counsel as always, and Piper Goodeve, Christianne Tisdale and Alan Gilbert provided valuable perspective as newcomers to Isobel's adventures.

I couldn't have written this one without the enthusiastic support of Caroline Luz, Beth Wiegard, Christiana Marran and Kate Koningisor, who encouraged my reimagined version of our shared history. I am also indebted to my extraordinary agent, Kari Stuart, for her boundless support, Jodie Renner for her editing expertise, Linda Pierro for her captivating cover design, and Ilene Goldman for her eagle-eyed proofreading.

Of course, none of this would be possible without my steadfast husband, Joshua Rosenblum, whose enduring love provides a ready antidote to his occasional impatience with my Isobel-like locutions.

Bluface Photography

About the Author

Joanne Sydney Lessner is the author of *Pandora's Bottle*, a novel inspired by the true story of the world's most expensive bottle of wine (Flint Mine Press). *The Temporary Detective* and *Bad Publicity* (Dulcet Press) feature Isobel Spice, aspiring actress and resourceful office temp turned amateur sleuth. No stranger to the theatrical world, Joanne enjoys an active performing career in both musical theater and opera. With her husband, composer/conductor Joshua Rosenblum, she has co-authored several musicals including the cult hit *Fermat's Last Tango* and *Einstein's Dreams*, based on the celebrated novel by Alan Lightman. Her play, *Critical Mass*, received its Off Broadway premiere in October 2010 as the winner of the 2009 Heiress Productions Playwriting Competition. Joanne is a regular contributing writer to *Opera News* and holds a B.A. in music, *summa cum laude*, from Yale University.

Look for the next Isobel Spice novel:
And Justice for Some

Coming in 2014!

www.joannelessner.com

Made in the USA
Lexington, KY
20 April 2013